CRITICS R... K!

"Shocking revelat... ever present in *Crimson*... ide to hell and back, run—don't walk—to your nearest bookstore and snatch up a copy."

—*Romance Reviews Today*

"Maverick provides an intense tale with complex characters to kick off a new series set in an original, dark and fascinating world."

—*RT BOOKclub*

"Liz Maverick's *Crimson City* is everything you could expect in a paranormal thriller. There's action, adventure, steamy romance, chills and thrills, and thwarted love. The action will keep you on the edge of every page and the romance is as hot as any summer day in L.A.... This is paranormal romance at its best!"

—Roundtable Reviews

"Ms. Maverick is a talented author who has penned a tale of love and vampires that I absolutely adored. I highly recommend it to fans of vampires and other things that go bump in the night."

—Coffee Time Romance

THE SHADOW RUNNERS

"If you like your heroines tough but tender, your heroes hard-edged and hungering for a better tomorrow, you'll love *The Shadow Runners.*"

—Revision 14

"A winning addition to the *2176* series, *The Shadow Runners* is sure to please. Full of suspense, adventure, and an explosive romance, it is a book not to be missed."

—*Romance Reviews Today*

"This third novel in the gripping and explosive *2176* series moves along at a breakneck pace as another tough, strong woman does her part in the fight for world freedom. Ms. Maverick writes a unique, taut, exciting tale."

—*The Best Reviews*

THE ROGUE UNVEILED

He stood there framed in darkness, and then he stepped forward into the light, his jaw set, his mouth a grim slash, a mixture of fear and fury in his eyes…

Naked.

He was entirely naked, and his body held an unholy kind of beauty.

Cyd gasped as he moved across the carpet and stood before her, a strange and fascinating combination of sleek metal and human flesh marred by shiny strips and plates, burn marks, gashes, and angry red and white scars where metal no longer lined up or had been pried away.

"What kind of secrets do I have? You tell me," he whispered.

Other books in the *Crimson City* series:

CRIMSON CITY *by Liz Maverick*
A TASTE OF CRIMSON *by Marjorie M. Liu*
THROUGH A CRIMSON VEIL *by Patti O'Shea*
A DARKER CRIMSON *by Carolyn Jewel*
SEDUCED BY CRIMSON *by Jade Lee*

Other *Love Spell* books by Liz Maverick:

THE SHADOW RUNNERS

Liz Maverick

Crimson Rogue

LOVE SPELL

NEW YORK CITY

LOVE SPELL®

April 2006

Published by

Dorchester Publishing Co., Inc.
200 Madison Avenue
New York, NY 10016

ISBN 0-505-52625-5

The name "Love Spell" and its logo are trademarks of Dorchester Publishing Co., Inc.

Printed in the United States of America.

Visit us on the web at www.dorchesterpub.com.

ACKNOWLEDGMENTS

Thank you, Marjorie, Patti, Carolyn, and Jade...we kicked some serious butt!

And a special thanks to our series wrangler and editor extraordinaire, Chris Keeslar. Yeah, you rock.

Crimson Rogue

Chapter One

Someone was definitely following him, but Finn made a point not to look over his shoulder. He didn't have to; he could tell. Picking up the pace, he pulled his jacket closer around him and cut across the street.

It happened no more than once a month, but it wasn't something a guy really wanted to get used to: Someone would figure him out . . . or at least think they had figured him out. And it wasn't just the B-Ops teams. They were the least of Finn's worries. He could track them on his black-market scanner, even tap into their comms and listen to them talk on the job.

It was the rest of them—the bounty hunters. And every time he found himself in this position, there were only two questions he had to ask himself. Whoever was after him, did they work for the humans, the vampires, the werewolves or the demons? And the second question was: Do they know what *I* am? Being robbed was one thing. Being revealed, something else entirely.

The longer Finn lived in the heart of Crimson City, the more experience dulled his once razor-sharp instincts. There were so many sensations and emotions competing for his attention. When he'd first hit the streets and slipped the Grid, he could hardly think for himself.

The Grid was the network that served as the technological backbone of Crimson City's enforcement matrix; it was how the Ops teams communicated. Ops—Crimson City's human government's intelligence agency. Part FBI, part CIA, part Special Forces, they were the ones who handled everything. The Grid was how their Battlefield division out on the streets connected to the intelligence division behind the walls of the base. It was how they supported their comm devices, how they linked up the computer systems . . . and how they controlled their mechs. Having escaped the Grid, Finn might be a wanted man, but he wasn't traceable and no one could tell him what to do.

Everything had been instinct, programming, training. Everything he was supposed to know had been drilled into his head and body so many times that he'd never thought he could escape. But then he'd found himself in the middle of a veritable war zone instead of the antiseptic calm of the Ops barracks. It had been an assault on the senses . . . and then he'd grown to appreciate it.

He'd spent most of his first free days rotating through the city's bookstores, attracting little notice as just another member of the city's large homeless population; then, rather quickly, he'd begun to assimilate to the new world. He wasn't living any longer on the few fragments of thought that some faceless organization allowed. Maybe that made him a weaker soldier, but it made him a better man.

"Drop your bag, put your hands on top of your head, walk into the alley, turn around and face the wall."

Finn froze in his tracks. *Hell.* He let the strap of his

bag slip off his shoulder and slide down his arm. His satchel hit the sidewalk with a dull thud. He could just whip around and have done with it, or he could give the man a chance to be mistaken. "You've got the wrong guy," he said.

"I don't think so. Move it."

Finn stayed where he was. "You've got the wrong guy," he repeated more forcefully. "Understand?"

Something blunt jabbed between his shoulder blades. Finn stumbled forward into the alley, pulling his hood up around his head more securely while raising his gloved hands. He heard the clink of the brass links on his bag's strap as the man picked it up and moved behind him into the alley.

And so it goes. Crimson City was more of a jungle than ever, the prospect of some kind of peace—real peace—far off on the horizon. The most anyone hoped for these days was less bloodshed.

With the kind of detachment that came from experience, Finn lay down on the ground at the end of the alley on his stomach—too slow, of course, for the bounty hunter's taste. A boot came down predictably on his back, shoving him into the slime, but allowing Finn to hide his hands underneath his body without attracting attention. Finn turned his head to the side, listening as the hunter fumbled with his equipment. Handcuffs, probably. Rope, perhaps.

It was more the simple lack of trust than a predisposition to hate that made the streets of Crimson City so very unpredictable these days. Which, in a roundabout way, was what had brought both Finn and the bounty hunter to this moment. In a world of "us" and "them," the lines of safety and inclusion were becoming muddy. Terrible things were happening. And rather than band together, the human, vampire and the werewolf inhabitants pulled even further apart, the vampires escaping into their old-world opulence and endless luxuries atop skyscrapers in the highest strata of the city, the werewolves burying themselves in a technological wonderland in the strata belowground, and the humans locking themselves indoors at street level.

Of course, maybe they were smart to do that. Urban unrest was the least of what Crimson City's citizens had to fear. There were also the demons who had broken through from Orcus to launch an offensive on the city. It had taken three government agencies to put it down, and not before a hell of a lot destruction had been wreaked.

How, in the middle of a problem of that magnitude, anybody could care about one failed experiment like him was hard to understand. But they did care.

A sudden weight came down on Finn's back as the bounty hunter knelt on top of him. Good. Now the man was close enough for him to do something about it.

"Hello? Can you understand me? I said, take off your glove or I'll put a bullet in your head."

"I can't move," Finn pointed out.

The bounty hunter shifted a bit, freeing up Finn's right hand. Finn squeezed his eyes shut, working to control his anger, and brought his hand to his mouth to pull the leather glove off using his teeth.

The bounty hunter grabbed him by the wrist. There was a silence. Then: "Holy shit. Holy *shit*! That's what I thought I saw. You *are* the one."

The hunter pressed Finn's arm back down on the ground above his head. Finn squeezed his eyes shut, working to master his rage. He didn't want to do it. He always gave them an out. Maybe this time, the guy would take it. "I'm going to beg here, okay? Please. Please, let me go. You've made a mistake. I don't know what you think you see, but you've made a mistake."

The hunter leaned over him, his mouth up to Finn's ear. "You're the biggest score in town. You're the Holy Grail. Do you even know how much you're worth?"

Finn frowned. He hadn't heard anything about that.

"Ops just increased the reward money. Those guys still want you, man. After all, you're what started this mess, yeah?"

They started this mess. I just couldn't stop it. But nobody controls me anymore. Nobody. "I'm a human being like you. Have a little mercy."

"I wouldn't know exactly what to call you, but you're definitely not human."

Finn's temperature instantly spiked, and wrath swept through him unfettered. "Son of a *bitch*. I *am* human."

The hunter snatched the hood off Finn's face, grabbed him by the hair and wrenched his head back, then ran the muzzle of an automatic weapon across the thin metal at Finn's temple. "My god." A greedy laugh burst from his mouth. "No dice, metal man. You're going down, and I'm the one who gets to take you."

With faster-than-normal-human reaction time, Finn whipped out his left arm, grabbed the hunter's ankle and pulled the man's feet out from under him. The hunter yelled in terror, releasing an arc of bullets into the air as he lost control and was slammed back down to the pavement. Finn rolled to one side of the alley; the hunter rolled the opposite way. Each man stared at the other as the shower of metal slugs rained down between them. As the last slug hit the ground, the two men sprang forward, the hunter going for his weapon, Finn going for the hunter and slamming the man's face into the cement.

"We're in a serious bind here, you and I," Finn said. His foe's chest heaved with big, uneven gulps of air. "Who told you about me? Who knows?"

"It's just me."

Finn slammed the man's face down into the pavement again. "I'll ask once more. Who told you about me?" He pulled the hunter's face back up off the ground. Blood was streaming from the man's nose and lip.

"It's just me! I'm working with someone, but they just know they want the mech that killed those vampire leaders, the Dumonts. They don't know who you are. I swear. I didn't say who you were. It's the only way I could guarantee they wouldn't take the job themselves. Dude, you gotta believe me. I swear I'll forget the whole thing if you let me go. I swear it!"

Finn gently pushed down the hunter's face and tightened his grip around the man's neck. "How do you know about me?"

"A month ago I was tailing this guy. Another freelance jobber," the bounty hunter confessed in a panicked rush. "He was on a job. He *was* my job. And, get this, you were in the mix. It was a fucking car wreck, with a three-way-intersection cat-and-mouse."

"Try making some sense."

"You hit him before I did the same thing. I watched you do it. And it was weird. The weapons you used . . . Dude, that thing came right out of your arm—I'd bet on it."

Finn swore. "Who sent you?"

"Does it matter?" the man gasped. "Everybody in

this town would kill for a piece of your bounty money. Kill or be killed, that's life in Crimson City, man."

"You're right," Finn said. *I can't let you go*. He stared into the bounty hunter's eyes.

Under the crush of Finn's grip, the man's eyes widened, and then suddenly his whole body relaxed, as if he were making a choice. He knew.

"What do you prefer?" Finn asked softly.

"A bullet," the man said, his voice cracking.

Finn raised his arm, then hesitated. "Like you said, it's kill or be killed. I'm sorry."

The hunter's lip curled. "You can't be sorry. You're not human."

The words themselves pulled the trigger. From the weaponry fused into the flesh of his forearm, Finn let the bullet fly, his aim true. The blast echoed down the alley. After a moment, Finn raised the back of his hand to his mouth, pressing the metal against his lips as he stared at the corpse at his feet. Leaning down, he gently swept a palm over the man's face, closing the eyes and then folding the arms over the chest.

"Yes," he replied. "I *am*."

Chapter Two

As the room seemed to spin around her, Cyd Brighton looked into pale green demon eyes and fell backward onto the bed.

Promises, promises, she thought grimly, pushing against Griff-Vai's shoulders with her fists. She should never have given in to him that first time. *You'll make everything better? Bullshit.*

"I said no," she spat out.

"I'll make everything better," Griff-Vai murmured, burying his face in her neck. "Just give in. Like you did before. Tell me you didn't enjoy that."

While it lasted. Sure. Before she'd realized that messing with her body equated to messing with her mind.

"Get. Off." Cyd stuck the sole of her foot against the muscled ridges of his abdomen and pushed as hard as she could, turning her face away from his and toward the window framed by shining panels of ornately embroidered silk. The midnight blue sky and the strange red-tinted moon served as a constant reminder of this strange exile she was living.

The cold desire Griff-Vai could evoke crept over her limbs, her body again begging her to surrender. She fought him that much harder. He was always persuasive, but she knew what it all meant in the end. The way demons like Griff bent and shaped reality . . . a mere human couldn't take it for long without something changing inside.

He'd made it clear what he wanted. He'd made it clear what he was about. He'd revealed that what he was doing to her mind was work he'd begun from afar, when she was still in Crimson City and going downhill fast. Before she'd been kidnapped. Before . . .

Griff-Vai had been watching her since the day her Ops team first summoned demons. He'd waited until she was at her weakest, and then in a whirl of glass and blood, had stolen her away from that phone booth in Crimson City, leaving only a mystery for her friends. He'd brought her through the veil to the demon underworld . . . to be his mate. All that studying, all the waiting had paid off. He knew her well, his arguments were persuasive, and even now, as Griff-Vai kissed her with a dark hunger, she was actually still tempted. But not enough.

Cyd struggled against him as she'd done ever since making the mistake of giving in the first two times. Squirming, she freed one arm, flailing out ineffectively as Griff-Vai caressed her body and she started to give in. The first time she'd surrendered, he'd promised her she'd never be alone again, that she could lean on him. But when she awoke in the cold morning alone and still a prisoner in a strange world, she had cringed with shame and fear. They were just words. Words he'd known from watching her that she would want to hear.

The second time he'd come to her, she'd resisted, and he'd said he loved her. She fell for it, of course—but in the morning she knew it was as much a lie as the words had ever been. Perhaps he wanted to believe them, but his was a cold desire. He'd chosen her to replace someone he'd lost. He might want to believe he loved her, but he didn't. And he didn't act consistently as if it were true. And that made him all the more dangerous. Because she knew he would do his damnedest to convince them both.

Oh, how he tried. He'd come to her again and again with his gorgeous, fake words and deceptively silken touch. He'd found she wouldn't be persuaded, would lose his temper and resort to the kind of violence that lived deep within his soul. And when she didn't respond to his words or his fists, he'd tried for her mind. He'd put thoughts into her head, tried to control her, tried to get her to come to terms with being his prisoner for eternity. But it never worked for long. Eventually she would always see through his lies.

Cyd knew that the only way she could ever get away from him would be to make him understand that she wasn't the one for him. And as he pressed his greedy mouth against her throat, she could only hope that the strange, frightening bond he'd forged between them with his mind and touch would die along with his desire.

"Cydney," he tried again. "We are perfect for each other. You belong to me."

She'd only just curled her hand into a fist to give him the answer he deserved when she was pressed flat against the bed in a surge of energy even more powerful than the bond Griff-Vai had worked so hard to forge between them. In the center of the burst of light in her mind's eye stood a man holding something in his hands—a disk swinging from a chain, like some kind of amulet.

The power he generated clearly pained him; the man

looked unable to maintain control. At his feet was a woman who looked to be dying.

Cyd stopped struggling, staring into thin air as the vision filled her head. Her heart was suddenly racing with terror. *That's Crimson City. They're back in Crimson City.*

"Shhh," Griff-Vai said, moving over her, mistaking her stillness for acquiescence.

"Get. Off. Me!" Cyd yelled to Griff-Vai as the stranger in her vision threw back his head in agony.

Griff responded with a nasty backhand to the side of her face. The pain of the blow couldn't distract her. She blinked away her tears and focused on the vision.

Griff-Vai raised himself off of her, and she and the demon stared at each other, gasping for air, Cyd wide-eyed and full of adrenaline. "Stop it," she snarled through gritted teeth. "Stop making me see things that aren't there!"

Griff-Vai blinked uncertainly, his eyes flickering between their glowing-red state and the palest green. "I didn't send anything to you."

She looked at him, pure and bitter hatred filling her. Swinging out, she missed him completely, but as he grabbed her by the wrists and easily trapped her arms above her head, the room suddenly flooded with blue light.

"No," Griff-Vai said. He looked up and out through the window. The view was gone, light pouring in. It blinded both of them. The vision came closer. "Not now. Not again," Griff cried out. "It's closing."

For the first time in a very long time, Cyd felt hope.

"Look at me," Griff-Vai said, his desperation giving itself away. Cyd could sense the real world close at hand, as close as she'd felt it since arriving here in the demon underworld. And with every bit of strength she had, she reached out into the energy and lunged for the one thing she could touch: the amulet.

Grabbing the chain with both hands, the entire weight of her body suspended from what seemed like the thinnest of strands. The man who held the amulet reacted to the weight. *I'm the Draig-Uisge. Let go, so I can fulfill my duty*. The energy dimmed for a moment, blue fading to white and back again. Cyd realized this was the opening of a portal between the two worlds.

Griff-Vai understood what she wanted. "If you leave me, I will seek to bring you back. You belong to me. It is because of me that you were ever spared." He tried to lock eyes with her, but Cyd wouldn't look. She held on to the chain for her life, knowing that her old existence was within reach. If only she could get there.

Holding on to the amulet chain with all of her strength, Cyd felt the moment Griff-Vai began to surrender. The air around her became lighter; the amulet itself came into focus. Cyd saw Griff's face as he watched the amulet gain detail. He looked shocked, greedy. He knew what it was. Even if she didn't, she knew it could lead her to freedom.

They exchanged a look one last time; then, suddenly, Griff-Vai reached out and pressed the amulet against her forehead, intoning some kind of oath in a foreign tongue.

Cyd screamed as the disc burned into her flesh. The demon grabbed her by the back of her neck, pressed his own forehead against the amulet so that it was between them, and then crushed his mouth down on hers in a cruel kiss. Finally pulling away, he held her face tightly between his palms.

"Don't think you've escaped forever," he said. "I

won't let you go. I brought you here once, and I can do it again. We may not be bound in the traditional sense, but we are bound together in my eyes nonetheless."

Cyd couldn't speak. She looked up at where the ceiling had vanished in a blue light. She closed her eyes and held on to the amulet chain with all of her strength. Griff-Vai cried out in anguish.

Terrified, Cyd felt her body burst through the veiled energy field. It was as if the glow formed a perfect barrier, with a single slim tear where she'd broken through. Pure white light slammed through her, as if she'd hit a brick wall, and she opened her eyes to find that she was falling, hurtling face-first toward pavement. She remembered to curl her body and take the fall on a roll. She tucked her head and took the impact shoulder to back, agilely leaping back to her feet, then stumbling over two bodies on the ground.

She thought one of them tried to grab her, to swipe the object in her hand, so when she regained her balance seconds later, she accelerated to a full-out sprint and ran like goddamn banshee-hellfire, not daring to look or absorb or think.

A moment later, her shoes hit new turf, and the unexpected change threw her completely off her feet. Legs and arms flailing, she sprawled headfirst into the ground. This time when she took the roll, she didn't get up.

Adrenaline washed over her in waves, and she stayed curled for some time after impact, her eyes squeezed shut. Her palm burned as though it were on fire. *I'll count to ten and open my eyes, and when I do, I'll be home.* A million times in the demon world she'd tried this childish trick; a million times she'd been disappointed.

A long twenty seconds ticked by. With her eyes still closed and her body tense, Cyd's quieted senses detected the total and complete change of atmosphere from where she'd just been. The acrid tar smell of hot pavement mingled with the organic freshness of . . . grass and flowers? A car was honking in the distance, and she heard the sound of a couple of kids laughing and kicking a metal can.

Slowly, Cyd unfurled her body and sat up, then staggered to her feet and ran shaking hands down her body. *I'm still wearing clothes. That's a bonus. I'm still intact, from a bodily point of view. I won't go into my mental state, particularly since I'm talking to myself again.* And, she noted with surprise, she was somehow wearing the same clothes she'd had on, when the demons came for her in the first place.

Looking around, she could see that she'd landed on a street corner on the edge of a sidewalk in a patch of ungroomed city grass.

The intersection was Jackson and Troubadour. Smack-dab in the middle of The Triangle. Cyd started to laugh, quietly at first; then she lost control of her emotions for a moment, practically crying as she realized where she was.

This was Crimson City. For better or worse, she was home.

As if someone were listening to her innermost thoughts, the pain in her palm started to burn brighter. Cyd looked down and found her fingers wrapped so tightly around a disc-shaped object, that it had imprinted a welt into her hand. She relaxed her grip and examined the piece.

The amulet was a thin carved disc, around which appeared some sort of sculpted ivy. In the disc's center was a raised crystal dome filled with red-black liquid. Cyd stared at the unfamiliar piece. Griff-Vai had recognized its power, even if she didn't.

She tucked the amulet away, keeping her hand on it inside her pocket, the thought of Griff-Vai sending a bolt of paranoia through her. She looked around wildly, expecting the demon to come for her at any moment.

Something cold curled around her heart as she processed what had just happened. She ran her fingers over her forehead, where the amulet had been pressed. Nothing but grass and dirt. She took a few deep breaths and tried to shake the woolly feeling from her head, where a dull pain thudded in a slow, periodic beat.

Suddenly desperate for something familiar and safe, Cyd started to walk. But even what should have been familiar wasn't quite the same. Large chunks of a freeway overpass lay crumbling at street level; burned-out storefronts and shallow craters spoke of military action. And a line of posters where the movies used to be advertised hung from a shiny new chain-link fence. White paper, red block print: QUARANTINE.

Cyd's exhalation of breath came in a fast huff. The sign didn't show any symbol for chemical or biological warfare, but "quarantine"—with or without explanation—wasn't the kind of word one wanted to hang around and analyze for too long. Something major had happened to her city while she'd been gone. Then again, something major had also happened to her.

The area called The Triangle had been her old partner's neighborhood, and the idea of seeing a friendly face was irresistible. Dain. A couple of lefts and a right put her on his block, and with a beating heart she picked up the pace until she was standing in front of his old apartment.

Except he wasn't there. No one was there. Nothing but a shredded FOR-RENT sign hanging askew off the door remained to greet her. She took the front stairs two at a time, then climbed along the dilapidated latticework trellis to peek through the side window.

The apartment was completely stripped. She winced at the emptiness, forced herself not to think about what might have become of him in her absence, then became incredibly angry with herself for running straight to the nearest man for help. She jumped from the lattice to the ground below and kept walking, shivering in her skin despite the temperate weather.

For god's sake, Cyd, don't you ever learn? Fix yourself. Two things. How long have you been gone, and what the hell are you going to do to get on your feet? She walked to the corner and stuck her hand into a green metal city garbage receptacle, tossing aside some fast-food wrappers and soda cans to reach a newspaper.

Her eye moved from the date to a secondary headline that screamed out in rage against the rogues: MORE GANG TROUBLE IN LA-LA-LAND. The rogues. That had once meant vampires—vampires who'd been "made" from humans instead of procreated; who were dangerously unpredictable. That was why the primary vampire leadership had banned such practice. Now it seemed Rogues were a group of vampires, werewolves *and* humans who'd refused to join with the leadership of their respective species. It seemed this rag-tag team of dissenters was finally taking advantage of the power in numbers.

The words blurred before her eyes. She'd buy a

new paper later; she couldn't even focus on the story if she wanted to. Cyd tossed the tabloid back as if it burned. She'd been gone for months. Months, stolen from her life.

Something brushed against her cheek, and she flinched, flailing wildly at her face with her hands before she realized it was just a scrap of paper blown up by the wind.

Now what are you going to do? Cyd started toward her old neighborhood, feeling its pull. She headed through the almost-empty streets, climbed a chain-link fence and dropped to the sidewalk on the other side. The sounds of sirens and yelling in the distance grew louder, and Cyd felt the pull even more. Walking faster, now jogging, she went down the familiar side streets and turned the corner toward the place she once called home.

Sticking her hands in her pockets, she went up to the window. The amulet heated her hand inside her jacket. A woman was in her old kitchen. A man came up behind the woman to plant a kiss on her cheek. Real things like a toaster and a blender were on the counter; real food, like lettuce and tomatoes, was on the cutting board. Her old apartment—rented to a new family and a new life. It was about as far from what she'd had in that place as you could get. Cyd backed away from the window and stood helplessly on the sidewalk.

What would she do? Go find her old partner, Dain? Go to her old team at B-Ops? Go to D-Alley and beg for an advance on something to numb the pain? Go fall at someone's feet and beg them for help? Go find a guy who would promise to fix everything?

Not this time.

Cyd wandered aimlessly down the pavement, away from her old neighborhood, ruminating on the past. When Griff-Vai had stolen her away from Crimson City that day, after he'd explained how he'd been watching, waiting for her, she'd asked him why he'd taken her when he did. "Why now?" she'd asked.

He'd answered, "You were at your weakest."

You were at your weakest. He couldn't have known how those words burned. Because they were the truth. She'd lost control of her world, pretty much: She'd leaned on Dain, her partner in the B-Ops division, to get her through the night shift, and used pop-drugs to get her through the rest. And every morning as she'd woken up in Orcus, a stranger in a strange land, she'd thought of Griff-Vai's words and blamed herself for giving the demon the opportunity.

She remembered the first moment she saw him: The demon turning to look at her through the double-sided glass. At first she'd thought he couldn't see her. He hadn't been with the group of demons who first came through, the murderers; he'd stared through the portal into the room. But with the crushed bodies of her coworkers at his feet on the other side of the glass, it was as if he was telling her she was next.

She'd lived in fear from that time, fleeing the research lab, the job, living life by the day, dreaming of that night and desperately trying to think of a way to forget. She couldn't forget. And apparently Griff-Vai hadn't forgotten either. He'd waited all that time for the right moment to bring her to him. He couldn't pass through the veil between worlds, so he'd watched. And he'd waited. And the unnerving sense of being followed by something dark and angry that never went away had burst forth now and again to scare the hell of Cyd so badly she had to call Dain on the phone to come over and sit with her.

It turned out, he *was* following her. Griff-Vai had had a mate once, a perfect bond the demons called a vishtau. A young, innocent human female—like the girl Cyd had been once.

But Griff-Vai's vishtau had died. And he saw Cyd as an ideal replacement. Except this time he'd chosen to wait for her innocence to change into something much darker, something that he believed could stand life with him in the underworld. And she knew he would do what he could to get her back to that dark place.

"Why me?" she'd asked.

"You know why." His voice had been almost comforting, his eyes not unkind.

"Is it because I saw? I never told a soul about what happened when I-Ops summoned those demons. I kept the secrets."

He stroked her face. "I knew you were perfect for me the first time I saw you through the veil. So fresh, so beautiful. And most of all . . . so innocent. You weren't there in that room. You were watching through the glass in your booth. You saw the others die.

"I watched your eyes the entire time. And as it unfolded, as you witnessed your nightmare unfurl, I watched something in you change. I think I saw the very moment when your innocence slipped away."

He caressed her chin. "One moment, you'd hardly seen anything in your lifetime. In the next, you'd already seen too much. The fear, the anger . . . the passion. It was almost as if there was demon in you from the moment you were born. I watched you turn inward—lose your mind a little, even. I watched you corrupt yourself. Remember that: You corrupted yourself. We didn't have to do it for you."

Griff-Vai, physically absent and yet very much present, kissed her neck, and Cyd turned her head away. It all fit the pattern of her life.

Why did she always give yourself to them? The men in her life. The ones who'd been there for years, the ones who lasted only a night. She let them take control; she let them be the heroes. Whether human, vampire, werewolf . . . even demon. They picked her up off the floor when she thought she couldn't do it herself. And she let them take control. She always let them explain what she had to do, explain how to get by. She didn't want to get by. And she didn't want to listen to anyone else anymore.

Whatever she wanted . . . it wasn't this. She didn't want to give herself back to a demon bent on possessing her body and soul, especially not for just another promise that he'd take care of things for her—not when what he really meant was that he'd control things for her.

Some days in Orcus, she'd felt as if she was losing her mind. She'd screamed and cowered on the ground, once again that same little girl of her past, shuttled from place to place, waiting for someone to take care of her and finding out that, just when she thought she'd got what she'd been asking for, it was a mirage. There was no love there. There was no love anywhere. It was all lies and false promises. Never anything like love.

Someone else's home, someone else's world. She'd rather be alone in the slums of Crimson City than in the most opulent palace in the demon underworld with a monster who had no true feeling for her. Who had done the things she'd seen him do.

You belong *to me.*

Pure fear leached into her bones as she heard Griff-

Vai's voice in her head. After walking a few more blocks at normal pace, still desperate for comfort, for the familiar, Cyd couldn't handle her fear anymore and finally just broke into a run.

Chapter Three

JB McCall was fried. Completely, totally fried. These days, all the shifts in B-Ops felt like doubles. Supposedly nothing had changed. That was how they were instructed to feel. *Instructed* to feel. He managed a wounded chuckle as he waited, slumped in the guest chair in the boss's office.

He and his partner, Trask, were the senior members of the team now, which said a lot. Too many people gone. But at least the new boss was cool; he'd basically ordered everyone to attend regular psych sessions—to avoid the whole stigma issue if anyone actually wanted to go but didn't want to stand out.

JB leaned over, stuck his elbows on the desk and put his face in his hands. He'd asked for this, of course. Government Operations—"Ops"—included I-Ops and B-Ops, and together the divisions were a blend of every law enforcement agency there was. If you wanted to hide behind secured walls, you went with I-Ops. But B-Ops . . . well, the real action happened here. This wasn't just some camera-ready front for deskwork. The thing was, at some point, when policing a city for paranormal crime became more of a war effort, a smart guy took the opportunity to rethink things.

So he'd been rethinking things. In between killing perps, destroying property in at-gunpoint searches and sacrificing informants to the promise of a better future, he'd definitely been rethinking things. Maybe it was because Trask was so extreme. A true glory boy. In comparison, JB felt like a total pussy. Trask said he was one.

At least he had the satisfaction of knowing he'd been right about former operative Dain Reston being a decent guy to the end. Now, months later, after those demons had gone shitfire all over the city, he'd seen enough to know that his instincts had been damn good. He'd been right to let Dain escape.

Lines were blurring and alliances shifting. The werewolves and vampires didn't hate each other anymore. Well, they didn't fight anymore. And there'd been rumors that a group had worked together against the demons. Of course, for Crimson City's human government, the softening of boundaries was reason for more fear, more instability, not more peace.

Only the rogues were seen to intermingle without concern, and as a result, the power of those multi-species groups was increasing. Where once JB had been seeing action involving one, two, or three individuals, fully formed rogue teams were fast on their way to becoming the norm. He didn't know what the primary vampires and werewolves might say about that, but it was a scary time to be a human.

Not that he was complaining about his job, exactly. Inside B-Ops, with its unlimited supply of weapons and his pretty powerful ID, JB at least didn't feel as though he was going to die at any moment. For a while there, the city had gone insane. There were the demon battles, and the levels of paranoia everywhere were at an all-time high—so bad that the police department had to ask for backup on 911 calls. Their lines had been swamped by freaked-out citizens convinced that the butcher they'd been buying their T-bones from for the past decade was possessed, just because he owned too many knives.

No, B-Ops teams weren't just tactical squads anymore. They were the police, military, animal rescue, psychiatrists and Zen practitioners of the streets. Well, that was JB's view of things. He'd seen this as an opportunity to do good. Trask took the alternate approach. Instead of getting warmer, he'd just seemed to get colder. But either way, the job was draining. You had to expend a hell of a lot of energy to maintain the image that you weren't the least bit scared, and that's what Crimson City's citizens needed to believe of their B-Ops operatives in order to stay calm.

JB had lost a little faith, though. The people he worked with weren't even the same. Most of the old squad was dead, in rehab or a completely different species. And, if he was honest, his partner was the dictionary definition of a loose cannon.

"What do we know? Any intel coming in?" the boss asked, entering the office and closing the door behind him.

JB shook his head. "Just the one preliminary message. The informant swears it's her."

"Was she in town somewhere all this time?"

"I think the question might better be, was she in this *world* somewhere?"

They exchanged knowing glances. "Demon?" the boss asked.

JB shrugged. "Sir, I really don't know."

"And she hasn't called in?"

"No."

The boss sighed and ran his finger over the time stamp on JB's report.

"I got the intel this morning and filed that paper just after," JB said.

"If it's her, she gets twenty-two more hours to call in."

JB reflexively looked up at the digital wall clock. "She was there at the beginning, you know. When we first made contact with the demons."

The boss nodded. "So I was given to understand. Did she ally with them? Were there any rumors about her becoming compromised?"

JB exhaled slowly. "That's not what we thought then. If anything, we thought she'd seen something that made her not want to have anything to do with I-Ops, paranormal research, demon stuff or any of that. From what I saw, she wished she'd never seen or heard a damn thing."

"Do you think it was an act? Was there any talk of her being a demon agent?"

JB shook his head with a laugh. "We wouldn't have even known what that was then. But no, I honestly don't think it was an act. Not Cyd."

The boss studied JB's face. "Did she ever tell you what she saw?"

"No. I don't even think she told Reston, her old partner. Look, boss, I'm not going to say she was a sweetheart, exactly. And everybody knows she wasn't 'clean.' But I will tell you that I think her fear was on the level. The word in the squad was that what happened to her in I-Ops was real, that the rest of her team were iced, and that the incident had freaked her the hell out.

Other than that, all I know is that she was good at her job and the informants trusted her—she got the goods and she was fair with them."

The boss frowned and looked out his window. "This is a tough call. She's the only member of that research team left. She was there at the beginning, and maybe she can help us get things back to normal. It's either a hell of a coincidence, given the problems we've had with those demon agents . . . or it's no coincidence at all. If she's been compromised, we have to take her out. We can't afford to hope for the best anymore—we've got to start anticipating the worst."

JB was as scared as anyone of the demon agent infiltration the two Ops divisions had been experiencing, but something about this stuck in his craw. This was someone he'd known as a team member. This was someone who'd watched his back in the field more than a few times. "I vote for assuming the best for as long as we can. If there's even a chance Cyd can help us make sure all the demons are gone—and if not . . . man, I don't know, help us get rid of them once and for all—god, I think we should take it," he said softly.

The boss shrugged. "Well, if she calls in, we'll bring her inside and put her to work, and I'll have someone keep an eye on her in case we've guessed wrong. Bridget Rothschild is still doing half days at I-Ops. We'll make her Cyd's admin."

JB had to laugh. "I seriously doubt Cyd's ever had anybody working for her. Imagine—Cyd with an admin!"

"She hasn't called in yet, JB." The tone of his boss's voice wiped the smile off JB's face. "She hasn't called in. And we don't know where she's been. At best, that suggests she may be going rogue. At worst . . . she's taking sides with someone or something else. We'll give it a while, see what she does, and then I'll have to make a call." He lasered a stare at JB. "And you'll have to follow orders."

JB looked out the window. *No way. No effing way I am putting a bit on one of my own team.*

"Operative McCall!"

The intensity of the boss's voice caught him by surprise. "Yes, sir?"

"I said you'll have to follow orders. You've seen what the demon double agents are capable of doing."

"Yes, sir. I understand," he replied.

"Let's keep the paper trail down. I'll send you an e-order on it one way or the other." The boss wheeled around in his chair and began attending to a stack of files.

JB stared at the man's back, then shifted his gaze to the computer monitor displaying Cyd's case file. He reached over and pressed the photo-album icon. The first picture was Cyd from before she disappeared, looking grim and tired, grown old before her time.

JB clicked to the text files and, not surprisingly, didn't find much he was classified to access. Just the short, euphemism-laden, coded blurb about her time in Paranormal R & D over at I-Ops before she'd transferred to the Battlefield-Ops teams.

"I'm out of here, boss." JB grabbed his helmet and left, closing the door behind him as he stepped out into the hall. He collided with his partner, Trask Spalding.

"Damn," Trask said. "Sorry."

"My bad." JB looked at the jacket in his partner's hand. "Going somewhere? Am I coming?"

"Um, I've got a thing."

JB nodded. "A thing. Okay." He wasn't going to argue. He wasn't going to nag. It was bullshit to walk out on your partner without letting him know, but Trask not only marched to the beat of his own drummer, he generally acted as though he were the only one marching at all. "The boss asked me about Cyd. Do you think it's really her this time?" They'd had quite a few dead-end leads about Cyd Brighton's potential whereabouts, all from lying informants trying to score a quick buck.

"What, you worried she'll want her old job back?"

Cyd as squad leader? "She can have it," JB muttered, leaning against the wall. "I'm exhausted."

"Oh, buck up. Maybe we'll get to shoot something today. It's been at least two days without a kill. I think I'm going into withdrawal or sumpin'." Trask grinned.

"Shut up, man. Just shut up. Don't you ever just shut up with the commando shit?"

Trask frowned. "You're jaded."

"At least I try to ask questions first, shoot later," JB snapped.

A muscle in Trask's jaw twitched. "You have a problem with the way I do business?"

JB shook his head. "It's just . . ." He rubbed his eyes and tried to relax, to simply ignore his partner. The city had gone crazy. He wasn't really sure what was what anymore. A lot of the guys were like Trask, had built defense mechanisms that basically established an us-and-them; and as long as you were working for the us against them, you were allowed to feel good about everything.

But that was a simpleton's version of reality. Everything was gray. One of his old teammates, the senior team leader for that matter, was a freaking vampire now, and JB didn't believe that made him any more good or evil than he'd been before. And since JB had taken Cyd's place, working primarily with the werewolves, he wasn't so sure that the dogs were so very different from humans, either.

The demons, of course, were another story. JB didn't have any reason to believe any good could come out of them. Not after the destruction they'd caused and the nightmare both Ops programs had gone through with their infiltration. And certainly not after Cyd had disappeared. Make that after Cyd had *been* disappeared.

Those who knew about Cyd's background had hardly been shocked when she vanished. Especially not when the demons next came into the city. Everyone in B-Ops and I-Ops eventually agreed it was the demons who'd done it, though they'd encouraged speculation that it could have been something else, like the fangs or the dogs.

But everyone had figured she was dead. The fact that she wasn't required an explanation. Or she would end up dead after all.

JB wanted to talk to Dain about it, but his old team leader was pretty much persona non grata in Ops these days and frequenting the same downtown corner market was as close as JB dared get. Sometimes they exchanged ideas in the cereal aisle, but things in the city had been just too unhinged for JB to risk his career trying to keep up the friendship. Not with someone now AWOL from both Ops and the human race.

JB sighed and waved everything off. "Never mind." He would have liked to talk about a whole lot of this stuff, but Trask wasn't the kind of partner with whom JB felt comfortable doing that. They were supposed to be a team. They were supposed to have a partnership based on mutual trust and respect. Unfortunately they really couldn't stand each other.

JB missed Dain and Cyd. Those two had been a couple of crazy bastards in their own ways, but they'd been good family. In this line of work, you had to be with people like that. Most of the time, your coworkers were the only family you got.

"Well, gotta run," Trask said. He headed off, then wheeled around, tossing his jacket over his shoulder. "I was going to call you. I swear. Let me know if we get a go-code." Giving JB a thumbs-up, he disappeared around the corner.

There was nothing to do but shake his head and let his partner go do his thing. JB stared down at the file in his hand. He had bigger things to worry about.

And so did Cydney Brighton. *Call in, Cyd. We don't want to hurt you.*

Chapter Four

Something interesting never failed to happen on a Friday night in the underground scene, and there were still plenty of hours left to go. Finn stared out into the blur of activity in Bosco's from the depths of his jacket hood. Watching. Waiting. He'd secured his customary booth next to the fireplace, which was never on and which probably hadn't worked for some time; but the number of bodies packed into the bar made the fireplace irrelevant anyway. He was sitting against the wall, of course, at the very end of the row.

Finn tugged the edge of his hood down a bit as a couple of guys passed his booth and took a seat in front of him. He knew the face of every regular, and, by paying, he found out about the ones who weren't regular. He also made sure that no one managed to find out much about him, and he had tried to kill any temptation to research him by carefully cultivating a reputation. As far as anyone knew, he was just a guy known for dispatching such jobs quickly and efficiently, and with deadly force.

No, no one wanted to piss off a guy who they might want to hire, and no one wanted to piss off a guy who would kill without remorse. Which wasn't precisely true, of course—the most recent death of that bounty hunter still darkened Finn's thoughts. But it was best this way. There were enough fugitives down here who didn't want to be found that Finn's habit of interacting with as few people as possible seemed reasonably normal.

He stuck to a routine that involved being indoors as much as possible, and he stuck to a few regular haunts for needed supplies and changes of scenery. Being very good at executing his jobs quickly and blending back into the bleak landscape of the city, Finn had managed to live in relative calm, mostly undetected alongside the shadier denizens of Crimson City.

He'd come to a kind of arrangement with Bosco up there behind the bar. There was a big tab system down here in the underground, once you'd proved you were good for the money. Paychecks were unpredictable, so barter was common. Most of the proprietors of whatever goods or services he wanted had let him open a tab—a *reasonable* tab.

Honor among thieves. Finn liked that. He liked the idea that good and evil could live in concert inside one person. He wasn't sure he really believed it; he wasn't sure anyone did. But it was a comforting thought that gave him hope. And without hope, he might as well just accept his fate and go back to B-Ops. That, he wasn't prepared to do.

Finn took another sip of whiskey and savored the smoky-sweet burn of the alcohol as it slid over his tongue. Eyes on the door, he waited. Friday night, party night. It never failed.

White plaster rained down on the scuffed flooring as the door was flung open. It slipped the hinge and crashed into the wall behind it. The attachment had dropped a couple of tiny nails sometime in the previous year, but since Bosco had negotiated for an alarmed iron gate that he slid down over the storefront at closing time, fixing the door apparently hadn't become a priority.

The door bounced back, shivering loudly, revealing a huge wound in the wall. But Bosco didn't seem too concerned about that. His hands, wrapped in a bar towel, had stilled on the highball glass he was washing, and the entire bar went silent as a new character stepped over the threshold.

Finn's adrenaline surged. Not a pair of jacked-up junkies. Not a desperate machine gun–wielding fugitive. Not even a suspected fang. It was just a girl. His interest turned more serious as she practically lunged into the middle of the bar, her brown eyes open wide and giving everyone a hard look that defied them to suggest she was even capable of being afraid. He could see that something had scared the piss out of her.

She held her arms up and out, every fiber of her body clearly ready to either attack or defend—it wasn't obvious exactly where her intentions stood on that score. Her chest heaved, a veil of sweat covering her exposed arms and face. Her dark hair was restrained in a limp, messy ponytail. She was dirty, covered in scrapes and cuts and bruises, and she reminded him of a wild animal that had stumbled into civilization. Finn knew something of what that was like. Intrigued, he catalogued every last detail of her as she turned and headed unsteadily toward Bosco, who slowly put down the glass he was washing and reached under the counter.

As the girl turned, Finn saw what she was wearing: a

thrashed, sleeveless, standard-issue military T-shirt, and cargo pants with a B-Ops imprint and serial number stenciled on one cuff. It took his breath away.

Clumsily, he set down his shot glass, sloshing a bit over the side, moved to wipe it up and noticed he'd shredded the bar napkin all over the tabletop. Smashing the shreds back into a ball, Finn soaked up the spill and tossed it into the ashtray, trying to force himself to relax.

She's just a girl. With a possible link to B-Ops, yes. But even so, B-Ops alone might not be enough to help him.

At the bar, Bosco took charge. He pulled an enormous weapon from underneath the counter and laid it where the girl could see. Almost as if obeying a signal, other people around the room cocked their weapons. Knives, guns, Tasers—a little bit of everything found its way out from boots and under jackets and back pockets in a quiet rustle of metal against fabric. The girl had to realize that Bosco could blow her away on the spot and not one person in the room would claim it was anything but self-defense.

The suddenly visible arsenal didn't seem to faze her. The girl stumbled over to the bar and leaned toward Bosco, who stuck the muzzle of his gun against her throat and pushed her back.

"Where you been, Cyd?" he asked. It was more of an accusation than a question.

Finn could only see the back of her now, but the girl didn't answer. Cyd. Cydney. The name seemed vaguely familiar, but he had no context for it.

"I asked where you been," Bosco growled.

Cyd swallowed and seemed to gain a little composure. She was still on edge, but it clearly wasn't the weapons, wasn't Bosco. She kept looking over her shoulder at the door, at the streetlights from outside glaring full force through the door frame. Wherever she'd been, it was apparently more unnerving than here.

In the eerie silence and faintly swirling dust, the girl put her palms flat on the counter, Bosco's gun still at her throat, and pushed forward so that the muzzle bored into her flesh.

"I have absolutely no fucking idea where I've been," she rasped, her smoky voice edged with forced bravado. "But I know I need a drink."

Bosco didn't move.

"A drink. A very large, stiff drink," she repeated.

With his free hand, the bartender ran an index finger down the bridge of his nose and considered the request.

A muscle in the girl's jaw rippled. "I've always covered my tab, Bosco."

"That was when you had a tab." Bosco kept his eyes trained on the girl's face, and one hand on his gun. His free hand reached for the steaming plate of steak and fries he'd just served to the guy propped on the bar stool next to her. He slid the food over in front of her, picked up a knife and fork and jammed them down into the grizzled piece of meat. "Eat up."

She looked up at Bosco, then down at the plate.

"I told you to eat it," Bosco ordered.

Cyd apparently didn't need to be asked a third time. She pulled the fork and knife from the meat and started eating as if this was the first meal she'd had in a long while.

The quiet broke, whispers ramping up quickly to a

low-level buzz full of the sort of murmurs and whispers from which underground informants made their living. Finn watched the girl drop the knife, jam some french fries in her mouth, then pick up the steak with her left hand and start pulling the meat off with her teeth.

She stopped eating as abruptly as she'd begun, her cheeks bulging with food. Finn almost laughed as comprehension flooded her face. Bosco wasn't feeding her to be nice. He was feeding her to test her, thinking he might get some clues about what had happened to her. Many people still assumed vampires didn't eat. Of course, she was ripping into the steak like a dog.

Finn personally didn't care who was what, as long as they weren't trying to kill him. He couldn't afford to distrust anyone based on species alone. When you were pretty much the only one of your kind, you needed all the friends you could get.

Bosco's intentions seemed to have dawned on Cyd; she slowly dropped the steak back onto the plate and picked up her knife again, chewing almost defiantly in the bartender's face. "Figured it out yet?" she asked with her mouth still full.

Bosco thought about it, then finally put his gun away. Cyd's posture relaxed a little more. If the girl really had been gone for a while, she probably didn't realize that things were always this tense in mixed-species environments these days; Bosco's, even at this level of tension, was still the most relaxed environment around.

"This place used to be a lot more mellow," she said, looking over her shoulder at the other patrons of the bar. "I thought you were an equal-opportunity vendor."

"I'm still equal," he said. "I'll ride anybody who comes into my place just the same. So . . . you still human?" he asked.

Finn flinched, grateful all eyes were up front, on the girl. But she seemed to find the question as unsettling as he would have. "Since when does that matter here?"

"It doesn't. But I like to know who or what I'm dealing with. When allegiances change . . ."

She mumbled something Finn couldn't catch, and Bosco's eyes flashed as he retorted. "You'd better believe I'm paranoid." He put his left hand on the bar, the one lacking a pinkie finger. "I got stiffed the other day, and I'm still not sure what the hell did it."

Cyd looked stunned. "Shit. That looks bad. I'm sorry."

Bosco seemed surprised by the sympathy. He and the girl eyed each other for a moment, and then finally he shrugged. "Now, how about that drink? You look like you could use one," he said, tossing a shot glass into the air and deftly catching it.

The girl's entire body heaved as she took a deep breath and slowly exhaled. "Yeah."

Bosco poured her a shot and slid it over. "This is the last you'll get without coughing up some green. If you want to pay off your debts in my kitchen, that's good by me. I'm short on the graveyard shift. If you need a place . . . you can crash in the back until you get on your feet."

Cyd reached for the drink. "You know I'm good for it."

"I know you used to be," he grumbled.

The girl downed the drink with a snap of her wrist, and slapped the glass down on the bar with a broad smile.

Well, this was how everybody got their start in the underground. It was how Finn had managed. You gained a little bit of trust from one person, and used that voucher to gain trust from the next. Soon you were moving from an alley and one change of clothes to an apartment with a full closet. Soon the money from the jobs added up, you built a reputation and you didn't have to depend on anyone else anymore. You could hide away, become just another freelance guy with an arsenal to handle just about any job, and if you lay low enough, people forgot that they had ever questioned you. Discreet, secretive, and under-the-radar were all assets for those interested in hiring here, and they acted as a protective shield against those who might want something else.

Finn remembered running through the streets of the city with his lungs burning, his fingers splayed wide, almost paralyzed with horror at what he'd been forced to do. He'd shot two vampires at almost point-blank range, with a weapon buried in the flesh of his arm. He hadn't been able to do a thing about it.

In all fairness, it wasn't exactly *what* he'd done that horrified him; it was that he'd had no control over it. *No* control. Which should have been fine, because he shouldn't have known the difference one way or another. But after rappelling down a skyscraper from the vampire strata, when he hit the bottom he didn't automatically follow procedure.

No, even with angry vampires filling the sky, searching for him and revenge, he was somehow able to compartmentalize what he was supposed to do next and also see very clearly what his other options were. And once he'd seen his options, he'd made a choice.

He'd run. He'd run in very much the same way, it seemed, that this girl was running: with secrets about where she'd been and what she was running from that seemed to confuse even her.

That Bosco trusted her enough to let her hang around his place on a regular basis spoke volumes to everyone sitting in the bar. Cyd clearly knew that. She turned and leaned her back against the bar as Bosco poured a second shot, and Finn watched her stare back pointedly at the curious onlookers. The room rustled with noise as most of them quickly turned away.

Finn would normally have done the same, slipping far back into his dark corner and drawing as little notice as possible. But this time he didn't. Her possible connection to B-Ops had his attention. He was getting a little desperate, and desperation had the nasty effect of forcing you to take more risks than you might otherwise be inclined to. From within the protective edges of his hood, he stared right at her—and she caught him looking.

He saw a bleakness in her eyes before they narrowed defensively, and he turned away. Finn knew that blank, lonely look. He knew what it had the potential to conceal. He might as well have been looking at his own reflection.

Chapter Five

As Cyd made eye contact, just about everyone looked away. Everybody except for the man in the corner by the fireplace, wearing that heavy black ballistics jacket with the hood shadowing his face. His careful stare met hers with no hesitation. She studied what she could of him, but couldn't remembering seeing those features before.

Raw emotions like open distrust or even hate, she knew what to do with. Measured stares like this made her uneasy.

Cyd picked up her drink in one hand and her plate in the other and slid into one of the booths that had been vacated upon her arrival. She'd come to Bosco's seeking the familiar, and a link to survival in the form of food, work and shelter. And while the normalcy of the scene was something of a relief, there was also a pure culture shock that made it all she could do not to reveal how shaken she was from the last few hours.

"Absolutely no fucking idea" was, of course, a clear-cut lie. She knew where she'd been. Amnesia would have been more convenient for a lot of reasons, but she wasn't lucky enough for that. Of course, while she knew where'd she been, she had no clue about what had happened in the city from the moment she'd been snagged from that phonebooth in a hailstorm of glass and blood. *Pleading general cluelessness would be fairly easy.*

This bar's patrons were like a litmus test for how just about everybody in the city would react to her. She hadn't gone out in a blaze of popularity, but she wasn't notoriously distrusted, either. In fact, she figured she'd once been known as an ultimately excellent, if sometimes erratic, B-Ops liaison. She'd been fair and honorable. And, of course, she'd had her partner's rank and pull to give her automatic acceptance with a lot of people who might have otherwise discounted her. It seemed she still got a bit of that respect.

If there was one thing Cyd was sure of, it was that she couldn't spend the rest of her life sleeping in alleys and eating out of Dumpsters. And if there was one thing she knew how to do, it was get information. The obvious next step was for her to plug back into the informant network. That would allow her to lie low, and it would give her some insight into whether she could, should or even wanted to try and reestablish herself at her old job.

Of course, lying low might not be so easy. It was almost as if the bar patrons were a bunch of animals getting reaccustomed to her scent. After half an hour, the stares weren't as long, the amount of personal space they left while walking by her booth wasn't as wide, and the tension in the air was transitioning from curiosity to commerce as each one considered how he might cash in on her very sudden and unexpected reappearance in Crimson City.

Cyd glanced at her wrist, forgetting she wasn't wearing a watch, then resorted to the old five-behind wall clock. She gave it fifteen more minutes before someone moved in for the kill. The sharks were already circling—even jockeying a little, as a couple of info runners ran into each other because they were too busy watching her.

Her first guess would have been the hooded guy in the corner fireplace seat. But he'd leaned back into the darkness, and his body language indicated he wasn't going anywhere.

She swept the room with her gaze. Ah. Tajo Maddox. She'd actually made out with him once, way back when she was in I-Ops and a total innocent. He'd seemed so dangerous, so badass. And that was before she had any idea he was a rogue werewolf. Now he just seemed like any of a hundred of the same guys she'd swapped info with on the streets.

Tajo made eye contact, inclined his head just slightly in a nod, as if to stake his claim; then, once decided, he beelined over from the opposite side of the room. There was a last-minute rustle, as though the music had stopped and everyone wanted the last chair, but Tajo had it covered.

He slid onto the bench seat opposite her and clasped his hands together. "You're not dead."

"That seems to be the case," Cyd replied—perhaps a little too flippantly, all things considered. She really couldn't explain her absence without sounding like a lunatic, which wouldn't be too smart, given that defending her mental stability had been something of a problem even before she'd been snatched. Likely everybody thought she'd been turned, which wasn't very good luck, given that anyone not totally human had it rougher these days.

"You a fang now?" Tajo asked.

Cyd gave him a look of total disdain.

"How about you tell me where you've been all this time, then." The werewolf jangled some coins in his pocket, and Cyd had to admit the offer of payment was tempting. The only thing she had in her pockets was a fucking demon souvenir.

She rested her chin on her palm. "Wish I could. I have amnesia," she said matter-of-factly.

Tajo leaned forward, very conspiratorial-like, the corner of his mouth turning up in a smile. "Then how do you know you're Cyd Brighton?"

Cyd calmly pulled a paper napkin from a rusty holder and wiped her mouth. She leaned forward. "Because it's *limited* amnesia. I don't remember anything after I disappeared."

"Do you really expect people to believe that?"

"Yes. I do. Anyway, if that's not good enough, there's always the asylum. Maybe I was there."

"Right. I might actually buy that. Always thought you were a little crazy."

Cyd rolled her eyes.

Tajo looked over his shoulder, then bent down lower to the table and closer to Cyd. "Okay. So, if you don't know what happened . . . how do you know you weren't bitten by a fang or a werewolf?"

She leaned forward. "That's an excellent question. I don't."

"Well, you look pretty good, Cyd." He studied her face close-up.

"I'm a disgusting, sweating mess, and I know you can smell it. Don't try that on me."

The werewolf chuckled and pulled back, drumming his fingers on the tabletop. "They say the fangs don't eat, but I saw a vampire eat once. I saw Fleur Dumont eat a hamburger in a diner—with your old partner, actually."

"Wow. A hamburger. Fleur Dumont ate a hamburger." Cyd raised her palms and waggled her fingers in mock terror. "Well, then, I guess we're back to square one. Because, obviously, you're right. With the amnesia and all, I can't guarantee one hundred percent that I'm completely human," she said pleasantly. Jamming the ends of some french fries into a blob of mayo, she stuffed them into her mouth.

Tajo's eyes shifted to the side, and Cyd followed his gaze to the hooded man in the corner—a man who immediately turned away.

Cyd gestured to him with her head. "He's staring at us? Who is that?"

"Changing the subject?" Tajo suggested, again all business.

"Was the conversation really going anywhere?"

Tajo leaned back in his chair and stuck his hands behind his head, a broad grin on his face that suggested he was enjoying himself a little too much. "Not a werewolf, a fang or a mech. A demon?" he asked.

Cyd choked. Badly. Tajo actually had to move around the table and give her a whack on the back. "French fry down the wrong pipe," she gasped weakly, her hands shaking and her eyes tearing up.

"No problem. The drama will probably drive up my price." He handed her another napkin and sat back down, his smile gone. "Cyd, I'm sorry. I was just kidding around."

"What the hell would make you say a thing like that to me? Everybody who knows anything about my background knows you don't talk about demons with me." Cyd wiped the sweat off her forehead, crumpled the napkin up and smashed it angrily into the ashtray.

"It wasn't really meant to be personal," Tajo said, looking at her askance. "Considering that beach battle was like from World War Two or something."

Cyd stared at him. "The demons?"

Tajo stilled. "You're not joking about this amnesia crap, are you?" His hands made a gesture of surrender. "When you disappeared . . . people said shit. Stupid rumors. You know, because of what you used to do before B-Ops. And then the demons attacked—hell, I was just making a joke. Forget it. I'm sorry."

"I guess I'm just sensitive," she mumbled, trying to wrap her brain around the idea of demons in Crimson City the whole time she'd been gone . . . and what that might mean as far as Griff-Vai coming back for her.

"Um . . . I guess you don't know about B-Ops, either," Tajo said.

She shook her head, a sinking feeling in her stomach.

"Let me put it delicately. A lot of your old team is . . . gone."

Cyd pushed her plate away, suddenly not the least bit hungry. "Is Dain Reston okay?"

"Cyd—"

"Is Dain *okay?*"

Tajo took an infuriatingly long sip of water. "You could say that," he said slowly. "He went fang."

So much for going to find Dain. Not even if she wanted to. Not now. Fleur had sunk her teeth into him after all. He'd taken sides. Fleur's side.

"He's up-strata running the vamp show with the Dumonts—Are *you* okay?" he asked, giving her a concerned look.

"Yeah," she said roughly, sitting slowly back in her chair. "Just . . . it's a little hard to take." So her old partner, Dain, had gone with Fleur in the end. She couldn't say she blamed him, and she couldn't say she hadn't seen it coming, but she couldn't say it was a welcome piece of news, either.

Tajo smiled a sympathetic smile. "I guess I'm used to it. Seems like everybody goes rogue these days."

"Technically, he didn't go rogue," Cyd snapped. It was impossible not to sound bitter. "Sounds like he *chose* to join the vampire primaries. That's different."

"I guess I have to agree with you there. But he went rogue from B-Ops, anyway. When *you* do the same, I'll be curious to see who you run to." The werewolf grinned.

"Nobody," Cyd growled. "I'm not running to anybody." When *I do it?*

Of course, Tajo wasn't that far off the mark. The idea of taking orders, of being controlled or running to anyone or anything—whether drugs, the government or men of any species—made bile rise in Cyd's throat. It was for that very reason that calling in to B-Ops and telling them she was home in Crimson City hadn't already been done. That was what she'd be expected to do.

Tajo shrugged. "Suit yourself. Well, for me . . . assuming I was running from something, the primary vampires and werewolves wouldn't be my first choice. You ask me, it's us rogues who will one day hold the power in this town."

Before Cyd could respond, a shrill whistle pierced the room. Tajo looked over, nodded to a guy waiting in the doorway of the bar, and pushed back his chair. "Got some business to handle," he said.

Cyd stared over his shoulder as he pulled out his wallet. "Is that who I think it is?" she asked. "You're working with Hayden Wilks?"

"Food's on me." Tajo peeled a couple of bills from his stash and dropped them on the table. "A lot has changed since you've been gone. Hey, I'll see you around, Cyd."

She watched him go, under no illusions about his apparent generosity with the cash: He'd left substantially more than the price of a plate of food. Like a paparazzo willing to scale an oceanside cliff to get a shot no one else had, the funds meant nothing more than that Tajo was willing to be the first to risk associating with her in order to get the scoop. They both knew he'd sell the information as soon as he could get outside. Maybe he'd already sold some. Most likely, to B-Ops. But at least he gave as good as he got.

He wasn't the only rat. Cyd knew that more than a few other barflies had stepped out within five minutes of seeing her to make contact with their B-Ops liaisons. Probably they were talking to JB or Trask. She could expect her old friends to pay her a visit any day now, and an audience with her boss to explain her absence. They were probably trying to figure out if she was compromised. Tajo would get good money for the details of his first-person contact. But, being anti-Ops, he'd choose his words wisely.

Leaning back against the heavy wooden wall of the booth, Cyd took a moment to absorb the shock of everything he'd just revealed—not the least of which was the total nonchalance with which two of the most individualistic rogues she'd known, from opposing species, were apparently teamed up for business. She looked out at the crowded bar filled with patrons bustling with purpose, and slumped weakly back in her seat. No real friends . . . no job . . . no money . . . no place to live. The cash in front of her on the table, the clothes on her back and the artifact in her pocket were all she had in the world.

Her fingers closed around the amulet. If she had to pick her poison, she'd rather side with the rogues as Tajo had implied, than step one foot in the B-Ops depot or on the I-Ops base where Griff had found her in the first place.

Her gaze shifted to the enormous bulletin board on the side wall, farthest from the door. The bulletin board at Bosco's was legendary. Anything and everything. Roommate wanted, shithole for rent, used-weapons sales, drug shopping lists, and of course the popular "job board."

All of it was in coded language and euphemisms, see-a-guy-about-a-guy, middleman city. "Dog needs good home . . ." Code for some unpleasant business involving a denizen of Dogtown, a werewolf. "Assortment of used exercise equipment . . ." Code for last-generation weapons, wholesale. "New books, must sell . . ." Code for fresh information. "Roommate wanted . . ." Code for looking for a partner, a pimp, a dealer or a mercenary. And the vague "Need problem solved" usually involved a killing. You had to read between the lines to determine when the language was literal and when it was figurative.

The mercenary trade was booming, if the number of listings was any indication. Cyd figured that her survival in Crimson City depended on this board.

Each listing only had one contact tab. Protocol was, once you were interested you removed the notice and stuck it in the shredder conveniently located just beyond the swinging half door of the bar. If you were hired, great; if not, a new notice would go up.

There might be a lot of listings, but there were also a lot of takers. Things were buzzing as people hovered around the bar, taking meetings over mugs of beer, and the notices were ripped down as quickly as they were posted. Cyd elbowed her way in and scanned the possibilities. Her best chance would be something in Dogtown, her old beat. No one could argue with her credentials for that.

The others at the board gave her plenty of space. She could almost guess what they were thinking: *Watch your back when it comes to that girl. She's former B-Ops, possibly compromised by another species, back under mysterious circumstances—in other words, nobody's ideal prom date.*

"Hey."

Cyd looked over her shoulder. It was Dougan, of all people. Her old dealer. Total cringe. "Sorry, Dougan. Not buying," she said.

He pulled at the sparse hairs on his chin that passed for a goatee. "Ah, c'mon. What, you been in rehab all this time?"

"I guess you could say I've been scared straight."

"Hmph. You need anything, I'll be in D-Alley. Come find me," he said, and slipped away.

"I'll be sure to do that," she muttered sarcastically. But she felt a little self-conscious as she returned to the board.

Scanning jobs for something in her area of expertise didn't take long; she found something right away. "Encyclopedia salesmen needed for Dogtown." Perfect. Someone needed her to go down to the werewolf underground and uncover some information. That played to her strengths. With her hand flattening the notice on the board, she looked behind her across the room, hoping to make eye contact with the middleman. She did. Cool. Manny. He was good to do business with.

She ripped the notice down, indicating she was applying for the job. But as she turned to face Manny, to discuss details and negotiate a price, she saw the hooded figure rise from the shadows and beat her to the punch.

Cyd narrowed her eyes; the sheer number of bodies in front of the board made it impossible to cross to Manny quickly enough. The hooded man leaned down and spoke in his ear. Both men looked over at her as she struggled like a goddamn salmon to get away from the board. She wasn't having much luck.

You didn't steal a meal from a starving person without a good reason. Not here, not anywhere. Not if you had honor. Nevertheless, this stranger was snaking the job right out from under her. And without an explanation.

By the time the bodies in front of her thinned enough for Cyd to get a decent view again, the two men were shaking hands and parting. Manny shook his head at her.

She wasn't sure whom to give hell to first, so she picked the guy she knew. Slamming the notice down on the table, she said, "What the hell was that? We had eye contact." She used two fingers to point to her eyes and then Manny's to illustrate her point.

"Sorry," he said bluntly. "Job's assigned."

"Nobody knows Dogtown better than me."

"Oh, Christ. Don't come whining to me, Cyd." He waved her off as if she were a fly, and went back to some paperwork.

"Manny, we've done business before. Don't give me this."

"Don't give you what? You're a goddamn ghost," he said, a cigar flopping between his lips. He didn't even look up as he slid over a file folder, put some documents inside, then put it in his briefcase and snapped the hinge locks closed.

Cyd had the urge to put him in a choke hold and ask if he knew any ghosts who did that, but it hardly seemed prudent.

Manny looked up. Without cracking so much as a smile, he said, "You're still here. Go away."

"You and I did good business," she complained.

"Like the man said, 'Where you been, Cyd?'" He mimicked Bosco's Italian accent. "We don't know you anymore. You're starting from square one. And at square one, you don't just waltz up and contract a job with a level-A boss like me."

Cyd sat down and leaned forward. "You trusted me."

Manny showed no signs of being swayed. "I already hired someone." He heaved his briefcase off the table and set it on the bench seat. "Why would I use you, Cyd? Seriously. Nobody's going to want to be the first to test you out."

"I'm the same as I ever was."

He twisted the cigar in his mouth, one eyebrow winging upward. "You're not a fang?"

"No!"

"Dog?" he asked dispassionately.

"No!"

Just as casually: "Demon?"

"No! I can't even believe this is a real issue here."

He gave her a skeptical look. "Everybody knows about that night, Cyd. They say your blood was everywhere."

Cyd shrugged dismissively, hiding her discomfort.

She saw the whole scene again, the look in Griff-Vai's eyes. "B-Ops just floated a good story; that's all. Do I look like I'm dead?"

"I'm more worried about whether you're *un*dead."

She rolled her eyes. "You want to test me? Bite me. Burn me. Whatever."

Manny drew back and studied her. "You are one messed-up girl."

Cyd stared back at him. "If I had a dollar for every time someone said that to me, and fifty cents for a variation on the phrasing . . ."

Manny reached out, and she flinched. He gave her a strange look, and when she followed his gaze, she saw that her hands were trembling. He pressed his coffee spoon down on the back of her hand to steady it, shaking his head in disbelief.

"I don't think you're faking this," he said, almost in surprise. "Let's assume you're not lying and you're the same old Cyd. You've been gone a long time, and you have no meaningful explanation for where you've been or what you've been doing. Nobody's gonna want to be the first to trust you. Nobody's gonna want to be the first to hire you out."

"Find me one person who thinks I did a shitty job while with B-Ops."

Manny's thick fingers dunked a sugar cube into the dregs of his coffee. He popped the cube in his mouth and asked, "If you did such a great job, Cyd, then why don't they ask you back?"

"I don't *want* to go back." The words came out of her mouth, and she felt a sudden clarity. She wasn't going back to B-Ops. She'd never liked working there; she'd never felt like she fit. She'd stayed because her partner was someone to lean on. But Dain wasn't there anymore. And going back to B-Ops would take her that much closer to where all her problems began.

Face it, Cyd. You're not going back. It's too close to the source of all this. It's where it all began. The demons. The deaths. Griff. And worst of all, everyone at B-Ops is gonna wonder where you've been, and you aren't going to want to answer that question.

Manny waved his cigar in front of her face. "You don't work for me again until you got someone to vouch. Get a subcon. Prove yourself. Then we can talk business." He yanked his metal briefcase off the bench and headed for the door.

Shit. "Hey, wait!" Cyd called.

Manny turned around.

"Who was that who got the job?"

Ask a stupid question, don't get an answer at all. Manny looked at her as if she was insane.

"Maybe I can subcontract, like you said," Cyd suggested. And she would give the guy hell for stealing the job right out from under her nose in the first place. "You know I'll find out anyway."

He shrugged. "I figure that's a fact. But the guy works alone, so . . ."

"Give me a name."

Manny laughed. "No skin off my back. Name's Finn."

"Finn? Finn who?"

"Just Finn."

"Where'd he come from? I don't remember any Finn."

"I don't know where he came from, and I don't care. I just know that he's good, and has stellar refs. You convince Finn to take you on subcon and vouch for you, you'll be in business in Crimson City across the board.

'Til then, uh-uh. And I'd get on it, if I were you—he's leaving."

Cyd whirled around in time to see Bosco's front door close, rattling on its loose hinges. Manny picked up his briefcase and headed out the back, through the kitchen. Cyd watched him go.

When Manny had disappeared, Cyd jammed out of Bosco's and looked both ways down the street. The man named Finn was pretty far away on the right, hunched into his jacket.

"Hey, Finn!" Cyd yelled at the top of her lungs, running after him as fast as she could.

The figure stopped, then turned around to face her, cloaked in darkness, his face so far hidden by the raised hood of his ballistics jacket that she could barely make out any features at all. She suppressed a shiver, a feeling of cold that stole through her bones, and steeled herself for an argument.

Chapter Six

"Finn! Wait!" Cyd sprinted down the block, stopping short as he turned. "Why did you do that?"

He stood there in silence.

"Why did you snake that job from me? You saw that I was going for it. That's not the way the job board works. You have something against me?"

He adjusted his hood slightly. As he shifted, a streetlight glinted off something shiny around his eyebrow—a piercing, maybe? But he didn't seem to have the thoughtless aggression of a street punk. She'd have preferred that type, actually. She knew how to handle a common street tough; this guy was a complete mystery.

"You're Finn, right?"

"I'm Finn." His voice was low, even, carefully measured.

Cyd crossed her arms over her chest. "You snaked my job. That's bullshit."

He shrugged. "It's done. How do you spell your name?"

"What?"

He didn't repeat himself.

"Cyd. It's short for Cydney. C-Y-D. Cydney Brighton."

"That's a B-Ops serial number on your pants."

She shrugged. "Yeah, I used to be B-Ops, if that's what you're wondering. It's no secret."

"I don't remember you," he said.

"Well, I don't remember you, either. When did you come to the city?"

"Recently."

She waited for him to elaborate. In vain. "You must have come just about when I was . . . leaving."

"Where did you go?"

"Where did you come from?" she countered.

"Was there something you wanted?"

He seemed about as humorless and emotionless as they came. She wasn't going to get anywhere trying to shame him on the point of job-stealing protocol. Cyd sighed. "Okay. Look. I needed that job badly. I know Dogtown like the back of my hand. How about you give it to me on a subcontract? I'll do all the work for sixty-forty. I'm the sixty."

He stilled. To her surprise, he seemed to be considering her offer.

She tried to see his eyes, peering into the hood without making it obvious, but he held himself just so, at just the right angle to keep himself concealed. The man was a pro. He knew just how much to give up and just how much to keep to himself. And clearly he knew just how much could be revealed in the eyes.

"Well?" she asked.

He cocked his head to one side, reaching toward her face with a hand clad in black leather. She flinched, cursed silently, then forced herself to steady. He put two fingers under her chin and gently tipped her head back.

When he leaned forward, Cyd thought she could see at least one eye inside his hood. Blue. And it actually didn't seem emotionless. Or humorless.

She should have lashed out, slapped him away, done any and all of the things she was used to doing when a strange guy tried to manhandle her. When any guy tried to manhandle her. But something about the way he looked at her . . . What the hell, he could mean anything by it. He could be checking her out as a fang or a dog, or in the way a farmer checked out a horse he intended to buy. He could be considering an exchange of this job for sex.

That, in and of itself, was new. She'd never traded on her looks. For that matter, she'd never done much with her looks at all. She'd never been one of those girls on the Ops teams whom the guys talked about. The fact of the matter was, she hadn't felt good back then, on the inside or the outside. And it showed. Walking around with messy hair, dark circles under her eyes, trailing punch capsules and candy bar wrappers in her wake—that didn't exactly make the boys weak in the knees.

But it suddenly occurred to her that things weren't what they used to be. She might be standing in her old cargo pants with greasy hair and dirt on her face, but something was different now. Maybe it *was* because of what she'd said to Manny about quitting the punch. Something told her it was more.

She remembered Griff-Vai touching her, how he'd seemed to envelop her entire body with his strange eroticism. There was no question but that he'd used seduction to manipulate her, but he'd been a master, a creature that truly understood desire. Now, as Cyd stood in the harsh, cool air in front of this stranger she'd never seen before in her life, she realized that something inside her had changed over the past several months. A heightened awareness. An awakening. For even through the leather of the stranger's glove, Cyd felt an intense desire that she had never felt before.

Finn's fingers curled abruptly into a fist. "Not interested." Whatever spell had bound them together was broken. The man turned and walked away as suddenly as he'd reached out for her.

Cyd pulled herself together and tried again, giving chase. "Fifty-fifty. I'll do all the work."

"No." He picked up the pace, not even looking back at her.

Bastard. "Okay, okay. Forty-sixty, I'm the forty."

His legs were longer, and Cyd quickly tired of walking. She was more tired of begging. She stopped in her tracks and called out, "Hey, this is a great deal for you. I'm a good person to know in this city!"

He glanced back at her over his shoulder and said, "Then how come nobody wants to know you?"

Cyd didn't have an answer for that. And with a quick quiet shake of his head, Finn turned a corner and disappeared.

Same old game. The reception would be the same no matter whom she approached. Cyd knew because she'd played it before, and she couldn't blame the others for refusing to take a risk on an unknown. Which she was. She headed back toward Bosco's.

Two guys heading into the bar gave her curious looks. Frustrated, Cyd turned away and ducked into the shadows of the overhang from the building next door. Hugging her arms to her chest, she leaned back and stared up at the night sky. A gray layer of smog was drifting low, with just the barest hint of a crimson sunrise peeking through. This would have been just about the time of her normal beat.

She was used to dealing with different personalities, adapting, reacting quickly to the rules of the different strata. And in a way, the demon underworld had been just another layer. But she had to confess that culture shock was setting in, and her usual facility at compartmentalizing situations was failing her. She'd been through too much.

And there were still so many questions. Had it been an accident she'd been allowed through the portal? Would Griff-Vai be able to find her again? Would he manage to follow her back?

He'd found her the first time.

The overwhelming starkness of her reality—what she knew and what she feared—began to panic her. And knowing she had nowhere to go and no one to turn to only spurred on the feeling.

Leaning back against the wall, she slid to the edge of the alley where it opened into the street. There she looked again at the night sky, noting the brilliant white of the moon.

When she went back into Bosco's, Cyd only had one foot over the threshold before Bosco tossed an apron at her head and told her start cooking. She had to work off her tab.

Finn took the usual circuitous route back to his apartment, checked the door traps for signs of entry and slipped inside. He locked himself in, double-checked the windows and storage areas, then finally allowed himself to relax a little, hurriedly shedding the layers of precautionary clothing that covered his body.

Stripped to the waist, finally able to breathe more freely without the heat and weight of his hoodie and heavy ballistics jacket, Finn grabbed a pitcher from the refrigerator and tipped up the entire thing, gulping the detoxified water nearly down to empty. He splashed the remainder over his overheated skin and stuck the empty container in the sink for a refill. His body was horribly dehydrated, as usual, and the alcohol he'd been drinking had made it worse.

Dripping into the sink and on the kitchen floor, all Finn could do was shake his head. *You're an idiot.* He'd taken that job out from under the girl in part out of childish spite, simply because he'd hated her flippant attitude about what was and wasn't human. He'd wanted to stand up in the middle of the bar and have a say, but he couldn't—with the bounty on his head it'd be suicide, and the last thing he needed was to draw attention to himself in an argument about relative humanity.

But he'd also wanted exactly the kind of collision with her that he'd got outside of the bar, and she'd given him more than he could have hoped for. Instead of putting her tail between her legs and getting lost, this girl—known to be associated with B-Ops; still likely to have contacts in both the Battlefield Ops and the Internal Ops divisions—had walked right up to him and delivered the perfect bargain . . . and like an idiot, he'd turned her away.

She needed someone to vouch for her, so that she could break into the underground job network; he needed someone from Ops to hand him the keys to a real future. Cydney Brighton had offered him exactly what he needed, and he'd choked. He should have taken her up on the deal, but he was afraid to trust anyone with his secret.

Don't be so hard on yourself. This is a matter of life and death.

Wiping his arm across his mouth, Finn looked around his spartan kitchen. He was always looking for clues he'd been discovered, was always on the alert. Satisfied that everything was in its proper place, he wandered into the living room.

To call the apartment a one-bedroom wasn't a lie; it might be small, but it had a separate sleeping area, which was a hell of a lot more than he'd had while living in the barracks. And he didn't own much yet, so there was plenty of space for just one guy.

He'd been thinking about getting something for the walls. The walls were what gave a place a sense of permanence. If he could find a discreet vendor, he'd try to get to that next week. It was important to believe there would be plenty of tomorrows.

Finn unlaced his boots and stood them up at the end of the couch, carefully lining them with their toes against a particularly heavy line of wood grain. Then he opened the window a crack more for fresh air.

If anyone had asked, he would have said that the fact he had no past didn't bother him in the least—if it was bad, he didn't care to know about it; if it was good, he didn't care to know what he'd lost. The past was past. It was gone. The future was all that really mattered.

Perhaps because the future was all he had, that explained why making it what he wanted was so important. To live on his own terms. To remove the shackles that still bound him in more ways than one to the people who would control his thoughts and actions.

Funny; he'd been looking for someone to trust for the last six months. Of course he'd tried to help himself, but he could only do so much. And as long as there was a bounty on his head, as long as he couldn't get rid of the evidence of what he was, his time as a free man in Crimson City was limited.

Until now. Until that girl had appeared out of nowhere. It was almost too good to be true. Of course, things that were too good to be true often turned out to be traps.

That girl . . . that girl . . . that *girl.* He couldn't get her out of his mind.

She was a true possibility, the first real chance he'd come across in a long time. He'd scoped out some other leads, but the specs were all wrong; they simply didn't have any incentive not to turn him in. He required someone who needed something as desperately as he needed their help.

From that scene in the bar, it was clear that this girl was pretty desperate. But did that make her more trustworthy than anybody else? On one hand, someone who had problems of her own could be drafted, but on the other, someone who had the kind of problems that put a look like hers in a person's eyes . . . well, she couldn't afford to solve someone else's problems first.

No, he had to forget her—to walk away as he'd already done. If he took it one piece at a time, maybe he'd eventually solve his own problem. Somewhere down the line, he'd need help for the areas he couldn't access himself, but if he could just get through most of it, that would be something.

Finn walked over and crouched down by the fireplace, turning on the gas. He lit a match, stared down at it as it nearly burned to his fingers, then tossed it into the small pit. The hiss of ignition was a comforting sound. The bottle of vodka on the mantel would provide even more comfort.

Finn pulled a tool kit out from under the couch and sat down, switching on the jeweler's lamp on a side table. The intense light illuminated his naked torso, the muscled planes covered by patchwork metal. There were scars where he'd already ripped some of the steel out of his flesh. Opening the tool kit, he withdrew a knife, a screwdriver and a small blowtorch.

His right forearm he'd always known he'd have to save for last—as a matter of self-defense. But the left . . . if he could just remove some of the metal from his left arm—hands shaking, he pushed up his sleeve—he'd be one step closer to contact with the rest of the human race without constantly risking discovery.

Bracing himself, Finn turned his arm to expose the underside, a crisscross of metal wire and plate running like map work over his skin. He leaned across and stuck the end of his tools into the fire, then laid them on the coffee table in front of him.

Inhaling, he let the breath out as slowly as he could, chasing it with a swig of vodka that sent a creeping warmth through his bones. Then he steeled himself, splashed vodka all over his arm and jammed the flat edge of a screwdriver down and in.

The metal was fused to his flesh like a second skin, and for the next twenty minutes all he got for his trouble was a white-hot pain that brought unfettered tears flowing from his eyes and sweat pouring down his chest. He worked the screwdriver and knife along the seams, a thin line of blood trickling up from the fresh wound.

Finn worked at it for another ten minutes, his body

shaking. *No. No!* He dropped the tools to the floor and hugged his bleeding arm to his chest, rocking back and forth in silent agony.

It was the same every time. He made a little progress, but never enough. Not without the kind of technical finesse the job really required.

Finn rolled onto his back and pulled his legs up to his chest. *Do I ask too much? Is this asking for too damn much?*

With the pain subsiding, anger took over. Finn leaped up from the couch and looked around. Still a prison. He might be living on his own, but he was still in a prison of someone else's making. He would be no matter where he lived or where he went—someone had made him what he was. Someone inside I-Ops.

He had no choice. If he hadn't found the courage to trust one of the shadowy figures that walked Crimson City's underground before, he was going to have to soon. He was willing to suffer and wait no longer.

There was a bounty on him, yes. And as long as he wore the evidence of what he was, he risked death. But that wasn't what bothered him the most. It was simpler than that. He refused to be defined by the metal invading his flesh. He refused to continue to be seen as anything less than what he felt he was deep inside: a man. A *human* man.

Finn fell to his knees and slammed his fists down on the coffee table, sending his tools flying in all directions. Still kneeling on the floor of his apartment, he gave up the safety of silence and roared out his pain like a caged beast.

Chapter Seven

Trask checked his watch, humming slightly off-key as he drove. He stopped at a red light and, in spite of the many official warnings not to take chances on such vendors, bought a dozen roses from a desperate-looking dude selling flowers in the middle of the street during rush-hour traffic.

The persistent honking as he completed the transaction didn't bother him—the fact that he had no intention of moving one second sooner than it would take to exchange the goods gave him a kind of a high. He was feeling good these days. Powerful. Deadly. He was a man with a plan.

His partner, JB, was a total pussy who let this state-of-emergency stuff bring him down. Trask let it empower him. One too many near-death experiences had only made him riskier, bolder, ballsier. He now drove as fast as he wanted, ran red lights, started confrontations. None of it mattered.

He gunned his engine, peeling out and racing down the streets toward Bridget's apartment. She wasn't expecting him, but he hadn't seen her in two days and he couldn't stand it anymore. A man had needs. A lot of different needs. They were a great match. She just needed to buy into his system.

He parked his car and ran up the stairs to her Melrose apartment. The lights controlled by motion sensors went on in the complex, making the water in the pool flicker and glitter. He knocked. No answer. Rang the doorbell. No answer. He stuck the cellophane-wrapped flowers in his mouth and pounded his fist on the door.

At last Bridget opened up and stood there, blocking the threshold.

Trask took the flowers out of his mouth and held out them out to her. "For my best girl," he said.

"Thanks," she replied, smiling sweetly. Then she moved to the garbage can and jammed them headfirst into the trash.

"What the hell!" he yelled, following her into the apartment.

"Yeah, what the hell! We have an understanding. And that means you don't subcontract jobs out from under me. You want to explain why you had someone else on the mech bounty job?"

There was one target universally known in Crimson City as the bounty of all bounties: the mech who several months ago had assassinated the two vampire leaders, the Dumonts, and failed to report back to base as it had been programmed to do. I-Ops was dying to get the thing back, and to dissect what had gone wrong. Until then, the entire mech program was on hold.

"The mech bounty job. Right. Well, turns out, it's back on." He shrugged, the picture of innocence. "Look, Bridge. Someone came to me with a hot lead. Other things . . . maybe I make an exception. But with the mech, I follow the intel."

"Unfortunately for you, your someone is dead—right?

"Um . . ."

Bridget shook her head, barely able to contain her outrage. "You've been playing me. You've totally been playing me! How many people do you have on this besides me?"

"Whoa, whoa, whoa. Let's not get excited," Trask said.

"Let's not get excited? *Let's not get excited?*"

"Okay, okay! It was just you and that one other guy. Like I said, it was hot intel, just a one-off thing. You and I are still on."

"How do I know you're not lying?"

"I didn't lie the first time. You never asked. By the way, you're getting awfully pushy. Without me, you wouldn't even be on this job."

She batted his hand away as Trask reached up to caress her hair.

"What gives, baby? I thought we had something going here."

"It's called acting," Bridget replied coldly. "And just in case you're still not clear, let me remind you that the potential for any real romance in our relationship got kind of lost when I had to shoot myself in the arm while you just stood by being amused."

"Oh, shit." Trask sat down in a chair, kicked his legs up on the ottoman and flashed a grin. "You going to milk that forever?"

"At least until the scar disappears. Are you going to be a total ass forever?"

"At least until that scar disappears," he replied with a wink.

Bridget rolled her eyes. "I am so over this," she muttered at the ceiling.

"Come on," Trask said. "You have to admit that shooting yourself was a total rookie move. Reston wasn't going to put two and two together."

"You don't know that."

"I didn't think you'd really do it! I mean . . . damn. I will say this, Bridge—you've got balls."

She smiled. "I know. So, it makes me wonder."

"What?"

"You trained me. You know what I'm capable of. It makes me wonder why you didn't trust me to bring in the mech."

A massive silence stretched out between them. "You know what?" Trask finally asked.

"What?"

"I'm incredibly thirsty," he said with a grin, leaping from the chair and making a beeline for the kitchen.

Bridget raised her hands, then dropped them back to her sides in total surrender as Trask blithely rummaged around in her refrigerator. If he didn't already have the title "master of deflection" on his combat resume, he ought to add it.

Theirs was a deal of convenience. As a member of an Ops Battlefield team, Trask wasn't supposed to take advantage of company intel for personal use, nor take the lucrative reward money that went along with capturing those on the bounty list. Bridget had been helping him handle business under the radar. As I-Ops administrative support, she was often underestimated and overlooked: she had neither official weapons nor professional training . . . but Trask had provided her with both.

In exchange, Bridget did most of the dirty work,

handling jobs herself under his tutelage or acting as middleman for third parties, laundering reward money through an outside source, and collecting her percentage of the take on the back end—a percentage that Bridget was quite certain should be split more equitably by now, except for the fact that Trask never seemed to give her the credit or respect she deserved.

Of course, she'd messed up pretty big on one of her first jobs. While swapping intel to Trask about the wanted mech, she'd panicked when one of his coworkers, Dain Reston, nearly discovered them exchanging classified information that wasn't even supposed to leave the base. Trask hadn't disappeared and Bridget had overreacted, shooting herself in the arm to distract him from putting things together. Being caught using Ops info to get reward money from freelance justice was grounds for dismissal, if not worse.

In all fairness, such a drastic measure might not have been necessary, and Trask still gave her crap about that. But Bridget hadn't made a mistake even close to that caliber since. She'd also concocted a story about dating Trask to conceal the true nature of their business relationship, which worked so well that sometimes it seemed like even Trask believed it.

The devil himself came wandering back into her living room, sucking down a beer. Bridget folded her arms over her chest. "You still owe me money for the last job. Did you bring it?" she asked.

Trask reached into the chest pocket of his coat, took out a bundle of cash and dropped it on the table in front of her. He sat down. She studied it.

"I deserve a bigger cut. You know I do."

He raised an eyebrow. "Don't let your head get too big. You're nothing without me."

"Don't let *your* head get too big," she growled. "I do all the dirty work. I'm beginning to think that some of the targets you've been giving me are more personal matters than true security risks." She plopped down in the chair across from him. "Hey, what happened to your face?"

"Nice of you to notice." He touched the scrape on his cheek self-consciously. "I tangled with a fang today."

Bridget raised an eyebrow. "What'd he do?"

"He looked pretty shady."

"And?"

"And, he deserved it," Trask snapped.

"Right. No, obviously," Bridget said in her most placating voice, though her gut knotted every time Trask mentioned taking out a fang or a dog without quite getting to the part of explaining the crime the target had committed. She knew he had a nasty streak.

He chugged the rest of his beer. "Okay, then," he said, standing up and slamming the empty bottle onto the coffee table. "Are we cool?"

Bridget's face softened into that of the sweet, adorable, tennis-playing receptionist she'd been portraying for so long. "We're cool," she said. But she didn't mean it.

Trask reached into the garbage can, pulled out the flowers he'd brought and gave them a little shake. He handed them over as Bridget stood up from her chair. She took them with a smile, pushed him away as she always did when he moved in for a kiss, and watched him see himself to the door.

She cocked her head and studied the bouquet. *Yeah, we're cool, you double-crossing son of a bitch.* I'm *going to find that mech. And I'm not going to give him to you. And once I've got him, it will prove I can play with the big boys, and I'm not going to have to work under anybody else's thumb. I'm smart enough to be part of a true B-Ops team, not just support. And now, thanks to you, Trask, I'm incredibly well trained.*

With a shrug and a quick flick of her wrist, she tossed the flowers back into the trash can and thought, You think you don't need me. I *know* I don't need you.

Chapter Eight

"Yo, Cyd, pick up the pace." Bosco pushed through the double doors to the kitchen and dumped a stack of dishes into the sink. He took one look at her, then pointed to a grease-spotted, dog-eared sign on the wall: NO ASH IN THE HASH.

"It's not lit," Cyd muttered, the cigarette flapping between her lips.

Bosco gave her a meaningful look, and she put down her spatula, removed the offending item and laid it carefully on a can of unopened Crisco. Then she used the spatula to slide a pair of bubbling grilled cheese sandwiches off the griddle. Arranging them next to ladlefuls of potato salad, she pushed the sandwich plates through the opening beside the stove leading back to the bar, then expertly adjusted the heat and checked the last outstanding order.

Pulling a hamburger patty from the freezer, she tossed it on the counter. In a way, this was good work to have. Simple, repetitive, it kept your mind from wandering as you focused on the next order. She'd been doing it since yesterday, and it wasn't so bad. The nights to come might be a struggle, but the job would keep her thoughts from getting the better of her during the day.

And at the end of the week, she'd have saved up enough to put some money down on a room somewhere, which was no small thing.

Of course, there were still a couple of unknowns. She hadn't called in to B-Ops. Tajo was right; once they knew she was back, if she didn't call in they'd consider her rogue. But she still couldn't bring herself to make the call.

Cyd picked up her cigarette and lit it in the pilot light, deciding Bosco could blow. She inhaled deeply and left it hanging between her lips, then added a ladleful of grease to the griddle.

A stubby hand popped through the order window and took the grilled cheese above the stove, and the palm slapped impatiently on the surface. "Where's the beef? I'm still waiting on a burger done rare."

Cyd scooped a handful of ice out of the pull freezer and jammed it into the server's hand. After a yelp of pain, most of the ice came right back at her in a shower of pellets, followed by a new order. "You're falling behind," the server said.

Cyd looked at the slip of paper and narrowed her eyes, then stormed around through the double doors and into the bar. Sticking two fingers in her mouth, she gave a shrill whistle that cut through the room. Everyone fell silent and turned to look at her standing with her legs braced wide and her arms folded across her greasy apron.

"Who ordered this?" Cyd demanded.

Somebody snickered.

"An organic salad with freshly picked herbs and fat-free lemon-basil dressing? You taking the piss, or what?"

"It's LA. Whaddya 'spect?" a voice called out. She looked over to see Tajo Maddox sitting at the bar with a beer.

"This you?" she asked.

He shrugged innocently.

"Let me make this clear," she said, addressing the room. "There's no 'organic.' There's no 'freshly picked.' And there's no 'fat free.' I'm not even making this. So get over it."

Tajo leaned over the bar toward Bosco and asked, "Is it wrong for me to be turned on by that?"

The barkeep kept his mouth shut, though a broad smile stretched across his face. Cyd scanned the rest of the bar.

The man named Finn was at his customary table, still covered up in that hoodie and jacket. A little odd, since it was fairly warm inside; but nobody else paid him any attention. The guy had been around each of the three days since she started, and she got the feeling he was studying her, maybe even reevaluating his position. Catching her eye, he offered a casual salute. Slightly unnerved, Cyd looked away.

"Well? Anyone have a problem with that?" she asked. "No? Good. We understand each other."

She turned away from the patrons and pushed back into the kitchen, leaving a chorus of laughter behind her. But as the door swung closed, she managed a smile of her own. It was a good sign when the boys hazed you. That meant they were beginning to accept you. She was beginning to feel normal. Beginning, anyway.

She dropped a hamburger patty onto the griddle and started scraping greasy scraps from the middle toward the side troughs with her spatula. The old analog clock hanging precariously from a wire sticking out of the wall clicked as :59 flipped to :00. Suddenly, Cyd's head went woozy and thick, her heart thumping wildly in her chest. She closed her eyes for what seemed like only a second, but the tool in her hand caught on a remnant stuck to the griddle and went flying. Her right hand kept moving, sliding bare flesh across the smoking stovetop.

Crying out, Cyd ran straight for the sink. Gritting her teeth and bracing for the pain she knew would come, she stuck her hand under the cold spray. Her eyes squeezed shut, and she sat there with her hand under the cold water and waited for the worst.

Until, she realized that she felt no pain. There *was* no pain. No throbbing.

She opened her eyes and pulled back her hand. And as the water gushed wastefully into the basin, Cyd just stared in shock as the florid blisters from the third-degree burn caved in and lightened, and her skin returned to normal.

Holding her arm out stupidly out in front of her like a zombie, Cyd backed away from the sink, hit her back against the center island and slid to the floor. Her hand was fine. Everything was fine.

She looked around the room. Had that just happened? Had that really just happened? Or had she taken a hallucinogenic on the way to work and forgotten?

Can't blame it on the punch, Cyd. You're clean now, remember?

Sure as hell she remembered. Just as she remembered Griff-Vai from her dreams last night. Even after she'd woken up, Cyd had thought she was still in the demon underworld. It had taken her a good ten minutes to accept that Orcus was the dream and reality was the bench seat in the back room of Bosco's.

Cyd studied the back of her hand and her palm. It was as if nothing had happened. But in her dream, Griff had been there, taking her in his arms. . . .

"I do not understand why you resist me," he'd growled. "We are bonded, you and I. And if you will not come to me willingly, I will make you come. I brought you here once, and I can do it again."

"You can't make me," Cyd had said through gritted teeth. She'd turned to go, but he grabbed her wrist hard and swung her around, pressing her into his body.

"I'm not meant for you. I don't belong in this world," Cyd had said, pleading with him.

"You don't belong anywhere, but I can fix that." He had spoken kindly, his body still hard but his eyes going soft. "You're mine. I saved you." He'd pressed his mouth to her ear as Cyd closed her eyes, fighting against his pull. "You will see that you cannot forget me so quickly. I'll make sure of that."

Shaking her head, Cyd felt the presence of the amulet in her cargo pants—just hanging out in her pocket. It was the reason she'd gotten out of Orcus, so she kept it on her at all times; but the truth was, she wasn't sure what it was capable of or even how to use it. That was very frustrating. Especially when she knew Griff-Vai was seeking her.

The double doors leading to the bar swung open. Spooked, Cyd jumped backward, knocking a jar of utensils onto the floor in a clatter. Finn stood in the doorway, watching a whisk roll into the side of his boot.

He gave her a quizzical look and quietly moved to the sink, where he turned off the water. Then he looked at the stove.

"You burn yourself?" he asked.

Cyd let go of her elbow and relaxed her arm, quickly

grabbing a dish towel to conceal her shaking fingers by the act of wiping them dry. "No, I'm fine. Almost . . . nothing happened." She didn't take her eyes off him.

"What do you want?" she added hoarsely. "I figured we'd covered what there was to cover."

The corner of his mouth quirked up. "I'd like a do-over."

Cyd nodded. "Okay. Um . . . could you just"—she raised her index finger—"just give me one second."

He nodded, and Cyd turned her back on him. She could hear him picking up the kitchen utensils and piling them on the nearby chopping block. Ignoring the sound as best she could, she closed her eyes and inhaled as deeply as possible, then exhaled as quietly as she could manage.

Removing her apron, she stuck it on a utility hook and turned back to the guy who'd essentially told her to get lost the other night. It was time to forgive and forget. "Okay, Finn. Do-over."

Finn chuckled. "I've had a reason to reconsider your suggestion to work together. The situation is, I'm looking for a partner on something big. Therefore, I'd like to start with something small. A day job. Just to see how it goes. We'll see how far we get with the trust factor."

Cyd chewed on her thumbnail, suddenly suspicious. "You didn't want anything to do with me a couple days ago. You totally blew me off. Who do you work for?"

"That's not a relevant question."

"Meaning, you work alone, or you won't tell me who you're working for?"

"Meaning, it's not a relevant question."

"You said you want a partner. In my world, that implies fifty-fifty—or if it's a skewed share, I get more."

Finn laughed. "Of course."

"Of course?" Cyd gave him a dubious smile. "You wouldn't give me the time of day yesterday. Now you're willing to bargain?"

"I gave you the time of day," he said meaningfully.

Cyd raised an eyebrow. She wasn't sure she was reading his insinuation right.

"Look, I apologize about yesterday," he said. "I just don't take kindly to getting accosted like that in the middle of the street. I don't make deals on the fly, okay? So I'd like to start over. And as far as I'm concerned, nothing has changed in your world since we talked—unless you consider being a short-order cook the answer to all of your problems."

"I appreciate your frankness," Cyd said sarcastically. "I love this job."

He ignored that. "The thing is," he said, looking surprisingly uncomfortable for a rogue mercenary used to making deals, "the percentage isn't really as important, because the money from this . . . bigger job is an enormous sum. And really, that's all I'm going to say about it, because it's a no-go if the chemistry is off."

They stared at each other for a moment in silence.

"You have a place to stay?" he asked abruptly.

"Um . . . I'm happy to report I've upgraded my prospects from park bench to a bench seat. Bosco's got me covered." *And if you invite me to come live with you, the deal is off, perv.*

But all he said was, "Good." He reached into his pocket and pulled out a small wad of cash, carefully folded and paper-clipped. He set it on the table between them. "An advance."

Cyd looked at the money, then back at the man's hooded face. Damn, if he didn't seem almost . . . sweet about it.

"If you're worried about trusting me," he said, "I can point you to five people sitting within a one-table radius in the other room who will vouch for me."

Cyd reached out and dragged the money toward her. "Obviously I don't have any armor or weapons," she said. "Or a car."

"I'll take care of that."

The questions Cyd should have been asking at this point were: *What's really behind this sudden change of heart*, and *Why me for this job?* The question she asked was: "When do we start?"

"I'll be in touch," Finn replied.

"Do you smell something burning? 'Cause I do." Bosco's hand suddenly gripped the back of Cyd's collar and pulled her away from Finn. She hadn't heard him come in. She let him steer her back toward the grill without a struggle.

Maybe Finn's sudden capitulation should be cause for major concern, but that's not what it inspired in Cyd. Part of her brain recognized that she was doing it again, letting someone else call the shots, letting them take care of everything. But she mostly felt sweet relief.

And also . . . Cyd felt a thrill. She wanted to work with this man. She wanted to work next to him. There was something about him—his mystique, his enigma—that drew her. She'd have to watch that.

Yes, she made the same mistake no matter which side of the veil she was standing on: falling too quickly, too desperately for the heartfelt promises or seductive tones of men. In both Crimson City and the demon underworld, she'd sleep with them, and if they even made it to the morning, she'd wake up to a cold bed.

She'd found herself falling for Griff once, had even

wanted his body over hers for a moment. But it hadn't lasted. The heat had faded and only the cold remained. The cold of insincere men and danger.

Keep it business with Finn and you'll be fine, she reminded herself. He hasn't asked for anything more. Just keep your body out of the equation and you won't risk losing your mind.

Chapter Nine

Jill Cooper, intrepid reporter . . . or something. Since being bounced out of her staff job at the newspaper, she was finding it a lot harder to get information out of her sources for freelance gigs.

The pink slip she'd received in her e-mail claimed her dismissal was for attempting to destroy newspaper-owned intel, but she knew the government was making sure she paid for her part in helping Dain Reston escape B-Ops. The paper still took her freelance stories on occasion, though, probably because the editor-in-chief thought of her as a nice girl who'd gotten involved in something way over her head.

Problem was, without Dain or his partner Cyd Brighton, who'd been "disappeared" as the term went, she'd lost her primary sources. Aside from the fact that she was out two acquaintances she liked, Jill had also lost her status as the totally connected go-to girl of the newspaper world. You couldn't get that back overnight, and she'd been grooming a new source for months, now: I-Ops administrative assistant Bridget Rothschild.

It was generally understood that few people in Crimson City were actually who they appeared, and

Bridget was no exception. And while Jill would probably have had little in common with the receptionist character Bridget played on a daily basis, she was becoming close friends with the real version.

Well, maybe "close friends" was overstating things. But it was hard to find someone who knew when to share secrets—and when to keep them. Since her disgrace at the newspaper, Jill had been finding out exactly who her true friends were in the intel world. There didn't seem to be as many as she'd once thought.

She pulled up at Bridget's place just as Trask Wilson was leaving. She took the man's parking spot and waved at her friend who was standing in her doorway.

"Hey, you," Bridget called as Jill hopped out of the transport and headed up the walkway.

"Hey, yourself. He never gives up," she noted, following her friend into the apartment and flopping down on Bridget's couch. "Has he been chasing you around the room or something? You look kind of tired."

Bridget slumped in the opposing club chair. "Tired of pretending I buy his macho crap, for sure."

"I'll bet. So, you got anything for me I can write about?"

Her friend looked up, her face a mixture of impishness and delight: the real Bridget, back. "Not anything you can print."

Jill sighed loudly for effect. "I had to ask. I need a damn story." She tucked her arms behind her head. "Suffice it to say that business is a wee bit slow. It's hard to make money when people know you won't sell out."

"It's not easy being a saint," Bridget agreed, shaking her head. "I don't know why you do it. The only interesting gossip I've heard lately is the Cyd Brighton thing, which is already all over the underground."

"Yeah, I heard that. Haven't seen her yet, though the boys at Bosco's have."

"When I heard, I was, like: 'How do you even respond to that?' Is she a dog or a fang now?" Bridget asked.

Jill shook her head. "Apparently she said she was neither. I know for sure that the dogs don't claim her. I don't know about the fangs."

"Does Dain know?"

Jill laughed softly. "The first question on everybody's mind, I'm guessing. I don't know. I expect he must. He's either treading softly, waiting for her to come see him or . . . I don't know. But it's weird, because he's with Fleur Dumont now."

"Good old Fleur." Bridget stared up at the ceiling. "I think about those girls like Keeli Maddox and Fleur. They've really got things figured out. They're the ones running the show. And then there's me, running around pretending to be a dimwit while the boys try and put their hands up my skirt. Not to mention, I'm starting to get really mixed up about who I'm supposed to be, when. My tennis game is improving, though."

"I guess it's not easy being a sinner, either," Jill said with a grin.

Sitting up, Bridget leaned over the coffee table. "But it's a lot more fun. If you get tired of being a good girl, come talk to me."

Jill laughed—but not without a kind of pang. She liked to pretend she was ballsy, what with the wigs and the makeup and the disguises she sometimes wore out in the field talking to informants and going undercover. But that was really all a bit . . . safe. She was just hiding, swapping words. Any real physical danger she'd ever been in had been more coincidence than not.

Bridget, on the other hand, was really out there. Sure, she was wearing a disguise of sorts and pretending to be something she wasn't; but she was also running jobs, packing her own weapons, and learning an operative's trade.

"I know that you've got your own kind of work around with Trask passing his Ops training to you, but did you ever think about trying to get into the Academy for one of the Ops teams?" Jill asked. "You still could, you know."

Bridget turned an unexpected shade of pink. "Um, yeah. Actually, I did apply. Didn't pass the entrance test."

A little surprised at the uncharacteristic embarrassment, Jill almost dropped it. But the reporter in her . . . "Well, it's not an easy test," she said softly.

Bridget's eyes narrowed. "It's not that hard. I was kind of stunned I failed it, actually. I mean, really, there's no way I should have failed. You start trying to find excuses." Her gaze shifted down. "It's not something I go around telling people. It's pretty humiliating. Maybe someone screwed with my results. Or maybe . . ."

"Maybe?"

"Maybe I just should have studied harder. Anyway, like you said. I've got my work around . . . such as he is. But look, whatever I think of Trask personally, he trained me well. He gets these assignments, ditches JB and takes me with him. I'm out there, doing this stuff. It's been awesome. It *was* awesome. It's just not so awesome anymore."

Jill cocked her head. Bridget's tone was off. "What *do* you think of Trask?" she asked. She'd always wondered.

Bridget stared at her in silence for a long, long time. Jill could almost see the wheels turning, the way it was when an informant was trying to calculate what and how much to tell. She kept her mouth shut and waited for Bridget to make a decision.

"Everybody knows the rogues are dangerous. Everybody knows they're unpredictable. You get a bunch of people who've been made into something they aren't sure they want to be, toss them in with a bunch of people who wish they could be made into something other than what they were born to be, and that's a lot of pent-up anger. That's a good starting point for revenge, violence . . . there's a reason they're the most controversial group in town."

Jill moistened her lips, itching to pull out her handheld and start taking notes. Demon agents, purported to still be hiding under assumed identities here in the city, were the hottest thing in investigative reporting. Rogue activity took a close second, what with the rumor about the formation of a truly organized multi-species rogue gang to rival the werewolf, vampire, and human leadership circles. Bridget here was delivering a nice fresh rogue angle right on a plate. And . . . it was totally off the record if she was going to do the right thing. Jill suppressed a sigh. This was what friendship was supposed to be about.

"Bridge? Is everything okay?"

Bridget was studying her manicure, an unsettled look on her face. "I think Trask is picking off rogues on a—how should I put this—on a personal basis. Fangs, dogs, humans, you name it. Sometimes he can justify it with the intel files from work . . . sometimes he can't. And it's possible that I've done some of the work for him," she said, her voice cracking at the end. "It's getting really creepy. At first I thought they were all on the Wanted list and that at worst he was just doing some vigilante thing on cases that would have the same end result through official channels. But I don't think that's actually how it is."

Trying not to reveal her shock, Jill said, "So he's just . . . deleting people? People of all species without official hit requests?"

"The rogues. The ones who ally themselves with the rogue movement. The ones that the bosses could probably be persuaded to turn the other cheek over."

"Can you prove it?" Jill asked.

"Can I prove it?" Bridget blinked and seemed to collect herself, focusing in on Jill's face. She grabbed a throw pillow and tossed it at Jill in a burst of laughter. "You sneak! You were doing that thing! Pulling me in! What, you going to write a story now, sell me out and make a million bucks?"

"No!" Jill dodged a second pillow. "I was not! We were just being friends. We're just sharing."

Bridget suddenly looked nervous. "Tell me you won't use it. I'm figuring out a way to handle it."

Making an X-shape over her heart with her index finger, Jill said, "I promise I won't use it."

Settling back into her chair, Bridget nodded. After a moment, her mood seemed to brighten and a wicked little smile bloomed over her face. "If we're just being friends . . . if we're sharing . . . then tell me about Marius."

Marius Dumont. Fleur's cousin. He was a Protector vampire, which probably involved all kinds of complex concerns revolving around Fleur's leadership of the primary vampires. For Jill, it simply meant that he wasn't free to love her. Even if they'd kissed. Even if they shared something truly special, something that they never spoke about.

"Nice change of subject," she sputtered.

"We should go up there," Bridget suggested. "Up-strata."

"What? Nobody's going up-strata right now. Things are way too unstable. It's not like it used to be. There's been the demon invasion, and the vampires are sure to be suspicious—"

Bridget gave her a look. "I hardly think you need to worry. The worst thing that could happen would be Marius gives you a nice big hickey—and then you'd have to be with him forever."

"That's not funny," Jill said grimly, not sure whether the idea of becoming a vampire bothered her more than knowing that Marius hadn't tried to make her one already. "It's complicated . . ."

There'd been silly rumors that maybe Marius Dumont had a girlfriend now. But those people didn't understand. Marius's kiss was like a promise. An unspoken promise. At first she hadn't understood, but he'd come to see her time and again and, though it was never anything more than a kiss, eventually she'd understood the depth of what was between them. What *could* be between them if they gave it a chance. However ridiculous it might sound to some, the fact of the matter was this: They were soul mates. He knew it. She knew it.

What she didn't understand was why Marius hadn't already made it a fact. Why did he wait so long between coming to see her? And always when she was in trouble, as if it were the only way he could justify it?

The Dumont vampires had long believed that making a human into a vampire was against some sort of code. But with Dain at the top of the vampire strata with Fleur, that was clearly changing.

Why, then, did Marius not do something about it?

Their relationship was a powder keg waiting to explode. Everything unsaid, but everything felt so incredibly deeply just the same. She knew she wasn't wrong about it. She *couldn't* be wrong about it. But all the same, she had the strange sense that time was running out. Marius had too much time to think about his actions and not enough to think with his heart. . . .

Jill squared her shoulders. "Okay, Bridget, if you were trying to get Marius Dumont's attention, what exactly would you do?"

"You're asking what a bad girl would do about Marius Dumont?" the girl murmured, curling the ends of her ponytail around her finger. "Make him jealous. Go kiss Hayden Wilks in front of him. *That* would get his attention."

Jill laughed. "That might work if those two were ever in the same room together."

"Okay, go get Hayden to bite you and make you a vampire. Then find Marius and voila! No problem."

"Marius wouldn't forgive me for that," Jill said softly. "I think even the idea of Hayden touching me would make him insane."

Bridget arched an eyebrow.

"That's so wrong!" Jill said, laughing. "I don't want it to be a game." She swallowed hard. "The thing is, I really believe we were meant to be together. I know he believes it too. I just have to be patient and he'll come around."

Bridget arched an eyebrow. "I hope so," she said. " 'Cause you've got it bad."

"I do 'got it bad,' " Jill agreed, standing up, as much to avoid further conversation as to get a head start on traffic. "And now I've got to go."

"Seeing what day it is," Bridget said dryly.

"Yes, today's the day I try to drum up assignments," Jill protested with a laugh. "It's not like you were any help."

Bridget checked her watch. "Lucky. You'll make it just in time for lunch," she teased.

Jill felt her face flush. "Girl's gotta eat."

"Absolutely," Bridget said.

She got up and walked Jill to the door. "By the way, I like your hair. Nice highlights. Must have had them done this morning. Looks good." She winked and closed the door after her.

Jill jogged down the walkway, hopped into her transport and kicked the ignition, feeling oddly bitter. She sighed. Always doing the right thing. Always playing the good girl. Looking out for her informants, putting her interests in jeopardy to protect theirs. Doing her job with integrity, for god's sake—not something that could be taken for granted in this day and age. Sharing information at the right times; holding back at the right times. And what did it get her except a pink slip?

But a good girl didn't just take what she wanted, when she wanted it.

It's not just about work, Jill, and you know it.

She should have seduced Marius. She should have found the courage to give herself up to being a vampire and seduced him, given him no choice but to make her one of his own kind. And putting highlights in her hair wasn't going to cut it. Pulling out into the street, Jill glanced into the rearview mirror. She ran her hand self-consciously through her hair, letting the blondish streaks stream through her fingers. Stupid, stupid. She was trying too hard. She knew it, and she hated that about herself.

But all the same, she couldn't help wondering if Marius Dumont really did prefer blondes.

For that matter, as she drove toward the newspaper building, she couldn't help wondering about a lot of the things that Marius would prefer.

It *was* a specific day of the month, and so Bridget had been justified in her teasing. It was the day that Jill made a point to eat lunch alone at the media complex commissary rather than with one of the editors who might be in the right mood to throw her a sympathy assignment. She did that for a specific reason. And while traffic was horrible, as usual, being late was totally out of the question. At least, it was if she wanted to catch Marius. Assuming he showed.

For the last six months, she and Marius had enacted a ritual, something they'd never discussed, something they'd just fallen into. Marius Dumont was a primary vampire, and while the species weren't doing a whole lot of inter-strata mingling in Crimson City these days, he made it a point to be at the paper on the same day every month. Maybe he did have a bit of business to conduct. Maybe it was part of a vampire agenda to show they would not be prevented from walking amongst all species in any strata of the city. But in her heart, Jill knew he showed up for her; and she enjoyed every minute of it. She'd choose the same table at the same time, with her back to the front door and an open seat across from her—in case he ever chose to take it.

Except, he never took it. That was the only kink in the system. Marius would walk inside the commissary for that totally fake lunchtime meeting of his, probably making the same boring small talk with the head of one of the news agencies who likely still wasn't quite sure what he'd done to attract the attention of a vampire leader.

Jill's entire body would thrum, as if Marius were tapping a tuning fork with a frequency set just for her. The words in the novel she'd be pretending to read would swim before her eyes, and she'd bask in the glow of the desire she could feel emanating off his body from across the room.

But he never came over. And she never turned around.

After circling the block a couple of times without any luck, Jill turned her transport over to a valet and headed into the building. She passed by a couple of her former coworkers and gave them a wave, running a few story pitch ideas through her head just in case they mentioned to their bosses that she was around and possibly available to take a job.

Once inside the door of the cafeteria, Jill could tell Marius was already in the room, at a table with his entourage. Her heart beating madly, she moved quickly down the lunch line, randomly piling food on her plate, and then headed to sit down. She pulled a book from her purse and opened it and then, without tasting—without even noticing what she was eating; with every fiber of her being focused on the presence of a single man in the room—Jill ate her lunch.

Unfortunately for her pocketbook but conveniently for her heart, none of her networking contacts peppering the cafeteria approached her to talk shop.

Feigning a need for extra napkins, Jill got up and went to the condiments table. There she got the equivalent of a sucker punch. Looking over at Marius's table from under hooded eyes, she froze.

A tiny blonde thing. A tiny pale blonde thing who wasn't Fleur Dumont sat next to Marius. It was the first time Jill had ever seen the woman with him.

She was openly staring now, and she knew it, but Jill couldn't stop staring and she couldn't move as the horror built up in her heart. And then he looked up, and their eyes met, and he must have seen the pain she was feeling. She couldn't have hid it if she tried. The napkins slipped from her hands and Jill took refuge under the table, picking them up as she blinked back tears. Was it true? Was that girl a fiancée?

Trying to hold herself together would have been difficult under any circumstance; it was nearly impossible as a pair of polished wingtips approached. She didn't even have to look. She could feel him walk up beside her.

Jill thought of the rumor that he was engaged, the rumor she'd refused to even contemplate seriously until now. And she thought of the way Bridget went after what she wanted without concern for things like propriety and neutrality.

Standing up, she tossed the napkins away, closing her eyes briefly just knowing that he was standing so close.

"Jill." Marius's voice wrapped around her like the most delicious beginnings of seduction.

"If you want to talk to me, you'll have to follow," she heard herself say. With that, she turned her back on him and pushed out of the cafeteria and into the VIP restroom off the lobby.

Seconds ticked by. Jill stared at her reflection. *Mar-*

Maybe I will come talk to you, Bridget. Or maybe I'll just talk to Hayden Wilks.

A strange dance this is, Finn thought. Usually in a situation like this, trying to feel out a possible new ally, suspicion and paranoia were the default. In this case, he and Cyd seemed to be falling over themselves to impress each other with their coolness and professionalism.

Cyd had driven up in the transport he'd rented her, precisely on time, in the city parking lot, bottom level, just as he'd specified, and then she'd offered up the ignition key without a moment's hesitation. Finn had responded in kind, simply unzipping his canvas duffle and offering up his entire arsenal for her inspection and selection. She'd given him a funny look, then dug in as if she were at the all-you-can-eat buffet at Harry's Hofbrau.

Leaning against the transport, Finn watched Cyd crouch on the parking lot floor, examining systematically, disassembling and reassembling a couple of different weapons, picking out and trying on some of the light armor, fitting out a utility belt. He still hadn't told her what the job was; he wanted to see how she'd prepare for the unknown. Too much info weighed you down on a job. Of course, too little could be worse.

One thing was becoming clear: Cyd Brighton might talk a big game and have no tangible proof to back it up, but so far she was acting like a true professional. One who wasn't likely to mess around on a job that had the ability to put her good reputation back on the map.

Yes, Finn knew he was her key, her all-important personal voucher back into the underground as a freelance operative. Someone had certainly seen them together—if no one else, Manny knew they were in touch—and there were probably a lot of desperate souls waiting to see if Finn would give her the thumbs-up. If he hired her and didn't get satisfaction—even if she didn't go as far as double-crossing or killing him—she was going to be out of business in this town before she started back up.

But she was a professional. The only thing that kept him from giving her 100 percent of the benefit of the doubt was common sense: she was ex-B-Ops. That, and the fact that she still couldn't or wouldn't account for her prolonged absence.

She finished fitting herself out. Zipping the leftover weapons and armor back in the bag, she looked up at him. "Your transport around here?"

"We'll leave it in yours." He flipped the backseat down, threw the bag into the hatch of her ride, and pocketed the ignition key.

Smiling to himself, he watched her slip on an armored vest and snap a utility belt snugly around her waist. She had to be dying to ask for job details. He would be. But it would be better to keep her on her toes this way, alert, by saying nothing and forcing her to assume the worst.

They walked side by side across the parking lot to the kitty-corner elevator. Cyd reached out and pushed the up arrow—the only arrow. As the door opened, Finn put his arm out to stop her as she nearly stepped over the threshold. Holding the door with his boot, he curled his arm around to the wall of the elevator car and stuck a large Post-it over the security lens; then he nodded at Cyd and she entered.

They rode up in a companionable enough silence. He glanced over at her; she smiled back. It seemed almost as if they'd done this together a million times. Finn swallowed and stared unseeing, at his blurry reflection in the warped metal elevator door. His shades, his gloves, his layers—she had no idea. He wondered if he'd have the nerve to do what he wanted in the end. He wondered if she'd still smile at him if he did.

The doors opened on the top level and, exiting, Finn took a sharp right, leading the way to yet a third corner of the parking garage. As high as this was, the vampire skyscrapers dominating the skyline soared that much higher. He stopped at the ledge, Cyd moving up next to him, not the least bit concerned by the height, nor apparently by the fact that he was readying a belaying line.

It was a blind corner, nearly butting up against the corner of the parking garage, with an odd little space in between that the city planners apparently hadn't argued with. He'd rappelled this building a million times. Because of the angle, you were nearly invisible to all, while having practically a panoramic view of the city behind you. They had to scale down and get to an adjacent rooftop.

They went for it. Cyd traversed the side of the building in good time, though he heard her labored breathing. But the girl was game.

If he'd been alone, it would have gone a hell of a lot more quickly. But he'd factored this into the time allotment—that he couldn't use the equipment built into his arms while in front of her.

He pulled himself onto the top of the other building and stayed low while he helped pull her alongside. She looked as though, if this hadn't been a tryout, she'd have something to say about his assistance; but she kept her mouth shut and crossed the roof behind him.

They worked the rooftop in a crouch, Cyd following

his lead as he went to his stomach at the midpoint and crawled across the gravel to the far edge. On their sides now, facing each other with the utility bag in between, Finn unzipped the bag and they began to assemble their weapons in silence. Cyd did the tripods; Finn loaded the ammo.

They dug in against the suicide barrier, and Cyd snuck a pair of field glasses out of her inside vest pocket. Finn mounted his rifle on the tripod and positioned it the way he always did.

Adjusting the telescopic sights on their rifles, the two of them settled in side by side on their stomachs, pressing close together to present as little viewable area to any who might observe. It really was like they'd been partners for a while. As the saying went, as comfortable as a pair of old shoes. Except, Finn didn't think that people who were like old shoes felt this awkward when their bodies touched.

Cyd was smashed against him from thigh to chest, and, feeling a jolt of arousal, Finn couldn't help thinking how little separated them. A few layers of cloth. That was all there was between them. Between truth and deception.

He'd thought before about revealing the truth of himself to another. Hell, he thought about it all the time. It seemed such a irony that now his temptation should be connected to something so basic, so personal. The phrase "the naked truth" was more than just a phrase for him. Nakedness would show everything he was, everything he risked.

Cyd was female; to reveal his body to her, to not hide what he was—that added an element he'd never considered. He didn't think anyone could imagine what it was like to crush down years of desire because the alternative was to reveal himself as not entirely of the flesh. And that damn bounty on his head . . . That damn bounty colored every single day of his life.

He stared at Cyd's profile, more than a little unnerved by the fact that if she was really the one he would allow himself to trust, there would be more he'd want from her than her connections.

Are you the one?

She glanced over, caught him looking and totally misunderstood. "Don't worry, I'm not going to give us away. Look, um, I think I have a right to ask now that we're in position. What's the job? Because this . . ." She gestured to his mounted sniper rifle. "Unless we're doing a scare, this is kind of . . . not a small thing. Especially given that this isn't exactly a clear area."

Grateful that somebody was keeping focus on the job, Finn peered through the slats of the suicide barrier. Below, pedestrians clogged the sidewalks. It was, after all, a Saturday night. And the main rule these days was safety in numbers. Apart from frenetic pockets of activity such as these, the city was dead.

Cyd looked down at their bodies pressing together in the confined space, thigh and chest. Finn caught her looking, and she flushed. "Bit tight, isn't it?" she muttered, and took refuge behind her field glasses.

Finn smiled to himself, watching her tongue run over the bow of her upper lip as she adjusted the focus she'd already adjusted. "See that restaurant down there?" he asked.

"Yeah."

"In about fifteen minutes, you're going to see Marius Dumont walk out of it."

Cyd flinched and took her hands off the tripod.

"Whoa. Dude. I'm not sniping Marius Dumont. That's *not* a small job. That's not even a medium job."

Finn casually turned on his side, resting his head on his gloved hand. "Why wouldn't you snipe Dumont? What's he to you?"

"Absolutely nothing. Believe you me, I'm not a big fan of the Dumonts. But assassinating people—vamps or not—isn't my thing." Cyd raised her hands. "I mean, I don't know what's happened since I've been gone, but that's just not cool."

" 'That's just not cool'?" Finn asked, fighting amusement. "Well, I'm glad to hear you say that. Because we're not here to snipe Dumont. We're up here to protect him."

"From whom?"

"From anybody who might try to kill him, kidnap him, you name it."

She shot him a suspicious look. "Sniper defense is pretty low-level stuff. I didn't think it paid very well. Any trained operative can do it."

He felt his face cloud a little, and he looked away. "I told you this isn't the big project. This is just a little repeat service I like to provide out of the goodness of my heart."

"What an angel," Cyd said.

He gave a bitter laugh. "Not quite. I have my reasons. But going freelance means you get blood on your hands every now and then. You need to be ready for that. Killing's part of the job."

Cyd looked through her sights. "Who hired you?" Suddenly she glanced over at him, as if she'd had a revelation. "Fleur Dumont."

He didn't answer.

"That's so sweet," Cyd pushed. "So, you don't kiss and tell."

"Do you know her?" Finn asked. A moment later he remembered. "That's right. Her husband is your ex-partner—here's Marius now," he interrupted himself. "I've got the ground; your eyes are on the sky."

Cyd blurted out a startled laugh. Readjusting the focus on her field glasses, she said, "Husband. That's just weird."

Finn watched her scan the nearby rooftops, tried to read her reaction. "You used to be with him?"

"No." Cyd rolled her eyes and laughed again, but he thought it sounded strained. "Everybody asks me that. Why, you jealous?" she asked belligerently.

Finn decided to ignore the question. He checked his watch.

"What's Marius doing down in the human strata, anyway?" Cyd asked. "And at this time of day."

"Just having lunch. He eats here the same day every month."

"Having lunch? At the news commissary?" She gave him a dubious look.

"He's not here for the food."

Cyd tried to puzzle out what he might be there for, and came away with zero. "Are you protecting or spying?"

"I'm just here to make sure the guy doesn't get shot or kidnapped on the way out."

"What about the way in?"

Finn shook his head. "Not my job."

He shifted his body and tightened a screw on the rifle tripod. His arm came to rest on the cement next to Cyd's. The contact surprised him, and he tried to ignore her right arm touching his left, tried to attain the kind of casualness he'd share with a longtime partner. He wondered if she was doing the same.

She was watching Marius Dumont head down the building's stone steps toward a limousine parked at the bottom. "Fleur really is paranoid," she muttered.

He didn't answer. After a moment, he asked, "You know Jillian Cooper?"

"Yeah. I like her. Nice girl."

"Seems she and Marius have some kind of almost thing. She takes meetings with the news agencies on certain days, eats in the commissary. Marius takes a once a month meeting with someone in the name of good human/vampire relations or something. He could afford to eat anywhere he wants; he eats in the commissary. You do the math."

"Oooh, Jill has a real secret life?" Cyd didn't know why she should be surprised, but she kind of was. "Damn. How . . . romantic."

"Word on the street is that Marius just got engaged to some chick."

Cyd frowned. "Oh. How not romantic."

"It is if you consider *Romeo and Juliet* romantic." He turned to glance at her. She looked sad.

"No. I consider it tragic."

"Well, there you go."

"There you go," Cyd repeated. "I wonder if she knows."

"Doubt it. I just heard, myself. Pretty fresh . . ."

They both fell silent as Marius traversed the last few steps. He glanced back at the building, then slipped into his limousine.

Finn moved the rifle to follow the car as it turned the corner, but he also noted how naturally Cyd backed him up, surveying the surrounding area and sky. He was impressed by her pattern, her thoroughness. The car disappeared. Cyd tapped Finn on the shoulder and pointed to a black-clad figure on an adjoining rooftop.

Finn shook his head. "He always stands up too soon. So obvious."

"Who is he?"

"I don't know." He shrugged. "He works that corner. I work this one."

"We clear?"

Finn stuck out his arm and they watched his chronograph tick. Finally . . . "Clear," he said.

"Clear," Cyd repeated.

He glanced up.

"Sorry. Reflex," she explained. "I wasn't mocking you. You can take the girl out of B-Ops, but I guess you can't take the B-Ops out of the girl." Her face suddenly clouded over and she muttered, "And I'm not sure that's such good thing, to be honest."

She had no idea how glad Finn was to hear that.

She stood up and stretched out. "Okay, what's the next piece?"

"That's it." Finn unscrewed his rifle from the tripod, folded the tripod and stood up.

Cyd was still stretching. Her hands on her hips, she ducked her head down. She was trying to get a look at his face; he could tell. "Finn?" she asked.

Unnerved, he knocked his shades, bobbling them, but he quickly recovered. "What?" He secured his hood.

"That was completely moronic. You did *not* need me. At. All. Why the hell did you pay me so much money for that?"

"I told you. To see if I could work with you," he said gruffly. "And I'm happy to report that I can."

"Yeah, but that was my best behavior." She stuck out her tongue. "I'm not always so good."

He chuckled. Putting his tool kit back together, he said, "Behavior aside, the important question is: Can I trust you? I feel like maybe I can." He did. It was scary.

A slow smile crept over her face. "Uh-huh." She checked her watch, clearly slower to trust him in return. "After less than two hours, you feel like you can trust me? 'Cause I sure as hell don't have the faintest idea what to think about you."

At least she was honest. Finn didn't answer.

It took a few minutes to rappel back up to the top of the parking garage. There, Finn had a surprised thought. Looking over his shoulder toward the elevator, he frowned. "I forgot the Post-it," he said. "I don't leave anything behind."

Feeling shy, he gave her a smile. "You distracted me," he admitted. Then he jogged off.

Chapter Ten

Cyd couldn't help but smile as she watched Finn run off toward the lift. "You distract *me*," she replied.

But her smile only lasted a second. It was quickly replaced by dread as a hand came down on the back of her collar and reeled her in. A low, gravelly voice murmured in her ear the very words she'd been hoping to never hear: "Griff-Vai asked me to stop by and say hello."

There were demons still in Crimson City. The ones hiding in the aftermath of their attack. She could not ignore that fact any longer.

She wasn't sure what kind of response the demon was looking for, but she decided on an elbow rammed as hard as she could into his gut. It was the wrong answer. The demon agent pushed her down on the hood of the transport. A gun hung easily from his other hand.

"No contest!" Cyd yelled as the demon latched one hand around her neck, squeezing his fingers together like a vise. "Tell me what you want."

The obvious answer was the amulet. She hadn't been back in this city a week, even, and getting jumped like this was just too much of a coincidence. If he wanted the amulet, why didn't he just say so? It was just hanging out in her pocket like a piece of loose change. She might not know what it was for, but she knew why she still had it; it was her only link to the route that had led her back to Crimson City, and some part of her mind worried that she might need it again someday.

The demon's grip tightened. Eyes watering, lips stinging as they began to go numb, Cyd gritted her teeth and forced herself not to completely panic even as he applied more pressure. Finn wasn't far away. All she had to do was stay alive.

Leaning over her body, the demon swung his gun up to her temple. "Cydney Brighton?" he asked.

She blinked. Looked straight into his eyes, and fear was all she knew.

Glowing red eyes. It wasn't the gun, or that he'd nearly choked her to death. What scared her most were those demon eyes.

"Take it! Just take it!" she screamed.

He didn't seem to process what she was saying, nor have any inclination to search her for the amulet. His lips curled back into a snarl. "I'm just checking up on you."

Cyd just let loose. For a moment, her flailing and screaming over the horror—horror at the idea that Griff might be watching her even now—drowned out everything else, sight and sound. And only in the brief silence as she took a breath did she feel the muzzle jam harder against her temple and hear the weapon cock.

Eyes wide, she waited for the bang, and instead got a thin metal blade barreling down at her out of nowhere. Using all of the power she could muster, she twisted her body up and to the side as the modified icepick missed her by an inch and drilled down into the car. It retracted from the hood with a painful whine, then came at her again.

The demon's hand grabbed at her face, pulling her jaw, trying to invade her mouth. Pinned beneath him and struggling, Cyd screamed and writhed in horrified anticipation.

And then, the demon's mouth opened wide. His eyes bulged, and the gun fell from his grasp and bounced loudly off the car to the pavement below. Cyd stared in terror as his other arm came down, but it fell limply to the side of her face without striking her . . . and without holding a knife. A thin trickle of blood from the corner of the demon's mouth hinted at his fate.

Just a squeak came out of Cyd's mouth. The full weight of her assailant had slumped down on top of her her, and Finn had been revealed towering above them both, blood spattered on his sleeve.

Finn reached down and shoved the body off her. It rolled off the front of the transport and hit the ground with a heavy thud.

"He only had eyes for you," he muttered.

Cyd slid off the hood and stood up on wobbly legs. "I'm better-looking than you are," she said, a weak attempt at keeping things light. Neither of them smiled. Things weren't light. They weren't going to get light. And Griff-Vai quite possibly knew how to find her when he wanted to.

Finn carefully wiped off the hood of the transport with his sleeve. "Getting jumped by dogs, fangs, humans—happens all the time. Never been jumped by a demon before meeting you."

The insinuation in his voice made Cyd incredibly nervous. Dazed, she took a step back and stumbled. He reached out and steadied her, warmth seeping through her sleeve where his fingers curled around her upper arm.

"Damn you," she said, tears sparkling in her eyes.

He pulled his hand away and held up his palms in a kind of surrender. "I didn't mean anything—"

"Damn you for being so nice to me."

Finn relaxed a little. "I wasn't going to let him put a bullet through your brain. I mean, come on."

Cyd pressed the back of her hand against her nose. "That's not what I mean. There isn't anyone to trust. You know?"

"I know," he said. But he looked completely bewildered all the same.

"And you go and do a thing like that. Act the way you do."

"We were looking for a reason to trust," he said softly, then shrugged. "You want to tell me what you think he wanted with you, I'd be interested to know."

Cyd looked up at the sky and prayed she was doing the right thing. Maybe Finn could help, even. After all, he'd been around when the demons had infiltrated the city. Telling anyone about Griff-Vai at this point was impossible without revealing where she'd been. But telling Finn about the amulet . . .

She put her hand in her pocket and touched the artifact lightly with her fingertips. "It's something I found. I think maybe he wanted it. I don't even know what it does."

Before she could talk herself out of it, she pulled the amulet from her pocket and held it out to him. Finn slowly extended his hand; then to her surprise, he winced as it neared the artifact. He pulled it back, turning his head away. His hood shifted away from his face to reveal a flash, as if of metal. "No idea. But it's got some fairly bad-ass juju if you ask me. Put it away."

She did, a little surprised by his reaction; but it looked like blood in the crystal center, and that could turn anybody off—though Finn hardly seemed like the type to get queasy over a thing like that.

"Did he ask you for it?" Finn asked.

Slowly, Cyd shook her head.

"Then I doubt he wanted to get at your toy. More likely he wanted to get at you." He shrugged and walked around to where the body had fallen.

Cyd stared after him, deciding she was a little relieved he didn't pursue the point. "Should we do something with the body?" she rasped.

Staring down at the ground, he said bemusedly, "That's not necessary. No body. The front of this transport is scorched, though."

Cyd rushed to join him. He was right; there was no body. And scorched was an understatement—the grill had completely melted.

"That was a demon agent," she said, trying to keep the tremors out of her voice. "I should get some sort of badge for this. I fought with a demon and lived. I wasn't here when they first went active in the city." *I was just here when they were thinking about it.*

As she stood there staring at the molten metal, Griff-Vai's face appeared in her mind. *You shouldn't have left me, Cydney,* he said. *I want you back.*

Cyd closed her eyes and shook it off.

"You okay?" Finn asked.

"Yeah. Sorry."

"Cydney?"

"Yeah?"

"You said you weren't here when they first went active in the city. Where were you?"

Biting her lips, Cyd couldn't think of a damn thing to say that he'd buy.

"Okay . . . okay." Finn folded his arms across his chest. "Let's go back a step. You *found* that thing?"

"I found it," she repeated through gritted teeth.

Finn studied her face, his suspicion obvious. He threw up his arms. "I think you might be lying about that. And if we're working on trust here, that's a concern. For all I know, you're a demon agent, too."

Cyd reeled back. "That's what you're thinking? I'm not a demon, Finn. I just . . . found it. Origin unknown. If I were a demon, why would a demon come after me?"

He didn't answer, but the suspicion and distrust in the air between them was palpable. And somehow, no matter how reasonable the suspicion was under the circumstances, Cyd lost her mind a bit. Because she didn't want to think it could be possible that she was a demon. Not after all that time with Griff, in that world. . . . And for someone else to think that it might be possible: that made her fear into something more than just silly paranoia. "Don't even think that. Seriously," she said.

"Okay, calm down a second. I'm just trying to put the pieces—"

"Do I look like a demon? Do I act like one? No! I'm not out here running around with an agenda for evil. I'm just the same old Cyd. Cydney Brighton."

He shook his head. "First of all, there are some who say not all demons are evil. And—"

She grabbed him and forced him to look at her, feeling as though her head might explode. He had to believe her. "I'm a human, got that? I'm *human*."

Finn sucked in a breath, as if she'd just kicked him in the gut. Good, maybe he got the point.

"Understand?" she asked. But her words were halting, because she was confused by his expression, confused by her own feelings, nearly desperate to make this man believe her, trust her again . . . help her. "I need someone to understand," she said, her voice cracking.

"*I* understand," he finally said.

And as if he could see what she wanted in her eyes, his mouth came down on hers. Cyd closed her eyes and surrendered.

It was a fierce kiss, but short. His mouth trailed away from her lips, along her jawline to her ear. "Come home with me," he whispered.

Cyd opened her eyes. She felt no sense of teasing, no hint of the kind of overeagerness that had always translated to one-sided satisfaction. She wouldn't have wanted that, would she? She reached out to remove his shades, wanting to look in his eyes. Finn intercepted her hand and curled his gloved fingers through hers.

"Come home with me," he said again. And Cyd knew without hesitation that she would.

Chapter Eleven

Barely out of the car, on the sidewalk, bursting in the front door as he pulled Cyd into his apartment, his mouth was the only way Finn could touch her without fear. He kicked the door closed with his boot and pushed Cyd up against it, pressing his mouth to her bare throat.

Her mouth, her neck—Finn didn't know what he wanted to savor first. He wanted it all. He wanted it *all.* He pulled her even closer, pressing the full length of his body against hers; then he brought up his left hand and pulled the leather glove off with a kind of flourish. He hoped that hid the true turmoil of what seemed like a simple act.

Eyes wide open, Cyd laughed. The leather had come off to reveal yet another layer of fabric, this one a fingerless glove. She couldn't know what it meant, Finn daring to bare enough of himself to be able to touch her skin on skin. The hot wetness of her mouth, the way it felt to trail his bare fingertips along the back of her neck. None of it was simple.

His glove fell to the ground between them; they

both caught the joke. "I throw down, Cydney Brighton," Finn murmured, challenging her in an age-old fashion.

It was all-consuming, his passion. He'd never let anybody over the threshold to his apartment, his world—he'd certainly never invited anybody in. But Finn seemed to have lost his senses somewhere in the haze of desire this girl evoked.

Perhaps it was because he felt so strongly that, after waiting for so long, Cyd would be the one to save him. And the way she'd insisted she was human . . . that meant she knew what it was like to live with that question. She and he were one. If she wasn't lying. But he didn't know why she would lie in that way. Not unless she knew. And he didn't know how she could guess what he was—and with her drab gray-green jacket and armor peeling away, falling to the ground to reveal more and more luminous skin and the shape of a woman not at all built to be a soldier, Finn didn't care.

Cyd slid out of his arms and backed toward the sofa, shedding more clothing on the way. She unzipped her field trousers at the ankles and pulled them off over her boots. She did some puzzling girl-thing and pulled her bra out through one sleeve. Finally she was wearing nothing but a gauzy white button-down garment, the layer between skin and armor . . . and a pair of combat boots.

She gave him a pointed look, stuck one boot up on the coffee table and slowly began to unlace it. Her shirt billowed open, and her leg up on the table seemed like an invitation to another world.

Finn couldn't wait any longer—in any sense of the words—and trying to control the intensity of his desire for her was like asking a genie to wait inside a few more minutes after centuries corked up in a bottle.

Cyd pulled both her boots off and sat down on the couch. She crossed her legs, the fabric of her shirt rippling across her breasts in an unbearable tease. Finn looked her body up and down and almost died.

He knelt on the floor beside her and ran his fingers from her ankles up the sides of her body to her breasts. There he made light circles around her nipples with his fingertips, and she sucked in a quick breath of air. His hands moved slowly, softly, teasingly over her barely clothed skin.

Pushing her back on the sofa, Finn pulled her shirt open and took one breast in his mouth. Cyd arched back and gasped with pleasure. Finn closed his eyes, gently running his tongue around her nipple.

It was amazing. Sweaty and smeared with dirt, Cyd Brighton still perfumed the air with a gorgeous scent, something he'd never been close enough to enjoy before. He didn't know if it was just because she was as willing as he, or whether he'd inhale the same sweetness with any other woman, but this subtle scent of her, this faintly salty taste of her skin . . . they were such delicate things. They were things that he hadn't known existed while in the stale confines of the government barracks. It broke his heart.

Oh, he wanted to touch her everywhere, to feel the completeness of perfect skin. He wanted to possess her. And some part of him had something to prove.

She tilted her head back, and as he stroked his fingertips across her white throat, he whispered, "Our chemistry's sure not off."

Exploring her body, he found his desire spiked even higher by the mere act of touching her, his curiosity and ego stoked every time he won a sultry growl or surprised cry of pleasure. He reveled in the smoothness of her skin, in discovering the incredible silky feel of the wetness between her legs. A corresponding sensation grew in his own body, an all-consuming lust; he wanted nothing more than to free himself and press his cock into her flesh and claim the pleasure that awaited them. But he held himself back.

Instead, he took his time. He listened to her body, to the racing of her heart, and rejoiced at the depth of her reaction. His fingers glided slowly inside of her and touched her very center. He watched her face, stroked the hair spilling out of her ponytail and tangling in the fringe of the blanket she lay back on. Her lips parted, her eyes closed and her cheeks were flushed; and as he worked her with his fingers, he nearly went crazy watching as he brought her to climax and she cried out, her body arching up off the sofa. Afterward she seemed to go soft, burrowing into the blanket, delicate and sated.

A moment of silence passed, Finn watching Cyd's face, almost mesmerized, his hand resting on her naked thigh.

Suddenly Cyd's lips curved in a smile, and she opened her eyes and sat up. Her hands flew to the zipper of his jacket, and adrenaline exploded through his system. A perverse fear of danger, of discovery, added fuel to the flames.

In the dark pools of her eyes Finn read both excitement and an intensity—and something new and base that he couldn't recognize. Her gaze was so specific, so present; he felt almost as if she already knew his secrets and that she wanted him no matter what, tomorrow be damned.

Her hands moved over the armored fabric covering

his utility arm before he even thought to stop her. Sitting up, she laughed, nuzzling her face at his neck and trying to work below the fabric. "You haven't taken enough off. You didn't even drop your weapons for this."

Finn was frozen in place.

"I don't know whether to be scared or turned on," Cyd continued, her mouth curving into a smile. He felt it against his neck. "I choose turned on."

If she's the one you believe can help you, you'll remove the layers and show her everything.

It was the most important decision of Finn's life, and he'd have to make it now. Cyd wanted him naked. She grabbed his shirt, pulling it up from his pants. He took her hands and put them behind her head, trying to hold them away from him.

She thought they were just playing a game. Cyd freed her hands and swept them back under his shirt, and along the ridges of his abdomen, less than an inch away from the unfamiliar coolness of a metal strip she'd never be able to ignore. Finn gasped and pulled away from her, nearly undone. The fiery sweep of her bare fingers against his bare skin—skin that no one but himself, his barracks comrades and a few technicians had ever touched outside of field exercises or a quick handshake—was overwhelming.

"Finn?"

What are you going to do—make love to a naked woman with every single layer of clothing still on you? Not going to happen, man. Not going to happen.

He wanted this more than he could possibly express, but he also couldn't let her see. She was right. There hadn't been enough time to learn trust. And this was his life.

She seemed to sense his shyness. "What's wrong? Everybody has battle scars."

Not like mine, he thought. And while Finn's body burned with want—she could surely see the proof of it, even with his clothes on—he stared in fury at her beautiful, willing mouth, and knew he had to give it up.

"Shit!" she blurted. "Did I totally read this wrong?" She scrabbled to the far side of the couch, her bare legs curling up under her, her arms covering her nakedness as best they could. "Is this some morality issue? Or . . . are you a fang? A dog?" She seemed shocked, as if she hadn't considered the possibility. "Is it—"

He shook his head. "No."

She moistened her lips, then reached out for something to cover herself with, her eyes not leaving his face for an instant. Finn watched darkly as her beautiful body disappeared under a plain gray military blanket, and he managed a bitter laugh.

"No, I'm not having morality issues. I'm not a fang or a dog. And it's not that I'm not attracted to you."

How could she believe that, anyway? The fact that his erection still pressed against the fabric of his low-slung utility trousers was not something she was going to miss. In fact, her glance shifted down and then back up to his face where he felt a muscle in his jaw twitch uncontrollably. The effort of his restraint was superhuman.

"I can tell," she said. "All systems go. Locked and loaded."

He picked up her discarded clothes, choking on his unsatiated lust. "I just . . . can't do this." He put the clothes on the couch next to her and watched a red flush sweep over her skin. "I'm the asshole here. I'm sorry, but that's the way it is."

She dropped the blanket and dressed almost as

quickly as they'd stripped her in the first place. He stepped back and watched her stumble to the door, only one arm in her jacket.

One hand on the doorknob, she turned back to him. "Right. So, if you . . . I dunno . . . if you still want to work together . . . if you ever really wanted to work together, you know where to find me."

And with one twist of the knob, she was gone. The door automatically locked behind her with a dainty click.

Finn ripped his clothes off. Tearing the shirt from his torso, he wadded it into a ball and slammed it down on the floor. Staring at himself in the mirror, he saw his chest heave, his face a grim knot of tension and desire.

"Could you handle this, Cydney? Could you?" He looked first at the gleaming metal embedded in his skin, then desperately around the room as if the answers were there. But there was nothing.

Two strangers, really. They were two strangers who wanted the same thing but who couldn't have it, whatever the reason.

What had she really wanted to happen in there, anyway? She knew. If she'd had the guts to tell him what was in her heart, she would have phrased it in the form of just one question: *Do you have any idea how much I need someone to hold me right now?* Just to hold her.

Finn had given her more. And he'd made further analysis irrelevant by taking charge, by touching her, by making the choice she wasn't sure she'd have had the balls to make. But then he'd put the brakes on. Why? He had some issue. He'd probably been wounded on a job and was embarrassed to show her the scar.

How silly. Frankly, if he had all his parts—and it certainly felt as though he did—the gift wrapping was irrelevant. His touch had made her feel as if she were engulfed in flame. It didn't get any better than that.

Cold drinks and a hot guy: the two necessary ingredients for getting over a bad day. That's what the girls in B-Ops used to say, anyway. But to call herself reckless would be grossly understating the facts. Sex should be pretty much the last thing on Cyd's mind. After Griff Vai and her past.

But, what the hell had just happened there?

Come home with me. Finn had breathed into her ear what should have seemed a cheap proposition, and had made it sound almost like a wonderful promise—an oath of loyalty.

Hurrying away from Finn's apartment, Cyd turned the corner and slammed her back against the wall. They *did* have chemistry, for god's sake. You couldn't fake that.

Maybe she should be pissed about the stop-go-stop business. It wasn't right of him to tease her that way. But if she was honest with herself, her biggest problem wasn't that some guy had thought twice about a one-night stand, but that she'd just messed up a job prospect. If Finn wouldn't at least vouch for her, she was back to square one.

Yes, the whole thing was a textbook error in judgment. The kind she'd made a few too many times before. Coming back from the demon underworld had been an opportunity for a fresh start. She wasn't supposed to use punch, and she wasn't supposed to fall into bed with men she knew didn't love her. That wouldn't make her feel better. And if she did fall into bed with them, at least she was supposed to admit—after it was over—that nothing was changed, so she could remind herself not to do it again.

But for some reason, this time, she didn't feel that old familiar shame, she felt only a lingering glow. And holy crap, he'd been *incredible*. Maybe it was the difference of being clean. She was doing better than ever, staying off the drugs. Was that what caused her libido to burn hotter than she ever remembered? She'd been a goddamn monk for a while. Now that she had a do-over in the city, she felt like the poster girl for a fucking public service announcement.

Maybe it was all in her head, the reason that moment with Finn had been so incredible. Maybe it wasn't some weird "connection." She *felt* incredible. Walking over to a nearby storefront, she stared at her reflection. Damn. She even *looked* incredible. Physically she was doing better than ever.

And then there was that whole griddle burn business at Bosco's . . .

Cyd looked up at the facades of the apartment complexes lining the street, boxy jack-o'-lanterns with brightly lit windows for eyes, and felt strangely optimistic. She turned the next corner and bought a pack of cigarettes at the neighborhood market, stalling to avoid a trip back to the bar. There was nowhere else to go.

She lit a match, enjoying the sound of the flare. Bringing the flame up, she lit the end of her cigarette and let the match fall to the ground. It lay there and flickered.

She played moments of their interaction over in her mind, reliving her interplay with Finn. The delicious feeling in the pit of her stomach came back. Okay, so the perfect scenario would have been giving back to him as good as she'd gotten, and then sharing a cigarette and a stereotypical but oh-so-meaningful cuddle, but that didn't mean she couldn't appreciate what she'd had.

Looking down at the sidewalk, she saw that the flame from her match still hadn't burned out, and a cold dread leached all the warmth out of her body. The flame flared like that of a blowtorch, and at the end of the stubby matchstick, in the blue-tinted combustion, she could have sworn she saw Griff-Vai's face.

Cyd dropped her cigarette, grinding it, along with the match, into the cement with her heel. Staring at the mess of shredded tobacco and paper, she felt a dark, familiar presence. Someone was behind her, watching.

Cyd whirled around to look behind her. Nothing. To the right? No. To the left? Nothing again.

She stood in the middle of the street and stretched her arms out wide, turning slowly in a circle. Opening her mouth, she croaked the first syllable, almost not daring to say the full name for fear it would be mistaken for some kind of summons.

"Griff?" she whispered. *Do you have to ruin everything?*

It was him. She couldn't see him nearby, but his presence was unmistakable. Or at least she had to admit the possibility. The demon who had watched her for so long as she made her halting way through life in Crimson City, the demon who had stolen her from this world, practically in front of the eyes of everyone who'd ever cared about her, the demon from whom she thought she'd just won her freedom, who had sent that demon agent on the top of the parking structure, would not give up on her.

He was watching. If not physically here in Crimson City, then somewhere in his different dimension.

Somewhere in that world to which she never wanted to return. Orcus.

The sound of sirens and the screech of tires as a transport took a corner too fast, a familiar sound from her past, knocked her from her reverie. Cyd dropped her arms and flattened herself into the darkened alcove of a closed storefront, and watched a B-Ops patrol car headed toward her at breakneck speed. Nearly falling to her knees in relief as it passed by, she saw Trask in the driver's seat. He was flailing one arm out the window like a hopped-up drag racer, and she discerned the shadowy figure of JB in the passenger seat, holding on for dear life.

Griff-Vai *isn't* here, she told herself. He can't touch you really, on this side of the veil, or he would have come for you himself by now. And you can beat any of his agents. Don't make yourself crazy. You have a new start, a new lease on life in this town. Somehow the misfire with Finn couldn't bring her down. In fact, it gave her hope. And so, wrapping her arms around her body for warmth, Cyd stepped out and walked down the middle of the empty boulevard, headed back to Bosco's.

Maybe it had just been her old teammates Trask and JB on surveillance, watching her. It was easier and kinder to believe that. Not Griff. No, she had a new life.

Chapter Twelve

"Hey, wake up!"

JB sat up straight in his seat. His partner slowed the car down, slowly flipped his phone shut and looked over at him.

"We've got a confirmation on the Cyd Brighton thing. We're on."

"On? Like, bring-her-in on, or delete-her on?" But JB already knew the answer.

"Yippee-kayyaaaay, motherfucker!"

Great. That was Trask's way of confirming the answer.

"What the hell is the matter with you?" JB snapped, smashing his hand against the dashboard. "She's one of our own."

Trask looked annoyed. "Hey, relax."

"Don't tell me to relax!"

"You're getting worked up over nothing."

"It's not nothing. What happens when they decide it's time for *us* to go? There's not going to be anybody in the department left on our side. Have you noticed we're losing our friends one after the next?"

Trask turned in his seat, his mouth screwed up.

"We've only whacked those who deserve it, JB. These are turncoats, man. They've gone to the wrong side. We're the lawmen. It's our job to take down the bad guys."

"Since when is disappearing a crime?"

"It's called going AWOL, you moron."

JB was silent. After a moment he said, "It's not going AWOL when something terrible happens to you. Her blood was all over that smashed-up telephone booth."

Trask sneered. "She could easily have staged that. And no one ever proved it was her blood. Not to mention that, whether she got injured or not, she should have called in by now. She's back, and she knows who she is. All the reports have verified this. If she's turned, she's turned. You can't just go rogue and expect to be treated like a member of the family."

Trask had a point. JB managed to calm himself down.

Trask took that as a "go" sign. He turned his attention back to the road and jammed his foot down on the gas, peeling a U-turn across two lanes and whipping the car back toward the worst neighborhood in town.

Reaching out a hand to steady himself on the dash, JB looked at his partner. "Dude. Just do me one favor. Let me handle this, okay?"

"No way. Are you serious?"

"C'mon, man. You owe me one. We play it cowboy all the damn time. Just let me take this situation. I can even drop you off somewhere, if you want me to take the blame."

Trask glanced over, a wide smile plastered on his face. "No way I'm missing this," he said.

JB shook his head. Grimly he looked out the window to where pedestrians on the sidewalk flashed by in a blur.

They were headed for Bosco's. Trask had one hand on the steering wheel, one hand checking his gun for ammunition.

"Watch the damn road!"

"Fucking pansy."

"Shut the hell up."

Trask flipped on the music player and turned up the volume on the Prodigy music chip—he liked his violence loud and with a pumped-up soundtrack. JB made a mental note to try to push his change-of-partner request through headquarters faster. Then he calmly loaded his own weapon with both silver and ultraviolet cartridges. There really was the possibility Cyd wasn't what he expected.

They parked a block away from the bar and geared up. JB slipped his protective visor down over his eyes and, after a sigh of resignation, gave Trask the thumbs-up.

A moment later they were quietly sliding down the length of the block, sticking to the shadow of the overhang along the edges of the buildings. Trask at his back, JB slipped silently toward a job he didn't want to do.

Finn's lungs burned as he sprinted down the city streets, leaped over upturned barrels, took the shortcut past a row of burned-out pits still under quarantine. This way was faster than driving around the roadblocks. Most people still wouldn't go near the quarantine areas, for fear they were demon-tainted. He himself was willing to chance it. The run-in with the agent after the job with Cyd had suggested he could take on a demon if he had to. He could take on anyone if he had to. He was a match for anything.

Unfortunately Cyd was not. The pirate scanner he

kept on at all times in his bedroom had broadcast a horrible message loud and clear: Cyd Brighton hadn't called in, and B-Ops was finally going after her. He didn't know what they'd do, but he was pretty sure it would be messy.

You should have trusted her. She's not an insider. They want her, but she doesn't want them. You should have shown her what you really are. You shouldn't have waited.

Bosco's was only two blocks farther, and he was running for his life, in a way. Though that should have been enough, there was an even greater impetus. Something in him was running for *her* life, and that was what kicked him into an even higher gear.

There was something so vulnerable about this girl. She probably had no idea what she meant to him since they kissed. Somewhere inside of his heart, beyond his determination to find someone who could help him rid himself of the things that made him mech, was a simple desire to hold her in his arms once more, to feel again the things that she'd made him feel. For a brief moment, he'd know joy.

He might find another person, another contact to help save himself. But what he truly wanted was a chance with her.

He kept running, nearly knocking the groceries clean out of some kid's arms. Bosco's came into sight with no B-Ops transport parked nearby. At least, not obviously. But that didn't mean they hadn't walked. He headed hurriedly around the back and went in through the kitchen, stumbling over a box of supplies as he tried to decelerate too late.

Cyd was standing there in the kitchen, water dripping off her elbows onto the grime-smeared floor. She held a dish she'd been washing.

"Cyd. Listen to me." Finn exhaled slowly, working hard to steady his breathing. "If you want to live, take this phone, call B-Ops and ask for your old job back."

She stared at him, her blank expression quickly morphing into something closer to anger. "What?"

"You heard what I said. You've got to call in to B-Ops. They've initiated SFQL. You're marked. If they get to you before you square things up, you're dead."

She shook her head, no words forming in her open mouth. Precious seconds evaporated. Finn reached out to take her arms.

"I don't know how to get this across to you. Just . . . do it. Do it."

"What's it to you? You're supposed to be freelance. . . . You're just supposed to be . . . some guy." She looked horrified, as though he'd betrayed her, and Finn wondered if he had.

"Who *are* you, Finn?" she asked.

Cyd stared at Finn, stared at the enigma who had made her feel so good—the enigma who was now pushing her to go back to her old life. "Just do it," he hissed. "They're coming for you, and they think you're an enemy."

"My inclination was to stay away."

"The inclination of the men on the scanners is that you have approximately five minutes before your personal inclinations become irrelevant—except to other corpses."

Cyd tried to get a good look at Finn's face, but he was hiding it in his hood as usual, only one side visible. There was no reason to trust him. What if he had an ulterior motive? But he didn't have the look of someone trying to work an angle. And she didn't sense that.

He put black leather-clad hands on her shoulders, crouching down to put his face next to hers. "Who you gonna trust, huh?" He was practically begging.

Cyd reached out to remove his sunglasses. He let her. She searched his eyes. One of them was bad; she could see it in the harsh kitchen light. One of his irises was entirely black. Weird.

"You looking at me? You seeing me? Who you gonna trust?" he repeated.

"Yeah, I'm seeing you. And I can't trust anyone," she hissed.

"You've got to trust someone."

Cyd thought she heard noises, soft voices behind the building. Finn gave her a shake to bring her attention back to him. She turned on him.

"Who do *you* trust in this city?" she growled.

"I'll trust you."

"What are you talking about?" She didn't believe him.

"I'll trust you. If you trust me." He broke eye contact to look over her shoulder. She noticed he wasn't as bundled up as usual. Something really wasn't right. He'd left home in a hurry. Whether he was dragging her into some kind of nightmare or saving her from one, whatever his fear, he truly believed in it.

Cyd's head throbbed as Finn shook her again. "Trust me. *Do* this," he pushed.

"I . . ." She trailed off helplessly. "You're asking me to trust you? You're saying you'll trust me? After what just happened earlier?"

Why can't everyone just leave me the hell alone? That's what I want, she thought. To be left alone. But another part said: That's not what you want. You lie to yourself. You're just afraid of him being worth trusting.

Finn thrust his cell phone into her chest and retreated toward the swinging doors into the bar. "I'll make things right between us. I swear it. Just . . . do this. And quickly. Take your old job back."

She couldn't afford to believe anybody, but from what he said, she couldn't afford not to.

"I'll trust you on this one thing," she decided. "But if you've lied, I will hunt you down and make you pay."

"I believe you," he said.

Cyd opened the phone and dialed the B-Ops red line. Her heart beat madly as she and Finn stared at each other, and as she waited for someone to pick up. It was a matter of only seconds. It felt much longer.

A female voice pierced the silence. "Red line. This is not an authorized incoming circuit. Identify yourself."

Cyd swallowed. Finn looked over her shoulder toward the back of the restaurant, then back at her. He nodded. Was it merely urgency in his eyes? Or something sinister, something evil?

What kind of a man are you, Finn?

"Identify yourself, or this call will trigger a hacking alert in five seconds," the B-Ops operator said.

Cyd took a deep breath and forced her voice to be steady. She said, "This is Cydney Brighton. Six-five-G-zero-two-seven. I'm back on-grid in Crimson City. Requesting reentry to Battlefield Operations Team, location Central City. Proof of identity, code number Bravo-India-six-oh-niner."

"Bravo-India-six-oh-niner. Pending . . ."

Cyd swallowed hard in the stretched-out silence while the operator checked her code and serial number against her name. She was supposed to remain silent, but the urgency of Finn's body language made the wait unbearable. "This is Cydney Brighton," she repeated. "I'd like to come back on-grid, B-Ops team central—"

"Please hold," the terse voice interrupted.

Cyd looked at Finn. He nodded his approval, then slipped through the swinging doors into the bar.

As the doors swung shut, a new voice on the other end of the phone line initiated the identity-check test sequence. It was Bridget Rothschild; Cyd recognized her chirrupy voice.

She didn't want to go back, the familiar tones only reminded Cyd of that. Even ignoring the fact that her disappearance itself was suspect, they couldn't possibly trust her completely ever again. And she didn't trust them, though she couldn't quite put her finger on which facet of allying with B-Ops bothered her most.

Cyd answered Bridget's follow-up questions by rote memory, her heart pounding. Once, she even thought she heard the scrape of boots against gravel outside.

She was right. Just as she put down the receiver, the back door to the kitchen opened suddenly, and a familiar face came into the light. The man stepped inside.

"Cyd?" he called.

"Cyd?" JB called again, when there was no reply. He moved farther into Bosco's, his hand on his gun.

A figure appeared out of the shadows of the kitchen. She looked pale, and a far cry from the girl who'd been working on his strike team just six months before, grease and some kind of batter were blobbed all over her apron. The grease on the griddle behind her was smoking and burning as if she'd just been standing there staring.

JB swallowed. "Cyd? You're . . . on grid," he said

lamely, taking a step forward and half expecting her to lash out with claws or bare a set of fangs, even though he'd just gotten a message to stand down. "You haven't called in for a long time. Where have you been? Did you know that we were . . . that we missed you?"

Cyd's eyes widened. She was clearly speechless. She wiped her hands on a dish towel that looked even dirtier than herself, and glanced around a little cluelessly. "Where have I been? JB, I have a feeling I'm going to have to get used to that question. The truth is, I don't know what happened to me."

"Okay," he said, inching forward with his hands out, fingers splayed, as if she were a wild animal.

She watched him approach, her muscles taut, obviously tempted to flee. But he'd cornered her, and when finally he couldn't advance any farther without backing her up against the stove, he stopped and they just stared at each other.

He waited a beat to make sure she didn't go for any weapon, then JB lunged and took Cyd in a huge hug that trapped her arms under his. "Everything's going to be okay," he said.

Cyd pulled away from him, and JB let her. He wasn't surprised. She'd never been the affectionate type, and if someone had been mistreating her, that would be amplified. He wondered again where she'd been.

"How about you come into the office with me?" he said soothingly into her ear. He took her in another hug that held her captive with her arms pinned down at her sides.

"I'll come back in tomorrow," she said. "I've got to finish the day here, or I'll lose credit with Bosco."

JB heard the back door swing open.

"Hello, Trask," Cyd said.

"Hello, Cyd," Trask replied. When JB glanced over, he got a nonchalant look. "You done with the nicey-nice?"

JB let go of Cyd's arms and cleared his throat. "I think you'd better come in now," he said to her. "We'll square things with Bosco. He'll understand."

"He and everybody else will understand the wrong thing if you drag me out the front between you guys," Cyd complained.

Doing his best to keep things sounding casual, JB shrugged. He said, "No problem. You go out the back with Trask. I'll square things with Bosco."

A muscle in Cyd's jaw twitched. "You'd better pay him off to get another cook and dishwasher, or I'm going to look bad. I can't afford to lose Bosco's voucher."

"You don't need Bosco's voucher if you're working for Ops," Trask said in a bored voice. Unwrapping a piece of gum, he popped it into his mouth. "You know, if you don't mind me saying, you sound pretty angry for someone who just called in to get their job back."

Cyd took off her apron and jammed the ball of cloth onto a hook. "Oh, you know me," she said sarcastically. "I hate Mondays at the office. And I'm moody, unpredictable . . . all that stuff. Look, if we're going to go, let's just go."

"Sure," JB soothed. "I'll go talk to Bosco. See you out front." He pushed through the swinging doors and headed for the proprietor.

He had to admit it was a pretty big coincidence, her calling in just as they were arriving to take her back under less pleasant circumstances. He'd give a lot to be a fly on the wall during her interview with the boss.

And there was no question in his mind that, despite the fact that Cyd had called herself in, right now she'd give a lot to be anywhere else.

Chapter Thirteen

JB and Trask handed Cyd over to Bridget Rothschild, of all people, which was odd because the last time Cyd had interacted with the annoyingly fresh young thing, apart from hearing her voice while reporting in, she was working admin out on the base for I-Ops.

"You transferred?" Cyd asked, using her peripheral vision to watch the boys file their report.

"I split time," Bridget explained, fluttering around in Cyd's personal space just a little too much. She directed Cyd to the back rooms of the depot. "They just promoted me to B/I Ops liaison."

As she passed through the B-Ops depot and glanced into the coffee room, it pained Cyd to see that only a few months were gone, and the faces were mostly those of strangers. And the room where Dain Reston had been such a fixture had a different tone, carried a different vibe. Everything was different.

JB managed a kind of a smile, following Cyd down the hallway. Most of the other team members looked at her blankly, curious, some a bit suspicious. One or two who were surely new to the team even managed a fair quantity of hostility.

I don't know what I'm doing here, Cyd thought. Finn better have a really good explanation for all of this. He'd better be right about what they planned.

As she passed the row of cubicles in the administrative center of the depot and headed toward the questioning room, she began to think he'd been right. Everybody looked up, frozen midact, watching her walk by. Cyd began to sweat.

Bridget reached out and opened the door to one of the hybrid interrogation rooms. Cyd stared inside at the furniture. She wasn't used to being on the flip side of this business, and getting questioned next to a bunch of medical equipment wasn't her idea of fun. Which was probably the point. They'd use the same punches they'd used on everyone else.

Cyd froze on the threshold and pushed back against what was apparently supposed to be Bridget's comforting palm on her back. "I don't need an exam," she said. "In fact, I don't need this first-day-of-school meet-and-greet at all. I *have* worked here before."

Bridget's shove was a surprise. As was the girl's iron grip as she led Cyd to the exam chair. "Sorry. Security measures." She whipped out an optical reader and shined it in Cyd's eyes, taking measurements and a retinal scan.

"I'm not in the system anymore?" Cyd asked.

Bridget pursed her lips, concentrating as she logged the various dimensions of the planes and angles in Cyd's face on the swing-arm computer. "They assumed you were dead." She looked Cyd straight in the eyes and smiled—the expression was a little saccharine for Cyd's taste. "I'm so happy you're not. Welcome home."

Cyd suppressed an urge to roll her eyes. "Um, thanks."

A man in a white lab coat appeared from a side doorway. He smiled. "Hey, Cyd."

"Hey, Doc."

"I think you know the drill. Stay in your seat. Everything's going to be fine."

"Yeah," she said, hugging her arms to her and fighting the urge to cry.

The doctor wheeled a seat over beside her and took her arm. He glanced up at her in surprise. "You cleaned up," he blurted.

Cyd stared at her knees.

"You know what's between us is confidential," the doctor urged.

Nothing is really confidential in Ops, Cyd thought.

Frowning, he studied the inside of her arm. "I'm going to be blunt here. I thought you used punch. You don't have any track marks. That's very odd."

Cyd was annoyed at his joke. She glared at him, then looked down at her arm . . . and saw what he saw: Nothing. The faint track scars were gone. Her skin looked, if not exactly fresh, then . . . undamaged. Forcing herself not to give away her shock, she tried to recall if Medical had ever taken pictures for their records. What did this mean, and how would they interpret it?

"Maybe you shouldn't listen to rumors," she grumbled, and then quickly looked away to stare at a chart of the digestive system hanging on the wall.

Shrugging the doctor held a heart monitor against her chest. His face turned to watch the green lights going nuts on the screen. Then he reached over and stuck something into her arm. Cyd blacked out.

When she came to, not much had changed. She slumped in the chair, the doctor was still beside her.

Next to him was someone else, someone she'd never met. His rank was clipped to the collar of his button-down shirt. Cyd frowned. He wore the same rank as her old boss.

"Where's Kippenham?" she asked.

"I'm the new guy around here," the man said pleasantly, helping her sit up. "Will Gaviola. You really gave us a scare," he added. "You weren't supposed to react to the test like that."

"What time is it? How long have I been out?"

"Two minutes or so. Enough for us to get the tests done." He turned to the doctor and nodded, and the man left the room.

She blinked and tried to clear her head, propping her elbow on her thigh and resting her head in her hands. "Well, I guess I'm cleared, huh?"

"You're not a vampire. You're not a werewolf. But that still leaves one question unanswered."

Cyd looked up, feeling suddenly vulnerable in the rather sterile medical room.

"Where have you been?" Gaviola asked. He stared at her, jovial but hard as steel.

Cyd shivered. There was no way she was telling the truth. Not with all that had gone on here, with the invasions. For her to have been Griff-Vai's prisoner, his love slave . . .

"I think I was in a coma," she said. "Something took me from that phone booth. I don't know whether it was intentional or accidental, but I feel like I've been out cold for a year. Suddenly I woke up in an alley, and I had no idea how I got there." She looked Gaviola straight in the eye, used everything she knew about lying suspects and made sure she didn't make any of those same mistakes.

"Amnesia?" he asked skeptically.

"Yeah," Cyd said, doing her best to look as muddled as she could. Lies, lies, lies.

The boss leaned back. "You asked for Kip. Kippenham, your old superior."

Cyd nodded. "I expected to see him."

"He's dead. I'm sorry. If you've only just heard, I understand it's probably a shock."

Cyd stared up at Gaviola for a long while, then moistened her lips and said, "It's all a shock. Where did you transfer from?"

"I've been monitoring species activity in New York City. I knew Kippenham on a videophone basis. They flew me in before the quarantine." He cleared his throat. "Your partner, Dain Reston . . . are you in contact?"

"No." Cyd fiddled with a rubber band, stretching it out, then letting it snap back into shape.

"Do you intend to be?"

"I don't know. Is he considered an ally or an enemy?"

"Would that matter to you?"

Cyd looked at him in surprise. "What the hell does that mean?"

Gaviola smiled. "Sorry. I forget you're not used to working with me. I prefer to be blunt. I'm not much for subterfuge. Your file clearly indicates that you have issues with authority, and that you were an excellent informant liaison because it allowed you to go off-grid on a regular basis, to shut off the comms and cut contact with the teams. You were a . . . loose cannon we could use mostly to our advantage."

She chewed on her lower lip and studied him. "That's true. But . . . JB has my old job. He's likely doing it differently, but I don't feel the need to take it away from him. He's earned it. He's a good guy. He can probably use the pay increase."

Gaviola laughed. "You'll have no argument for me. That's not where we want to put you anyway."

Cyd felt a sinking sensation in her stomach. "You want me to work with the vampires? You want me to do surveillance on Dain or something? You say you prefer honesty? Okay, I'd rather not work against my old partner, for what it's worth. Is there—"

"You're not working the fangs," Gaviola interrupted. "I'm putting you on a new B-Ops/I-Ops tandem project. It hasn't really been official until now. But it seems to make sense."

Cyd shifted uncomfortably in her chair. "Um, I'm not really the I-Ops type."

"You were once." He flipped open her file. "Paranormal R & D division. You graduated first in your class and chose demon research. Administration ended the project, but the circumstances were top secret, which is why I have no details. I do know that whatever happened . . . changed you, and that you requested a transfer to B-Ops to work the streets."

"I appreciate your delicacy," Cyd said. "But the details are that everybody's dead except me. And I have no plans to revisit the past." She shuddered just thinking about it.

The boss leaned over the table. "I believe you don't know what happened to you over the past few months. However, I think we both have a suspicion."

His insinuation hung in the air. Cyd didn't rise to the bait, though; she wasn't planning to give an inch.

Gaviola went on: "All right. My question for you is, if you won't work the dogs because of JB, and you won't work the fangs because of Dain . . . then what did you plan to do for us? Why did you call in?"

Because a guy I chose to trust told me you were planning to kill me. Choking, Cyd said, "I never had a chance to give official notice. I wanted to quit."

Gaviola just stared at her. She knew he'd never let her quit.

"The demons? Is that what I'm here for?" she whispered.

The boss played with a paper clip. "That's correct."

Cyd focused on his face. This was her worst nightmare. "I don't know anything," she said hoarsely. "I can't help anybody." She unfolded her arm and stared at the smooth skin, once scarred and marked. *I can't help anybody. I can't even help myself. For god's sake, what's happened to me?*

Gaviola studied her file and then folded his hands over the papers. "Let's talk about this veil. The demons have been passing through it to get to us and our world. It's been ugly. Real ugly. The last few months . . ." He stopped and stared at her, and asked, "You're not bullshitting at all, are you? You don't know about any of this."

She just shook her head.

"The fangs and dogs have become the least of our problems. It's these demons we've been doing the serious battle with. The demons came in, and they pretty much decimated half of the city before B-Ops, I-Ops and a whole squad of mainline government troops came in and did a full-scale deletion. We've got a whole new trade in demon bounties."

Her heart leapt into her throat. She was glad they'd stopped the heart scan; she was sure the thing would look like a 9.0 earthquake. What were they going to ask her to do?

"Before B-Ops, you used to work in Demon R and D. Your file is pretty light, for obvious reasons. Afterward, that entire department was purged. Which, in hindsight, was a bonehead move. You're our only known link to that team and everything that happened. Frankly, you're our only friendly." Gaviola shook his head and sighed. "We're also having some issues with double agents, Cyd. Do you know anything about that?"

A crawling sensation made the hairs on the back of her neck stand up. "What kind of double agents are you talking about?" she asked. Her mind was still whirling. Were they really going to pull her back into her worst nightmares?

"Demons." He glanced up, noted the surprise on her face. "We're talking about demons. Haven't you been paying attention?" He gave a rueful laugh. "If only we'd known that no amount of document shredding and pretending we didn't just see what we thought we saw could prevent them from coming back."

"What . . . ?"

The boss frowned, and Cyd realized she'd mouthed the words, but no sound had issued forth. "What do you need from me?" she rasped out.

His eyes looked so kind, so sympathetic. He reached over and lightly touched her wrist. "The demons got through the portal. They're not just something for research teams to worry about anymore. We were able to stop their invasion attempt, but just barely. We think we've weeded out the double agents, but we're not sure. Nowhere is safe. But you're going to change all that."

Gaviola stood, clearly indicating that the discussion was over. Tossing her the human resources employee-welcome kit, a temporary government ID, and a Glock, he said, "We've got the National Guard, B-Ops and the cops to try and take down any others we can identify. But we need somebody to stop them from sending anyone else. Our experts say the portal is closed . . . mostly. We need someone to find a way to close it for good."

Cyd couldn't breathe. She couldn't breathe. Couldn't breathe. Her temperature rose, she was sweating . . .

"What exactly is it I'm looking for?" she finally managed to say.

"I want the demons blocked from ever coming back here, Cydney. And I think you do, too. I want you to get everything together, reassemble everything that's left of the research done by your original team. I want to know what we did to let the demons in . . . and I want to know how we undo it. You may not wish to revisit history, but that's exactly what you have to do. I've assigned Bridget Rothschild to you; she's at your disposal. Anything you need to put that lab back together, let us know."

"I don't think that's a good idea," Cyd said.

"Well, you'd better start getting used to it. Welcome back, Cyd."

A fury rose up inside of her. She'd wanted a chance at a fresh start. She'd wanted a chance to put her past behind her. "Sir," she asked, "can I ask you a question?"

"Shoot."

"If I hadn't called in . . . would you have had me killed?"

Gaviola laughed. "Don't be ridiculous. We might have threatened, but we wouldn't have done it. You're special, Cyd." He nodded. "And we're glad to have you back." He went out into the hall, called the doctor back into the room, then smiled kindly down at her. "A few more tests. Standard practice."

Another needle prick. Cyd closed her eyes and, for a moment of sluggish peace, remembered what it felt like to be able to numb the pain. Then all went black.

Chapter Fourteen

Cyd didn't know how long she'd been out, but she woke with a gasp, as if she'd stopped breathing for a moment; and she realized it had been long enough—and she'd been out of it enough—to now find herself unceremoniously installed in I-Ops base housing. The unmarked white of the ceiling scared the hell out of her. She got tangled in the sheets and catapulted out of bed to the floor.

"Christ."

Well, she was wide awake now. She unwound the sheets from her ankle and stood up. It took her a few minutes and a glance out a window to deduce that things weren't exactly as she remembered them here, and it was all she could do not to make a SWAT run-through of the apartment just to make sure she was safe. Then she remembered how long she'd been gone, and all the things that had probably happened.

She staggered out into the living room and noticed a piece of paper that had been slid under the front door. She picked it up, her heartbeat racing, but it was just a memo from the housing department apologizing for the new-paint smell, but they were rebuilding and refurbishing properties in the aftermath of the demon destruction of LAX.

Jesus H.

She crumpled the paper into a ball, looked around for a wastebasket, and then went into the kitchen to toss it into the garbage there.

There were the usual appliances, everything in the sort of beiges and browns that were supposed to offend the fewest number of people. She was, of course, completely offended. The antiseptic smell in the kitchen made her faintly nauseated. She lifted one of the slats in a nearby blind and peeked out. Across the street was a row of identical, newly built apartment buildings. She lifted the slats a little farther apart. Looking west, she should have been able to see the LAX traffic-control spire. It wasn't there.

She took another look around the apartment, finally wandered back into the kitchen and stared down at the pristine coffee machine; then she backed out and headed for the bathroom. She stopped halfway over the threshold, turned around and went to the apartment's comm unit. She opened the bottom of the device, poked around amidst the wires, found the bug and pulled it out. She went back to the bathroom and flushed it down the toilet.

The shiny glass, white tile, and gleaming metal—it all gave her a headache. Sure, when she'd had a place, it had looked like crap, but at least it had been her own; she wasn't being forced into a job that would mean her downfall.

She washed her face in the sink, then grabbed a towel that felt somewhat like sandpaper, apparently having been washed in Central Cleaning about a billion times. She dabbed dry and stared at her face in the mirror, and did a double take. Damn. She still looked pretty good, all things considered. And, like the marks on her arms, it looked as if the scar on her cheekbone from the broken phone booth glass was finally starting to fade. Part of her was glad. She didn't want any reminders of that night.

Dressing in clothes that were provided for her, she stepped out into her brand-new Stepford neighborhood and looked around. It was dead silent. Not a soul around. Everything looked and smelled new. Chewing on her thumbnail, Cyd surveyed the area, taking in the details of the place. Everything about this side of the fence—the world of I-Ops—made her skin crawl. She remembered it too well.

As she stood there in the unnatural silence, it took only a few moments for her anger to return. She remembered Gaviola's denial. He had seemed sincere, she had believed him. Just like she'd believed Finn.

Finn. Finn. Finn.

I don't know if you set me up or what, but it sure looks that way. I'm going to find everything out about you I can, and at the next possible opportunity, I am going to kick your ass.

Finn checked himself in the mirror. Nothing that wasn't supposed to be showing was showing. He was wearing two or three different layers of fabric everywhere except his face and hands. He traced a finger along the silver thread running from the corner of his screwed-up eye to just behind his temple, then slipped on his wraparound sunglasses and checked his face from every angle to confirm that he was covered. A generic bully hat, the kind he usually never wore, and, also out of character, he donned a long coat he'd picked up at the Goodwill the other day, with a raised mandarin collar he could sink behind.

Those in the business might guess who he was, but the average citizen couldn't possibly peg him for anything other than an anonymous street punk. These days, there were a lot of those. And thank god there were; Finn had made an art of going unnoticed in the middle of any crowd.

Satisfied, he put on his leather gloves, practicing removing the right one with lightning speed. The leather slid away, and he raised his arm and fired—a blank from the metal weapon cunningly built into his arm. Pleased with the functionality, he put the glove back on. He'd keep the arm intact until the very end. He had no choice; he couldn't afford to live without it. But when he finally got access to the mechanic and was at the end of this journey, one way or another he'd get it off himself. Pry it off, rip it off, or burn it off, he'd do whatever had to be done, until he was just a man.

Finn set his alarm system and laid out a couple of "tells" to let him know if anyone broke into his apartment; then he stepped out into the streets and headed for Encino.

People were definitely out tonight. He tucked farther down behind the collar of his jacket and picked up the pace as he hit Ventura Boulevard. It wasn't a particularly cold evening, and he was overdressed, but no one seemed too interested.

He was working a multiple tonight, a group job, which he hated. At least it was a ladder scheme: He had no idea who the others were, how many there were or how his job linked with theirs. He'd purposely moved up the food chain of crimes and misdemeanors at Bosco's, and taken the sort of thing he usually tried to stay away from. But that was his only option. It was the nature of the business. You pulled a job off the bulletin board and you earned your living, and it was nobody's business but yours and the guy you had to take for a ride.

On the surface, it wasn't a good idea to take a job when you didn't know the other participants. If you didn't know them, you didn't know if you could trust them. But Finn tried not to know anybody; not while he was still like this. He didn't dare. So since he'd slipped into this relatively normal life in Crimson City, he'd been forced to become something he might otherwise have spurned. At least there had been no shooting the shit, no clinking beer mugs after work. Nothing that might let his guard down and reveal his secret.

No, he didn't want anyone to know about him, and he didn't need to know about anyone else. Whatever the jobs were, whomever they were for, that had nothing whatsoever to do with his problems. The fangs stealing intel off the dogs, or the humans doing it to the vamps or vice versa—no matter what kind of truce, what kind of pact was being discussed in the city, everyone still worried and plotted. And where there was plotting, there was a market for intel. He would know. Hadn't he been an instrument of human offense? Hadn't he killed those two vamps on the orders of Kippenham all that time ago, forced to by his implants?

He didn't like not being in the know tonight; there was a similar feeling of helplessness. But it beat being discovered himself. A multiple was used to make a job less traceable, more difficult to puzzle out.

He allowed himself a brief moment of optimism. If luck was with him, he'd finally found someone who could help him with his secret. That was the point of taking a blind job like this one; he needed money to bribe the girl. He needed to have enough both to bribe her to do what he needed . . . and then bribe her not to tell.

Of course, there was no way around it: He was going to have to tell her.

Heading up the block, Finn could smell his destination before he even got there. Mulberry's Pizza. The smell of the food almost made him smile. Something about the smell of pizza smacked of normalcy. Brilliant normalcy.

He checked his watch again. Early. He walked straight past the restaurant and turned the corner at the end of the block, blending himself in among the patrons at the nearby newsstand. There he waited.

After a few minutes of browsing, Finn stole a look at the watch on the wrist of a guy reading a magazine next to him. Time to go. He paid for the magazine, turned the corner and dumped it into the first trash can after a quick glance behind him. Then he headed into Mulberry's.

Burly guys in stained aprons stacked to-go orders on the counter. A delivery boy with a bicycle wheel tucked under his arm compared an order to a tower of boxes. The phone rang off the wall as a sweating cook used a giant spatula to lift pizzas in and out of the double-stacked ovens.

Finn leaned over the counter toward the surprisingly scrawny guy manning the register, and asked for his phone-in order; a medium pepperoni with extra sauce. Ordering a small for himself would be suspicious, and the extra sauce gave the order a little extra legitimacy. He didn't want anyone questioning his visit.

As he paid for his pizza, he watched the orders pile up next to the register. Sullivan, Jenny, Chris, Voransky, Wilks . . . *Wilks*. His mark. He'd been told Wilks. The first person he'd thought of was the rogue vampire, Hayden Wilks, but he didn't actually believe that would be the man to show.

The door opened as the register guy handed Finn his pizza, and Finn headed toward one of the small tables lining the side of the restaurant, pretending to fuss with his wallet. From his vantage point via the mirrored beer sign on the wall, he saw the Wilks pizza come down off the stack. He glimpsed a bit of swagger and heard some foul language from the pizza's recipient, and Finn turned, catching sight of a figure with dark hair and pale skin leaving the joint. The door closed again with a cheerful chime.

Finn slipped out after his mark, not above a moment of regret as he ripped the order slip from the side of his box, dropped the fresh pizza next to a bum on the sidewalk, and kept moving.

As he reached his mark, he threw him to the ground as though it was a mugging, rustled in the groaning guy's coat pockets, searching hurriedly for the item in question.

"Where is it?" he hissed.

Wilks looked at his pizza box. "You didn't really think I was going eat all that fat, did you?"

Finn rolled his eyes and grabbed the box. "Try to act like you're hurt," he whispered.

"I don't think that's going to be a problem. Ease up next time."

Finn didn't answer; he just got the hell away. Nobody seemed to be around, to be watching, but he knew better than to assume that if you couldn't see them, they weren't there. After all, one of his specialties was to be present without seeming to be.

His piece of the job had been to do a soft beat-up of a guy named Wilks and get this transfer, whatever it was; then to go sit on a park bench three blocks away.

Just before he turned the corner, he looked back over his shoulder. Wilks was just now crawling off the ground, putting his hand on the wall and getting to his feet. He'd be fine.

Finn ducked into an alley and took a moment to quell the fire inside him. He didn't quite like doing violence, but something primal inside of him fed off it. Something he hoped could be removed with the right set of tools.

His was a strange way to earn a living, he realized, but it served dual purposes. The more he established himself as someone to fear, the more likely people would leave him alone. He hadn't had to kill anyone yet for realizing what he was—no one except that bounty hunter who would have done the same to him—but it seemed inevitable unless he got rid of the evidence. He didn't want to have to hurt the innocent.

The small city park wasn't far. No more than a fifteen-minute walk. Finn made it there without a problem, and settled onto the designated bench.

He opened the pizza box, a little disappointed when he saw the vegetarian topping, but dug in. He sensed the presence of someone after about three bites. Pretending to be completely engrossed in his food, he was unsurprised when a few moments later a gun barrel was placed at his temple.

"Don't move."

Finn made a mental note, cataloguing the low growl of the voice. He looked straight ahead, but he also used his peripherals to watch his assailant reach over the bench toward the pizza box, rip some cardboard off the spine and remove a flattened, sealed envelope. The guy stuffed the object into the breast pocket of his coat, grabbed a piece of pizza and jogged away. Mission complete.

Finn took a moment to register the fact that the growl and the general body shape of his assailant undoubtedly made him Tajo Maddox, that this was the second job he'd been staffed on with both Hayden Wilks and Tajo, and that on both of the jobs neither of them had been too concerned with maintaining their customary level of attention to detail and security.

He sat there in the park, staring at a very small patch of intensely green grass—a dividend of the city's rebuilding initiative—and finally just shrugged and scraped bell peppers off another slice of pizza.

A strange way to earn a living, indeed.

Finn finished the pizza and tugged at the sides of his collar, sinking into it as far as he could. He rose and tossed the box into a corner Dumpster, then cut across a darkened parking lot. His plan was to go straight back to Bosco's and pick up another job.

Cyd Brighton was probably trying to track him down by now, undoubtedly pissed off. He knew she wouldn't understand. She hadn't wanted to go back to her B-Ops team, and he didn't blame her; the last thing he would want himself was to be under the government's thumb again. But they would have killed her—that was clear enough from the talk on the scanner. And Finn wasn't going to let that happen.

If he was honest with himself, it wasn't just because of what he needed; it was also because of what he wanted. The memory of his fingertips, his mouth against her body, her mouth open in a pleasured moan—it was never far from his thoughts. He wanted another chance.

So, she would come around. And when she did—

Bam!

Chapter Fifteen

Finn went flying into a concrete wall, courtesy of a full-bore body slam that he hadn't sensed coming. His instincts kicked in, a little late he supposed; but in a split second he had a choke hold and a swift knee in his opponent's stomach before he realized whom he was about to beat the living crap out of.

He let go immediately, stepping away with his hands up, palms out in full surrender. Cyd Brighton slid to the ground, gasping and wheezing. He let her catch her breath, then reached down with a gloved hand. She managed a smile and took his hand, and he heaved her to her feet.

She bent over slightly, still recovering from having the wind knocked out of her, then casually lifted her hand as if to brush the hair back from her face. Her hand detoured, and instead she delivered a mean right hook to the side of his cheek.

Finn grunted and turned just in time, catching only a fraction of the force of the punch, but her sheer fury propelled him into the wall. He heard Cyd yelp from the pain of impact against the metal in his face, even as he struck his other cheek against the brick. He instantly covered the injury with his hand.

Facing the wall, he touched the area gingerly, gently pressing against his cheek and jawline. It wasn't bad. She hadn't broken the skin; she wouldn't be able to see anything. But her knuckles were probably bleeding.

"We're not going to get anywhere like this," he said. He turned back and found her once more doubled over, this time holding her fist in her hand.

"Let me see," he said, fishing in his jacket pocket for something in which to wrap her hand.

"I'm fine," she managed to say, turning away from him. She inhaled sharply and released a quick, harsh breath, as if she'd been holding back her anguish, and then forced herself to stand upright. Shoulders back, defiance written all over her face, she stuck her injured hand into her jacket pocket and pulled herself together.

Stubborn. Damn stubborn. Finn calmly reached out and wrenched her hand out of her pocket.

"Hey!"

She struggled but couldn't match his strength, so he studied her knuckles at his leisure and then let her pull away. No blood. For a minute they'd looked quite bruised, but it must have been the light. Upon closer inspection, she seemed fine. She must have delivered the punch on an angle as he turned.

"I said I was fine."

"That was a hell of a punch," he said grimly, his hand moving up to his jaw.

"You'll get over it." She took a step forward, obviously trying to crowd him against the wall. Her boldness surprised Finn. He had cultivated a reputation for being the kind of guy you didn't work idle threats on.

He'd even had to break a couple of limbs in the beginning to get the right message across. Apparently Cyd didn't see him as too dangerous; she'd been willing to attack him.

"You owe me an explanation," she snarled, advancing on him as much as possible without their bodies touching.

Finn's instinct was to swat her away like a fly. She had no idea how easy it would be for him to crush her, to simply put her lights out. But something else in him was stronger: a sense of protectiveness toward her, a sense of affection. Yet that affection didn't overpower his sense of self-preservation.

"Back off," he said.

"Are you afraid of me?"

She gave him a hard look, and he snorted. "I just don't want you to hurt yourself."

"You don't want me to hurt myself? It's okay if you set me up and drive me into the arms of an agency I want nothing to do with anymore. It's okay if you pretend that you want to give me a voucher, when you get me naked in your apartment and leave me hanging. All you want to do is gain my trust so you can use it against me. But that's all okay . . . as long as I don't *hurt* myself?"

She was apparently pretty furious. She jammed her palm against his shoulder blade. "Why did you want me back in B-Ops so badly? Huh, Finn?"

"First, calm down."

"Oh, don't tell me to calm down!" Both her hands shoved him backwards. "I hate when people tell me to calm down."

"Don't touch me again," he warned. He made his voice cold.

She cocked her head, then reached out with her index finger and poked him in the chest, a how-'bout-them-apples look on her face.

Finn forced himself to control his temper. He didn't like being manhandled. He didn't like being condescended to. Not many tried.

She made a move to grab for his hood—to pull it down off his head, it seemed—and that was more than he was willing to take. That old sweet instinct—violence, violence—burned its way up in him to the point where he thought if he so much as opened his mouth to try to reason with her, he'd breathe fire. Her fist came at him once more, and this time he lashed out physically. Grabbing her by the wrist, he twisted her arm to the point of fear.

"I saved your life," he growled.

"Says you," she said, sucking in her pain. "They told me they weren't planning to kill me."

"Then they're lying to you."

"I think *you're* the liar." She lashed out with a well-placed kick, aiming for his groin. He dodged it, loosening his grip on her, and she wriggled out of his grasp. She grabbed for his jacket and his hood slipped, the shades knocked from his face and clattering to the ground.

All Finn could think about was concealing the truth of what he was. He couldn't let her see him again up close, couldn't let her examine the metal threads visible near his temple. He ducked his head, but the wall prevented complete escape. He turned and grabbed her around the waist, hauling her body into his tight enough so that she could see only over his shoulder. She yelled, and he hauled her closer, smothering her cries in his jacket.

"Are you really this fearless? Or just stupid?" he asked her quietly.

She struggled furiously, but he had her immobilized in his bear hug. Finally she gave a muffled curse and stopped moving. She exhaled, her hot breath smoking through his jacket.

Then she was talking again, asking for answers, but Finn didn't comprehend the words. He lost track of the conversation for a moment, distracted by the sensation of holding her so close. Of her smell, of her feel. She was so soft, and yet so hard.

What would it mean to tell someone? To tell her? To trust her? Just the idea that someone else knew, someone who wasn't trying to kill him—it was a desperately appealing concept.

Slowly, Finn lowered his forehead to rest on her shoulder, and closed his eyes and let his breath come out long and slow. He felt her body tense against him, and he released her, embarrassed by the pleasure he'd felt in something so silly. In holding a female body. In holding someone who didn't even want to be held.

Cyd stepped awkwardly away, clearly recognizing his desire and confused by it. "Whoa. We went there, remember? It didn't take. As I recall, you pushed me away." Her tone was still as confrontational as ever, but her body language had relaxed some, almost as if their brief moment of contact supplied a kind of welcome familiarity for her as well as him.

After a funny little pause, she said more calmly, "Okay, let's clear something up. What that was . . . what we did . . . that was, like, a one-time shot. That was that, and this . . . this is business. Right? Do I have this right?"

Finn nodded, struggling with a smile in spite of the seriousness of his situation. She could play it off all she wanted to; he knew better. He could see her naked perfection in his mind as clearly as if she was still lying sprawled out in ecstasy on the sofa before him.

Cyd cleared her throat. "So, here's the thing. I want some answers. I *deserve* some answers. And if I like the answers, then I think we'll come out of this okay. But you need to start talking. If you can't trust me, now who can you trust?"

Her words echoed in his ears, the vision of her vanished. She was right, of course. This was business.

This is your shot, Finn. You haven't come this close to someone who can make things happen for you since you slipped the Grid. You're going to have to tell her everything. She's as good as it's going to get. You've done your research. You've got her where you need her and, even better, she has no true allegiance to anybody—not B-Ops, not I-Ops, not anybody. She's a rogue at heart. It doesn't get better than this.

"You're right." His voice sounded strained and hoarse, and he struggled not to show the weakness or the fear he felt. "I owe you the truth."

She swallowed, looking almost as sick as he felt.

"I do need you in there," he said. "I still stand by the fact that I am a hundred percent certain that those B-Ops guys would have killed you if you hadn't called in. I have equipment at home I use to tap into the official comm."

"Okay. Fine. Stand by your story; I'm not sure they were honest with me anyway. But if it's me in B-Ops you wanted, you're out of luck. I've been reassigned to the other side. I'm I-Ops now. Does that still work for you?"

"Better, actually."

She cleared her throat and folded her arms across her chest. "You're going to tell me what you need me in there for, right?"

"I'm going to show you," he agreed. "And once you see for yourself what I'm dealing with, there won't be that much more to explain." He moistened his lips. "You were right. I have . . . scars. They're not what you think."

He didn't expect any kind of mercy or compassion; he didn't think he particularly deserved it, though he wouldn't have done things differently. But he saw a kind of sympathy on her face that gave him hope. So, when she nodded and they headed back toward his apartment without even having to say anything in words, Finn knew that she had to be the one after all. He just hoped she could handle things once she'd seen what there was to see.

Believe me, Cydney Brighton, it's not at all what you think.

Chapter Sixteen

They walked to Finn's place in silence, every muscle in Cyd's body tensed to flee in case the whole thing turned out to be some kind of bizarre scheme. Either way, she wasn't going to get sloppy and let down her defenses like she had last time. This time she'd handle the situation like an operative. And Finn seemed to be on the same page. Going to a strange man's home wasn't the smartest thing to do; nor for that matter did a smart man show a stranger into his home, his sanctuary. But in his repeated and willful breaking of this unspoken rule, Finn was offering up something meant to be interpreted as an exchange of trust. He had serious hopes for her, or was serious trouble. Maybe both.

Cyd took the time to look the place over better than she had before, when she was admittedly preoccupied with a bad case of lust. She could see it wasn't anything special. He'd picked a unit hidden from the street in a slightly sunken alcove, and used many of the same techniques for securing his property that she'd learned back in B-Ops. In a way, the familiarity gave Cyd a sense of comfort, though not enough for her to totally drop her guard.

At last Finn finished inspecting his door for signs of entry, and waved Cyd in.

Ideally she'd have a gun out, but at the moment she'd have to make do without one; she didn't want to seem too anxious. Slamming the door forward, she slipped inside the room and pressed her back against the wall. She assessed her surroundings, flicking her glance to the four corners of the room, keeping her weight on the balls of her feet.

Finn put his hands up in mock surrender as he followed her over the threshold. The two of them stared at each other for a moment, just standing together in the middle of his living room, and then he nodded.

"Okay," he said, heaving a sigh and nodding to himself as if gathering strength. "Okay. I'll just be a minute." He opened the door to what Cyd guessed was his bedroom and closed it behind him.

Okaaay. Cyd didn't waste the time. She began inspecting the apartment, looking for clues about his identity, his secrets, his life, anything.

The only artwork on the wall were two enormous maps side by side, one representing what Los Angeles used to be, the other representing what it was now. Small touches of color dotted the room in the form of secondhand objects he'd obviously purchased on the street to cut the sterility of the gray, greens and browns that otherwise dominated. A pillow here, a glass bowl there—it all made for a slightly retro and very bachelor effect.

She moved to the small kitchen area. The refrigerator was plenty full. Not overstocked, the way it might have looked if this had been a setup; not understocked, the way it might have looked in hers. She opened one of the drawers, noting the precision with which the various kitchen accoutrements were ordered and carefully lined up. Finally she ran her hands along the wall and the windowsill, noting the absence of dust.

And then Cyd noticed the appliances: an old-fashioned French press instead of a coffeemaker; a whisk sticking out of a pitcher full of kitchen tools but no blender obvious on the counter; a radio with an analog face.

She stuck the whisk back with the other tools, opened the cupboard door under the kitchen sink and pulled out the garbage. Food remnants, packaging, of course, and some clumps of torn paper. A sudden static-filled squawk coming from Finn's bedroom had Cyd freezing in her tracks for a moment. She quickly put the trash can back, washed her hands and returned to the living room.

He had the radio system on high volume; obviously he didn't care if she heard. And what she realized she was hearing was a pirated B-Ops scanner—she recognized the codes the operatives were swapping over the airwaves.

Cyd backed up uncertainly on the carpet, standing in the middle of Finn's living room, wondering if she should get the hell out. But if he was undercover B-Ops and she'd guessed wrong, he would have no reason not to tell her now. If he wasn't B-Ops, there were only two reasons she could think of to pony up for a serious piece of equipment such as that: either listening in so he could effectively stay out of their business, or listening in so he could get involved in things he shouldn't be involved in. She had a feeling she was about to find out which.

The sound went dead; he'd switched off the radio. She just stood there, with the strange sensation that he was right behind the bedroom door facing her. The doorknob turned, and Cyd's heart skipped a beat. The light at the threshold went out, and Finn finally opened the door.

He stood there framed in darkness, and then he stepped forward into the light, his jaw set, his mouth a grim slash, a mixture of fear and fury in his eyes. . . .

Naked.

He was entirely naked, and his body held an unholy kind of beauty.

Cyd gasped as he moved across the carpet and stood before her. He was a strange and fascinating combination of sleek metal and human flesh marred by shiny strips and plates, burn marks, gashes, and angry red and white scars where metal no longer lined up or had been pried away.

"What kind of secrets do I have? You tell me," he whispered.

It took her a moment to process what she was seeing. Part man, part machine . . . she didn't have to draw her conclusion out loud. They both knew what he was.

A mech.

Cyd swallowed hard and slowly walked around his body. On a uniform, there was a serial number inside the collar. On a mech, there was apparently a silver plate embedded between the shoulder blades. That's where it was on Finn. MADE IN FINLAND. BETA CLASS XG8.

"Finland . . . Finn," she whispered.

She heard him swallow, as if he was trying to make a lump in his throat go away. Reaching out, Cyd touched her fingers to the plate and then dragged them across his shoulder as she circled around to face him once more.

They stared at each other for a moment, Finn looking as though he'd like to jump right out of his skin.

Cyd laid her bare palm to his chest; he flinched as if she'd just burned him. But his eyes told her not to stop. She'd never seen anything like this before. Like him. She dragged her fingertips back and forth across his chest, absorbing the magnificence of his body, noting the contrasts of smooth and rough, wondering who had hurt him so badly or if he'd done it to himself.

She guessed he was less uncomfortable with his nakedness than with the destruction wreaked on his flesh. Yet for all the damage, he was . . . fantastic.

What a perfect build, what perfect musculature. Cyd looked down and caught herself blushing at his perfect everything. Reaching up with a index finger, she drew an invisible line over the thin strip of metal running like silver thread from the corner of his dark eye up to his temple.

His hair was longer now than would have been allowed if he was still working as a government soldier; and as she ran her fingers through his locks, she could feel the change in grade between metal thread and flesh.

Finn was not immune to her touch; his labored breathing and the tremor that wracked his hands that he forced himself to keep at his sides told her as much.

She swept her fingers gently over his lips; he closed his eyes, his fingers curling into fists. Try as she might to maintain an objectivity, a scientific demeanor, when she touched him, Finn's body seemed to radiate with suppressed desire. And though she fought equally hard, she could no more stop her own racing heart or the damp flush on her skin. She'd wanted him before. The feeling was stronger now.

"Cyd," he said, his words clearly intended as a protest, but his body indicating otherwise. He turned away from her—but he couldn't hide what he felt. She knew that the number of people who'd run their fingers through his hair, who'd placed their palms against his bare chest, who'd so much as held him close even clothed could probably be counted on one hand.

"I'm sorry," she said, for lack of something better to say. Pity wasn't so much what she felt. More of an agony on his behalf. The sheer loneliness. She knew how that felt. And she had even been lucky enough to have a few people she could trust in her past. Whom had he had?

She leaned close, and her lips brushed against his earlobe. "I understand," she said in a whisper.

She reached up and cradled his face in her hands, forcing him to look directly into her eyes, and saw that the pitch-black iris was a prefab lens. At just the right angle, you could see a light behind his retina.

And then Cyd saw the light pulse, and she jerked away. *Oh my god.*

Finn bowed his head, obvious disappointment sketched on his face. "Was this a mistake?" he asked gruffly. His muscles were tense.

Cyd opened her mouth, but no sound came out. Finn was off the Grid, but he wasn't decommissioned or labeled as dead. He was technically still active, and that meant he could become traceable again. That was surely his problem.

Before she could answer, Finn wrenched himself away from her. "You get the picture. I'll go change," he said.

The bedroom door closed, and Cyd took an unsteady step back before snapping out of her daze. His nakedness, his vulnerability, the intensity she'd experienced when their bodies came into contact with each other—this wasn't like anything she'd experienced before.

She rummaged around in her jacket pocket and pulled out a slightly squashed cigarette, looked around for matches and finally settled for the pilot light in the stove. She was supposed to have quit. In fact, she'd almost managed it, once. Now was clearly not the time.

So. He was on the run from B-Ops. He was the mech with a bounty on his head, the one who'd killed the Dumont brothers and escaped. The one who'd spared Fleur. And he wanted Cyd inside B-Ops so he could do something. What that "something" was, she was about to find out.

Cyd stared at the wisp of smoke coming off the end of her cigarette. The thing was, in order to help him get rid of his demons, she would have to face her own. Her very literal demons. And it was hard to see what was in all of it for her.

"Was it good for you?" came a joking voice.

Cyd stared wide-eyed at Finn, who now leaned in the doorway of his bedroom, reclad in pants and a T-shirt, the engineered mess of his arms still on full display. She followed his amused gaze to the cigarette in her hand, and quickly stubbed it out in the sink.

"Let's just say I've never experienced anything quite like you before."

"Or I you," he said quietly.

Cyd had to look away from the heat in his eyes. She moved to the couch and sat down. "You know, I was there that night. My old B-Ops partner, Dain, and I were on our beat, and we see this thing on the comm that we've never seen before. Some strange code. Dain realizes that it's a mech. Obviously they'd never sent one out before—we didn't have the right software loaded. But we get to Dumont Towers, and it's obvious something's up." Cyd looked up at him. "I guess it was you up in the vampire strata. You killed Ryan and Christian Dumont, didn't you?"

Finn sat down next to her and pulled at the newspaper lying on his coffee table, shredding the paper until tiny fragments pelted the floor. "Yeah. I killed them. That was me."

Cyd swallowed hard. "And then you disappeared."

"Then I disappeared," he echoed. He pushed the newspaper away almost angrily, and turned to face her on the couch. "I couldn't go back to the barracks. That place is a prison."

"But . . . you're a mech. You're not supposed to have thoughts about what you want or don't want."

He heaved a sigh. "I'm a human, Cyd. Let's just get that straight. Whatever I might look like, I'm a human. They just had control over me. I was blank for a long time, and I still don't know what snapped the link. Maybe that face. Fleur Dumont's."

Fleur again. Cyd just shook her head, thinking of what the vampire leader must have done to her old partner.

"Or maybe it was the hit itself, the very thing I was programmed and ordered to do," Finn said. "I wasn't supposed to have control, but out of nowhere I did. She wasn't in the kill program, that vampire girl. But she was a witness, and I was supposed to delete any witnesses. But I saw her face and she wasn't just a target anymore. And I couldn't . . . *didn't* do it."

"And you didn't finish any of the rest of your orders, did you? You didn't go back to base, and you didn't call in after?" Cyd asked.

Finn shook his head. "I didn't call in. I was supposed to do something, and I didn't, and then . . . it seemed so simple. Before I really even knew what I was about, I just continued not doing what I was supposed to." He shrugged. "I never called in. They put out that bounty on me, and then it was far too late to go back. Not that I would have."

Cyd exhaled loudly and stared up at the plaster ceiling. "What is it exactly you think I will be able to do for you?" she asked.

"I want out," he said. It wasn't his answer so much as the intensity behind it. The desperate, intense longing. It half won her over right there. "I need a mechanic to get this"—he gestured angrily at his arm, the one that expanded to a full-fledged weapon, the one that was part gun, part knife, part cobbled-together mechanisms—"off of me." He touched his temple and added angrily, "*Out* of me. I want all of it gone!"

"You want to take the man out of the machine," she murmured.

"You make it sound almost simple, but it's not," Finn said, his voice straining as if he was working overtime to keep his emotions from bubbling over. "The minute someone who knows mechs sees me, I'm a dead man. The only people who can help me are those who are most likely to want to turn me in. Even if I knew exactly who could do the work I need, I couldn't risk asking myself. I need a go-between. And I need someone with access. That's you."

She stared down at her hands in silence.

"Will you help me?" he finally asked. "It goes without saying that I'll owe you. More than I can even begin to express."

Cyd managed a laugh. "That's a nice change."

"I need this, Cyd. I'm trapped."

Cyd's gaze shifted to his arm. "It's pretty incredible. I mean, Finn, you're like a goddamn superhero. And to try and remove it . . ." She put her hand over some of the scars on his left arm. "It obviously hurts, and could be dangerous for you. Why not just let it go? Concentrate on finding a way to get rid of the bounty notice itself. Flee the city."

Finn shook his head angrily. "If I knew of a way to get rid of the bounty, I'd be working on that. But you're missing the point. We mechs are supposed to be nothing more than cyborgs that the humans in Ops control. I have a computer in my head that used to tell me to do things like, 'Kill vampire leaders,' and I did them without questioning. Do you have any idea what it's like to have some foreign construct in your mind, determining your fate, telling you what to do, stripping any sense of self-control away?"

Cyd froze for a moment, thinking of the way Griff-Vai had tried to mess with her head, to get her to think and see and do things she didn't want to. "I don't know why I should help you," she said quietly. "You've manipulated me. I'm in I-Ops now, for god's sake, the last place I want to be."

"They would have killed you if you hadn't called in," he repeated.

Gently, he reached out and took her face in his hands. "Don't you have some unfinished business there?" he asked.

She looked at him askance. What an odd question. But he was right. She couldn't run anymore. She should take a cue from Finn—fight back. And in all fairness, being assigned to research the demons for the boss would allow her to research demons on her own behalf as well. To destroy Griff-Vai and win peace of mind for all time.

"My first job in Ops was in Paranormal R and D. I'm just back where I started," she murmured. "It all moves in a circle."

"What happened to you there?" Finn asked.

"I know what you're doing," Cyd suddenly realized. "I've had access to the same training you have. You're trying to get us on an equal playing field. You're trying to make yourself into my confidant so I'll want to help you." She pulled his hands away from her face and tried to shrug his question off. "I've been asked that question a million times, and I've never answered."

"Maybe you've wanted to, but never found the right person to tell," he replied.

She looked at him as if he was insane. And then she thought about it for a minute. Thought about what it would be like to tell someone. To tell someone like Finn. Few people could truly understand the magnitude of what she'd seen, but that was before the demons had come to Crimson City. It was before she met a man who'd been built and controlled. Maybe now was the time to talk.

"I literally just laid my secrets bare to you," Finn said. "If ever there was a time—"

"I saw a room full of people die horrible deaths," Cyd blurted out, almost in spite of herself. The minute the words were out, she felt a rush of relief and just kept talking. "I saw it from a room separated by a couple of glass plates that would have been like reaching through a wall of dust particles for these guys. I know they say some demons aren't evil. But every one I ever saw was. And I saw what I saw. Ops must have guessed."

"This was your research team that was killed?" Finn asked.

Cyd nodded, forcing back the tears that pricked at her eyes. "The evidence was all over the walls and the floor. The bosses looked at me like I was possessed or something. They brought in a team of cleaners, had them sanitize the room, and then I found out that every single one of them had been disappeared by the end of the week. The only witness, the only person who had seen the whole thing, was me, start to finish. See, the cleaners, they'd been told to get in and get out. It was a rush job. You should have seen it. Four terrified bastards in white suits running around to clean up a paranormal crime scene as if the authorities were coming."

"Except the authorities had demanded the cleanup," Finn murmured.

"That's right. They took everything out in hazardous waste disposal bags—bloody clothes, body parts, broken glass, everything in one big jumble. I don't think you could make it any more horrific."

Finn reached out as if to take her hand, but Cyd dodged. "Then they sat me in a white room—I don't know, I just remember very distinctly how white that paint job was—and they talked to me for a while. I don't have the faintest clue what they said, except at the end, when they handed me a pen and told me to sign a transfer to B-Ops. And then they told me to go clean the wall in the hallway. There was a trail of blood smeared all the way from the door to the exit. There was no one left to do that job, it seemed, but me. So I got a bucket and some disinfectant spray, and, still wearing my stupid skirt and pumps, I scrubbed my old team's blood off the hallway wall.

"I didn't actually start throwing up until I got back to my apartment. I didn't leave that damn apartment for what seemed like a week. I'm not even sure. I had . . . friends, I guess, who did their best. And I had D-Alley." Cyd shot Finn a defensive look, daring him to judge her drug use. "You don't see what I saw and forget. It takes something else to make you forget."

"Why were you the only one Ops spared?" he asked.

"Because I was the only one the demons spared, I suppose. I'm the only record of what went on before, during and after. I'm the only researcher from that time, that first moment of contact, left. As much as it's something they wanted to cover up, they also needed someone who would know something about it if the demons came back. They did come back; and judging by the mess this city is in right now, I just wasn't around when Ops needed me the most, I guess." She threw up her arms and said in a voice calculated to sound light, "So . . . that's my big secret."

A weighty pause filled the air between them, and finally Finn asked the question he'd probably been dying to ask for a long time. The question she least wanted to answer. "Have you been with the demons all this time, Cyd?"

She whirled and stared at him. What the hell was he looking for? How could she avoid talking about Orcus and Griff-Vai and—"Don't start with that. Everyone wants to know that. Was that your plan? We share some deep inner thoughts, and that means we have some special connection?"

"Yes," he said simply. "You know it does."

Cyd huffed. Anxious to get away, she stood up and headed for the exit. Finn followed, and placed a palm against the door to prevent her escape.

"You know it does," he repeated. "Why be so angry about it?"

She stared at the whorls in the wooden door, overly conscious of the heat radiating off Finn's body against her back. He leaned in, his mouth hot against her ear. "Okay, then. Don't tell me. But will you help me, Cyd?" he whispered.

She closed her eyes. "You know I will. If I were you, I'd kill me if I didn't. You can't afford not to."

That wasn't the only reason she was going to help, but it was the only reason she would cop to.

Without another word, Finn dropped his hand and Cyd made her escape.

Chapter Seventeen

The headquarters for the human government was visible from the road leading out of the housing complex, but distance didn't do the place justice. LAX might have been significantly damaged, but the massive I-Ops compound still gleamed proudly out of the scorched wasteland all around. There was something creepy about its survival in the face of so much destruction; it was like a whitewashed cockroach that refused to die.

Liquid silver ran up and down a transparent piping system built into the glass and stucco. A web of red lasers and blinding floodlights remained in place—security measures designed to combat vampire and werewolf intruders. It made Cyd wonder what new security measures they'd implemented in her absence to combat the demons . . . and if those could somehow detect where she'd been.

She might be able to sympathize with Finn's reasons for leading her back here, to this job and life she'd so wanted to escape, but that didn't stop her from resenting it; it didn't stop her from fearing what lay in front of her; and it didn't stop her from fumbling in her pocket for a drug-popper. The action was out of habit more than desire.

You don't do that anymore, Cyd. Meet life head on. You can do this. You have to do this. Forget about what Finn wants for a moment, and for that matter, forget about what your boss wants. Remember that some of your own answers might lie inside this building.

Cyd took a couple of deep calming breaths and headed inside, silently cursing as she submitted to a battery of security checks and was finally allowed through the gates. Hoisting her bag over her shoulder, she entered, mumbling a stream-of-consciousness pep talk as she went through all the old familiar motions: plugging a security chip into her comm device, running her new I-Ops badge through the reader, flashing it at the latest receptionist, heading down a familiar hallway.

Doing fine, doing fine, keep going . . .

A couple of turns, through the double doors of the Department of Paranormal Research & Development, down the hall once more to a faded black door labeled CLEANING SUPPLIES, through that closet and out the back into the secret lab for demon research.

It wasn't secured, and Cyd didn't give herself time to get psyched out; she just pushed the door open and walked in. Most of the things that had been in the room before still seemed to be present and accounted for, though it was now significantly more organized. There was one notable addition: A long card table had been set up against the wall, and was currently piled high with file boxes.

The books in the small library were dusted and shelved alphabetically. The Bunsen burners, chemical testers and forensics equipment were cleaned, rinsed, labeled. Small mechanical parts and miscellaneous bits and pieces of machinery were sorted in a row of clear, labeled boxes. The broken glass that had littered the floor the last time she was here was now catalogued and placed in a covered plastic bin.

Apparently everything in the room was considered research now. The higher-ups had made sure that nothing got thrown away. Nothing at all.

Including, Cyd thought with a grim smile, me.

Sitting down at her old desk, she sifted through some artfully arranged personal effects, including a photo of the team when she'd joined as a rookie researcher. She picked that up, running her index finger over the faces. Dr. Stowe, smiling. And Riker. She'd had such a crush on him. And there was Allison, front and center, of course.

Cyd put the photo back down on the desk and pulled open the top drawer. Dark fingerprints still marred the inside, where someone had gripped the wood to steady herself. They were so faded into the grain, only Cyd would really know what they were: Allison's blood.

It was Allison's death that had really triggered Cyd's downward spiral of self-destruction. It could have been me, she'd thought. *It still can.*

Granted, her research team had summoned those Bak-Faru demons on purpose, but they couldn't have known what they were dealing with. Allison had been a Bak-Faru's play-toy. No matter how much of an arrogant bitch the girl was, she hadn't deserved to die like that. No one did.

Cyd couldn't help recalling that if it hadn't been for Griff—a member of a separate demon faction known as the Vai—cutting a deal with those her team had summoned, Cyd would probably have died that day, too. It was no glass wall that had separated her from the death and destruction; it was Griff-Vai.

Behind her, the door was suddenly flung open, and Cyd nearly had a heart attack. While personnel were clearly allowed in to clean, she wasn't used to the place being so open to visitors.

"Hey, Cyd," a familiar voice chirped. Bridget Rothschild peeked through the cracked door and did a double take. "Wow. You look bright-eyed and bushy-tailed."

Suck-up, Cyd sneered. She stared at Bridget, once again contemplating the girl's meteoric rise through the ranks. Same perfect white teeth, same ivory skin. Forever young and pretty and innocent. But Cyd grew conscious of the fact that a big part of the reason she found herself unable to like the girl was that she herself had been just like Bridget once—before this job wreaked havoc on her life.

"I have top secret clearance," the former secretary said, apparently misinterpreting Cyd's stunned expression.

"You must have been a very good admin," Cyd said dryly.

Bridget smiled. "Somebody's got to type up all the important stuff. It helps when that person is clever. Do you want me to get the cleaning crew back in here?"

"No. It's cleaner than it's ever been. Step back and close the door. I'll be right out."

Bridget looked at her curiously, but she did as asked. Cyd took a moment to herself, then joined the girl outside.

"I didn't mean to bug you," Bridget said. "I just wanted to tell you to call me if you need anything."

Cyd stuck her hands in her pockets, absently running

her fingers over the surface of the demonic amulet. "Actually, there is something. I need a division roster. You know, everyone in I-Ops. The one that includes job titles."

"Sure." But Bridget didn't move; she just stood there staring.

"Is something wrong?" Cyd asked.

The girl snapped out of it. "No, of course not." She actually giggled. "This is stupid, I know, but . . . can I ask what you use on your face?"

"Soap," Cyd snapped. Then she walked back into the research room, shut the door abruptly, and turned and leaned her back against it.

Well, then, she thought to herself. *Let's get started.*

She pulled the boxes down so that they were all lined up on one level on the card table, and started systematically browsing through the tabbed files. There was no way everything was here; with all of the information her team had collected, they could have filled three times as many boxes. The good news was, it wouldn't take long to see what she had to work with.

One of the boxes was full of research books, which was a welcome surprise, and one contained the encyclopedia the team had been developing, a resource book of their own making.

Cyd pulled out the enormous white plastic binder and scanned through it. Descriptions of every known species; of every known family, clan, order, faction or what-have-you within each species; every term; every weapon or form of "magic" known to be in use, summaries of known methods of summoning . . . it had everything they'd known.

She flipped through it and found descriptions of the Bak-Faru and the Vai. She also found sections on the paranormals of Crimson City proper, nondemons: the Dumonts, the Maddox clan, big-name rogues such as Tajo Maddox and Hayden Wilks, and notes on whether each character had been born or made. The data went on and on.

Cyd brought the volume to her desk and started searching for the one term she'd never seen or heard before. Draig-Uisge. The man from her vision. The man with the amulet.

Her finger froze on the line in the index. It was there. Or "Draig" was. Flipping wildly through the book, she found the entry, but immediately sighed with disappointment. There were just a few penciled-in notes where a detailed description would normally go.

Draig: Associated with neodruids. San Bernardino. Found near nature. Check parks, beaches, gardens, etc. Bend energy. Santa Monica Pier.

"That's helpful. Not," Cyd muttered. Not to mention, according to the newspapers, Santa Monica Pier was apparently still in a state of abandonment after the beach was essentially bombed out by demons.

At least someone on her team had been aware the Draig-Uisge existed. She rummaged around for a serviceable notepad, found one, copied the thin clues down, then flipped back to the front of the encyclopedia to look for something about amulets. In the *A*s she found an entry and could only roll her eyes at the listing: "Cross-reference Artifacts Manual."

Pushing the binder away, Cyd took the amulet from her pocket and laid it on the desk. Okay, so the Draig-Uisge had wielded this. He'd said something about fulfilling his duty. He knew what to do with the thing. If she could find more out about the amulet, maybe she could get to the Draig and figure out how best to use the artifact to protect herself from Griff-Vai. Until the portal was closed for good, while she was standing on the right side, Cyd didn't think she'd ever feel safe.

The deal was this: If she closed the portal for herself, she'd be fulfilling her obligation to Ops, and then maybe the boss would let her go on her way. So she just needed to understand the amulet.

Cyd leaned back in her chair, turning the artifact over and over in her hand. What had Griff-Vai done when he pressed it to her forehead and said those foreign words? What was this thing capable of? Was it just an energy conduit, or was it something more?

She suddenly sat straight up. Who could say for sure that the thing had been protecting her? Sure, it had appeared at the time she'd escaped Orcus, but the fact was, Cyd had found herself in the middle of something that wasn't about her. What if she'd been reading this all wrong? What if the amulet was something negative, something that tipped off the demons to her whereabouts? That would explain the immediate visit from that demon agent who'd claimed Griff sent him to deliver a message.

A sick feeling came over her. *What if he's watching me right now?* Cyd looked around the empty room. "Griff?"

No answer. And she had no more sense of him inside her than she'd ever felt since leaving the underworld.

A new, frightened urgency came over her. For the next several hours, Cyd sorted through the boxed material, pored over the encyclopedia and read as much as she could get through, from printed text to handwritten scrawl. And finally, finally, in box four she found the amulet information.

The manual gave what was listed as unverified information in a blurb signed and dated by Riker about a month before they'd summoned the demons in the first place. He noted that there were thought to be six amulets of different shapes and sizes, but all with similar symbology invoking earth, fire, water and air. One was apparently believed to be in Cambodia; another in Egypt. The others had no known provenance.

Cyd studied several illustrations, one per page, feeling herself freeze as a final page flipped back to reveal a precise line drawing of the amulet she held in her hand. She read the accompanying text, this time official and in typewritten form:

> *. . . and we now know that the amulet manipulates energy. In the center is a crystal with dark liquid. This is demon blood. The more energy the amulet retains, the brighter red the liquid. In calm state, it is a black ichor tainted with red. We are still learning more about how this instrument of energy replenishes itself, but note that it is considered painful to the touch and impossible for the average human to wield. Should a team member find such an artifact, she or he is instructed to leave it where it is and call the emergency line, and request protective gear.*

"What the hell?" Cyd shook her head. She was surprised: it hadn't been painful for her at all. Of course, Finn had seemed unwilling to touch it.

She read through the remainder, part scientific description and part alarmist warnings, but she learned nothing more about a connection between the amulet and the druids or a Draig-Uisge. It also failed to go into any depth about a connection between the amulet's ability to bend energy, and the opening and closing of portals to other worlds.

Whether someone had known the information but had not documented it for security purposes was a valid question, but Cyd didn't remember the team using an amulet when they'd summoned the demons that day. Of course, with other information in the manual slightly off, she wasn't sure how much she'd be able to take at face value.

The fact remained: The only reason she could imagine she'd gotten out of the demon underworld was because of this amulet.

She came back to her previous conclusion: *I need to find this Draig-Uisge to get accurate answers.*

She heard the door crack open, and a sheaf of papers fluttered through and to the floor. The door closed again, silently.

How about that? Cyd thought grudgingly. She's actually not half bad as an admin. Cyd picked it up the papers. It was the I-Ops roster.

Grateful for a break, Cyd immediately switched gears and scanned the list of names of technicians working in the Body Shop, the department that would know the most about the mechs. At first glance it was a bunch of unfamiliar names, none of whom had probably worked on any of the original models. But there was one . . .

Valerio Dagama. She vaguely recalled the name. He'd been around at least as long as she. Which meant, she hoped, that he'd been around long enough to know about the various mech prototypes. If they were lucky, he'd been around long enough to also be in possession of a nice dose of anti-Ops cynicism, and an open mind when it came to being bribed.

Bringing in Finn would be the easy part—though not exactly a cakewalk. Getting him out once Valerio had seen him and understood there was a juicy bounty available, that would be something else. But enough money could solve any problem.

The question of why she was helping him passed through her mind once more, especially as she thought of all the risks involved. Did she really believe he'd kill her if she didn't? Actually, she did. It was the only possible thing to do with someone who knew a secret of that magnitude, a secret that could destroy you.

Cyd looked at her knuckles, reminded of how she'd told him her own secret, and how he'd implied there was something more between them. She wondered if he realized just how intense that pressure had been for her. He was either a brilliant strategist, or he had no idea how lucky he'd gotten in hitting a nerve. Deep inside she understood that a big part of why she was so touched by Finn's revelation about losing control of his body and mind to someone else was because she feared that what had happened to him might be happening to her.

Physically, she'd escaped Griff-Vai. But she didn't feel the same. And a tiny part of her mind wondered . . .

But that was impossible. Demons didn't "make" humans the way vampires and werewolves did. It just wasn't done. You were either born with demon nature and abilities, or not. There was nothing in between.

Stop it! There's *nothing* in between, she repeated to herself. He could not have changed you in that way.

Sick of the fact that her mind kept bringing her back to the one subject in the world she wasn't keen on thinking about, Cyd decided to head down to the Body Shop to talk to Valerio.

Halfway out of the building, she stopped dead in front of the mirrored surface of a corporate wall hanging. She thought of Bridget's effusive compliments, and stopped short to see if she could see what the ex-admin saw, what she herself had been seeing lately.

Reflected back were her own flawless skin, bright eyes and lush, full lips. She hadn't really thought about her appearance in a while; she'd had bigger things on her mind. But Bridget was right in one respect: Cyd looked better than ever.

Well, she wasn't using drugs. She was cleaning up her life, and both mind and body were showing the positive results. It was that simple.

Cyd turned her back on the mirror and headed out to the courtyard. *Please, let it be that simple.*

Chapter Eighteen

Hayden Wilks was enjoying himself thoroughly; Jill could see that quite clearly. No matter how threatening his expression, how dark the look in his eyes, he was getting a total kick out of throwing the entire patronage of Bosco's for a loop.

"The rumors are already starting," he growled, leaning up against the wall with his long legs sprawling open along the rest of the bench seat. "Us meeting here like this."

Jill leaned over the table. "I don't think you really mind."

He gave her a quick look up and down. "What do you want?"

"Are you sure you don't want to talk somewhere private?"

"Here's fine," he said. But he lowered his voice.

Jill hesitated, unsure how to begin, and inexplicably nervous around the vampire. On the job, she'd done interviews with guys like him a million times before, but somehow, because the issue was personal, it wasn't the same.

She just had to remember that there was strategy to

these things; there was a strategy to Hayden. And as long as she remembered what drove him to do the things he did, she'd be fine.

Hayden's eyes focused in on her like lasers, but nothing else about him could stand to be still. He was a man in constant motion. Not the typical restlessness, either. Though it had been years since Fleur Dumont had made him vampire, Jill read him as man who still didn't feel right in his skin. A man who hadn't come to terms with what had been done to him, and one who still had a taste for vengeance.

Revenge was the key to an alliance with Hayden Wilks.

Jill cleared her throat. "I've been collecting a lot of information about you. You and your . . . friends." She shrugged, affecting an air of nonchalance. "It's an old habit. I like doing the research."

"For an assignment?" he asked.

She leaned over the table. "I'm sure anyone would buy an investigative report about the rogues. I could even get my job back if I were really . . . thorough."

His eyebrow arched upward.

"I know about the rogues, Hayden. I know what you guys have in mind. It's always been my business to know things. Now I want to make it my business to *do* things."

"What guys? What guys have what in mind?" He kept his expression carefully blank, but his voice lowered further.

Jill smiled and folded her hands neatly in front of her on the table. "Don't be coy. It doesn't suit you at all."

Funny, his coloring was so very similar to Marius's yet the package as a whole read so very differently. Marius was sensual yet subtle, powerfully built, could burn an imprint on her of what was inside his heart just by reaching out with his body or mind. Hayden was the opposite: lean, overtly sexual, all cold danger, glowering looks and mixed signals.

Thinking about Marius at all gave Jill a pain. She looked away, knowing it probably seemed odd, but she couldn't hide it; the heartbreak was simply too fresh.

Hayden shook his head and shrugged. "What's this all about, Jill? You're known as a straight shooter. So give it to me straight."

She cleared her throat. "I'd like to be known as something else. And I want you to help me do it. I've got friends who've earned vouchers from people like you, and who are going into business. That's what I want. I want you to train me to take the kinds of mercenary jobs you do down here. I want you to train me to be a street operative." *I want to be more like Bridget, not afraid of anyone or anything. Not needing or wanting so much. And I want to show Marius up. I want him to hurt like I hurt.*

Hayden stuck a toothpick in his mouth, playing it around with his tongue. "You know what that would mean, right? You're saying you want to start taking sides. You're saying you're willing to say good-bye to the reputation you got as a journalist?"

Angrily, she tossed her hair back. "I'm sick of that reputation."

He studied her face and then said, "What do *you* know about us rogues?"

"Come on, Hayden. I know you're creating a new kind of group. Whatever you're calling it. A gang or a council or whatever. I know you've got something cooking. Some kind of interspecies alliance."

"Who do you think is involved?"

She gave it all up. He wanted to know how serious she was? Well, she was completely serious. And so she gave up her info, confidential or not, to prove it. Because that's how it would be without the constraints and benefits of neutrality.

"I've heard about Conor McCabe, Dave Fagin, Korzha, Tricky Simons, the Krolls, a bunch of the girls from downtown . . . Trish, Veronica. . . ." She had to think for a moment. "You, obviously. Which means Tajo's got to be involved, because you guys are doing tandem jobs all over the place. And that guy, Finn. The one who's always wearing a billion layers even in the summer. I know you've pulled him in on a couple of multiples. I think the lot of you are putting something together that will stand alongside the vampire primaries, the werewolf alpha clan and the humans. The Society of Rogues, if you will." She stared pointedly at him, challenging him to prove her wrong.

His mouth twitched; he almost smiled, but forced his expression back into something blank. "What else do you think you know?" he asked.

Not so fast, she reminded herself. Don't give the grid without the quo. "What do you know about Marius's engagement?" she blurted.

Hayden raised an eyebrow.

Jill chewed on her lower lip. They were treading in deep water.

They stared at each other for a moment. Hayden gave her a noncommittal shrug. But then he cocked his head and gave her something better: "I know that Marius is engaged to a werewolf."

Jill's throat constricted and she choked, unable to

find words at first. Finally, she asked, "She's a werewolf? Why would he do that?"

"The Dumonts are apparently rethinking their long-term strategy. With Fleur on the vampire side and Keeli Maddox on the dog side, they're actually working together on some fluffy peace initiative. It seems Marius is meant to seal the alliance by marrying cross-species. Effing medieval, if you ask me, but he always did have a overdeveloped sense of honor."

Jill gripped the table hard enough to crack the wood, as if it were an anchor. "If Marius doesn't care about being with a dog, why does he care about being with a human? And if he doesn't mind being with a human . . . why doesn't he get one of his brothers to seal this alliance so he can marry his soul mate?" she cried.

Hayden's mouth dropped open. After a moment, he closed it and leaned over the table. "You don't think Marius is your soul mate, do you? You actually believe in that crap?"

It was too much. The look of delight on Hayden's face as he processed the information was too much to take. He knew why she'd come. She'd set up this meeting for the very same reasons she knew he would take her proposal seriously: Payback. Something to prove.

"Whoa. Hey. You're not going to cry, are you?" Hayden looked totally nonplussed for a moment. Then, to her surprise, the rogue grabbed a bunch of napkins from the metal holder on the table and held them out. "I'm not really the cry-on-my-shoulder type," he said gruffly.

"You're doing pretty good," Jill laughed. "And don't worry. I already cried." She squeezed the damp wad of napkins in her hand, blinking rapidly to hold back any more tears.

Hayden sat right across from her and waited patiently.

"I don't think anyone could possibly understand how lousy I feel right now," she finally mumbled.

A bitter look came over Hayden's face. "I can probably get close," he said. Then he shrugged the sentiment off as quickly as it had come. "Different circumstances. Look, Jill. You're in a bad way. But before I agree to get involved with you, ask yourself if you're willing to put yourself in mortal danger just to get Marius's attention."

Jill steeled herself. "Whether you admit your team exists or not, I know what I know. I want to be a rogue. I want to be part of your group. So show me what I have to do to earn my place."

Hayden took a long pull at his beer. "We both know there's nothing I'd like better than to put the Dumonts in their place. You'll do just fine. There aren't any rules, and I'm not confirming that what you're describing really exists. But let me put it this way: To be a true rogue in this city, you have to be running away from something. I guess, in your own way, you qualify."

Jill held her hand out to him. Hayden shook it roughly to seal the deal, a wicked grin on his face.

"You might have some overfancy ideas about all of this," he warned. "But I know I'm going to enjoy seeing Marius squirm."

You and me both, Jill thought. *You and me both.*

Chapter Nineteen

Using a combination of a forged guest pass and some pretty questionable black-market fingerprints and lenses, it was easy to get through the Ops security system that spanned the government compound. Almost too easy. Finn had to wonder if mechs were coded for automatic clearance so they could enter and exit their "home" in between missions, and the idea of having anything is his body automatically coded to do anything made him that much more anxious to get the components removed.

The last time Finn saw the inside of the Ops complex, he'd been a different person. Trying to remember the substance of his time as a virtual prisoner in the military barracks there was like replaying an old movie—a movie with a one-dimensional actor playing someone who only looked like him. He wasn't even sure he accurately remembered how he'd felt or what he'd thought. Standing next to Cyd in a tiny little alcove about ten feet from the entrance to the Body Shop, the cluster of work spaces where the mech technicians exacted their craft, the extent to which he'd changed during his time in Crimson City seemed clearer than ever.

The door opened, and a group of workers piled out in a haze of gossip and fresh cigarette smoke. It slammed shut, and Finn watched the men pass the side of the barracks building and head toward the cafeteria.

"A few more minutes," Cyd murmured. "In case there are any stragglers."

Training for combat behind these gates, off back behind a maze of whitewashed walls, had been his life at one time. He knew no past beyond that. Then, in comparison to what he knew now, his emotions had been dulled, compartmentalized, made irrelevant, really. He'd lived a world of green fatigues, white paint, and metal. Back then, he would have looked at Cyd and felt nothing, experienced nothing in his head but cold reaction to threat. He looked at her now and felt a million different emotions, none of which had existed for him before.

"Not my favorite place either," Cyd said suddenly, checking her watch and staring out into the empty courtyard. She wasn't even looking at him, must have just felt the anxiety in his body.

Finn looked over at her and smiled a little. The arm she held behind her, her fist pressed against his arm like a safety barrier; the crinkle in her forehead; the way she instinctively understood that his discomfort was just as much about the place itself as what it stood for, the procedure he faced: All the little things about the way she related to him, the mech he'd once been would have missed them all. And wouldn't have even known what he was missing.

"Cyd?" he said.

"Yeah?"

"Thanks," he said quietly, knowing the word wasn't even close to enough.

She turned and stared at him, not even trying to hide the fear in her eyes.

"What is it?" he asked.

She reached out and clutched at his shirt. "Finn, listen. This is dangerous. Really dangerous. And I'm not just talking about what might happen to me if anybody finds out what we're doing. I'm talking about trying to get the metal and the programming out of you. Are you sure you can't live with it inside? Because if there's any possibility that—"

"I'm sure," he said.

"You're sure. Because I'm . . . I'm really . . ."

"You're really?"

"I saw what you were doing to yourself. This isn't snap on, snap off," she blurted out, then looked away. "You're going to bleed, Finn. It's going to hurt. And I'm—And that's going to be really, really bad."

Finn pulled off his left glove and liner, and offered her his bare, scarred palm. She put her hand in his and he gave it a squeeze. "This is what I've been waiting for all this time," he finally whispered.

"Okay," she said simply. "Then let's get it done."

She turned away, but then thought of something and turned back. "Hey, Finn?"

"Yeah?"

"You're welcome."

It took a moment to process; then Finn grabbed her and pulled her into his arms, closing his eyes as her body relaxed into his. He pressed his lips to the top of her head, then let go, shrugging his emotion off with a smile.

"For good luck," he said.

She smiled back, then stepped out of the hidden area of the alcove. He followed her across the courtyard up to the back door and pushed in. Finn immediately recognized the place. He'd been here before. The names on the various doors meant nothing to him, but as he followed Cyd around a maze of hallways, a sick familiarity coagulated and wouldn't leave.

Cyd drew up short at a door stenciled VALERIO DAGAMA. She gave Finn a question mark of a glance, a final chance to back out. But he just nodded, and she went ahead and knocked. A flap covering the window in the door from the inside lifted up, and a round, mustached face appeared on the other side. Valerio Dagama's eyes flicked from Cyd to Finn and back again.

Finn's adrenaline went suddenly haywire. He grabbed for the knob. Cyd's hand clamped down around his wrist.

"Easy," she said.

Valerio unlocked the door from the other side, opened it and ushered them in, rebolting the door behind them. "Valerio," the man said, jamming his thumb into his chest. He cocked his head, the strap-on headlamp there bobbing a bit, and studied Finn. "Why no uniform? Which team is he with?"

"Valerio, do you remember what we discussed over the comm when we made the deal?" Cyd asked.

The technician shifted his weight from one foot to the other, his mouth twisted into a dissatisfied pout. Finn quickly heaved his duffel bag onto the mess on the desk.

"I think you do," Cyd continued. "I think you recall the part about me paying you a lot of money, and you not asking questions. Am I right? You've done this before. So there's your money," Cyd said. "Let's do this."

Valerio stared at Finn a little too closely for a little too long, as if he was trying to work out something in his mind. Finally he moved to the duffel bag and unzipped it. His hands pawed around in the bag, counting out stacks, which he carefully thumbed through for additional assurance. Finn watched a sweat break out on his face. Greed was good; this tech would do it.

"I'll go: arms, front, control panel and back, legs," he said, gesturing to the rigged-up work chair behind him.

Finn immediately stripped to the waist and lay back in the chair. Valerio zipped up the duffel and gave it an affectionate little pat. Then he turned to Finn, making no attempt to censor his reaction to the piecemeal surgery done to-date. The technician walked up behind Finn and slid his fingertips down between Finn's shoulder blades to the identifying plate.

"Beta Class . . . X . . . G . . . 8? Why do I know that identifier?" he muttered.

Finn exchanged glances with Cyd, but Valerio let it go. Instead he turned to the control panel to adjust the chair for surgery. Different parts of the apparatus shifted, accommodating Finn's body, and a set of iron half-arcs clamped down to restrain his legs, arms and chest.

Though they were probably just to stabilize his body for the work, as Finn lost his ability to move, a horrible claustrophobia settled in. "Not the right arm. I want it free. Do it last," he said.

Valerio glanced at Cyd for some kind of approval, and when she just shrugged, he pushed a few buttons on his panel and the restraints over Finn's right arm slid open. Finn breathed a sigh of relief and focused on compartmentalizing both his emotions and his imminent pain.

Moving to the sink on the other side, Valerio scrubbed, and the unmistakable and welcome scent of disinfectant wafted through the room. "I get a lot of modification requests when the new betas come out," the tech said to Cyd, "but nobody's ever asked me to try and take it all out. And they usually come in alone with order papers."

"This is a special project," Cyd said.

"Rare, though. Nobody ever wants stuff removed unless it's for an upgrade—or if certain parts are on the fritz."

Finn gritted his teeth as Valerio babbled on. *Betas, orders, upgrades, parts . . . for god's sake!* Suddenly he hated that Cyd was there. He hated that she was watching this incredibly demeaning experience. He hated to hear her talk about him as if he were merely a collection of metal components, hated that she was seeing him more like a machine than ever before. He thought she'd be seeing him the way he wanted, as fully human. But exposed, rendered powerless, what she was really seeing was his ultimate dehumanization.

Valerio turned on his headlamp, sat down on a wheeled stool next to a carefully organized tray and began to work.

In all fairness, though the man wasn't particularly gracious about taking the job, he was clearly a skilled technician. He expertly removed the metal remnants peppering Finn's left arm from fingertip to shoulder, then moved on to his torso, clucking each time he came across a new scar remaining from Finn's less-skilled attempts at surgery. A virtuoso with the tools, delicate with the medi-surge and gauze that would numb the area, prevent infection and keep the blood flow to a minimum, Valerio made quick progress on Finn's arms and chest.

The thin wire along his temple was next, and Finn felt a kind of crazy elation in spite of the dull pain. No more hiding his face. To have that piece gone would be no small thing.

"This bit's tricky," Valerio muttered. "But I've just about got it. . . . *There*."

Suddenly an electric shock had Finn pressing back hard in his chair, his breath stolen completely away as blue code flashed along the inside lens of his left eye. He hadn't seen that code since the Dumont assassinations.

Cyd flew to his side, her hand pressing down on his chest, trying to keep him steady as he jerked in the restraints, gasping for air.

"What was that?" she asked.

Valerio was frozen, holding his tools suspended in midair. "He's still connected to the Grid," the tech finally whispered. He looked up at Cyd. "I thought he was decommissioned. I thought he was dead meat. Out of service."

"I never said that," she snapped. She looked at Finn, total confusion and panic in her face. "Finn, tell us your exact status so we can do this right. What's going on?"

Finn stared at the technician and took a chance. "I slipped the Grid. End of story. Fix it so I stay off the Grid, or you're a dead man."

Valerio cocked his head, slowly moving closer to stare at the retina of Finn's left eye. Finn wondered if the tech could see the code scrolling across the lens.

"Whatever you did, undo it," he growled.

"Whatever *I* did?" Valerio snapped, rising panic audible in his voice. "You came in half-baked. You could have rewired yourself in any number of ways with the number of parts you've already taken out. The better question is, what did you do to yourself?"

"Get it off me. Get this *out* of me," Finn whispered, his breath coming in fits and starts. The blue code continued to scroll along his retina.

Valerio cursed and pushed a couple buttons to raise Finn to a sitting position. Then he slid a component out of the chair to allow access to Finn's upper back, and he began working away at the metal bar between Finn's shoulder blades.

Finn's hands clawed at the armrests. "Get in there, and make sure I stay off the Grid," he ordered through gritted teeth. "Get me off for good."

Finn felt the moment the screws popped loose and the metal strip fell from his body. His tag. His identification tag. He wasn't a number any longer. It should have been a moment of pure euphoria.

"XG8," Valerio murmured. "X . . . G . . . 8 . . . Oh my god."

He knew. The tech knew. The metal tag striking the ground sounded to Finn like a death knell.

"You're the one," Valerio said, his voice thin with wonder.

The room went dead silent. Finn's left hand shook violently in its restraint; his right hand curled into a fist. Red fury and blue code swam before his eyes, and every emotion that he'd ever had to suppress was building up inside him.

He heard a weapon cock behind his ear, and Cyd's voice careful and low as she held her gun on the technician. "You don't know XG8. Understand? Now finish what you were doing. Make sure he's still off the Grid, and make it so he stays that way."

But Valerio didn't go back to work. With his hands held palms-up in surrender, he edged away from Finn's chair as if Finn were an unpredictable animal ready to pounce. Their eyes locked.

"You're the one," the technician finally said. "The one who fired the shots heard around the world. You were the one on the Dumont mission. They said you never came in from the cold. You have a bounty on your head worth twice what you gave me."

Valerio's face swam before Finn's eyes, mocking shades of blue and red. All he could focus on was that this man was taking away his self-control, was clearly threatening him. He was supposed to help. He was supposed to help!

With single-minded fury, Finn lashed out with his right arm, grabbing Valerio around the neck. As he choked the technician, for a few seconds he was only faintly aware of Cyd pounding her fists against his wrists, yelling into his ear to make him stop.

"He's your only chance!" he heard her scream. His only chance.

Finn let Valerio go, and the technician crumpled to the ground. Cyd knelt down beside him, her gun pointed at the technician's temple. The man gasped and sputtered, one hand at his neck, one hand in the air as he tried to scoot away from her.

"There's nowhere to go," Cyd said, simply.

It took a few moments for Valerio to find enough oxygen, and then he said, "He was never truly off the Grid . . . System in a kind of hibernation . . . when . . . machine slips the Grid . . . during mission. . . . Not automatically deactivated. . . . Would . . . mean . . . total reprogramming or scrapping. . . . This one just flatlined . . . different."

No. No! "No! No! No!" Finn felt the blood roaring in his brain. His vision skewed. The cold blue light of his past was scrolling down his retina. The machine in him was trying to take him back. He couldn't even hear the sound of his own voice anymore; he just knew that he was screaming.

The gun in Cyd's hands was shaking. Valerio was shaking. The two of them were kneeling on the floor, yelling at each other in a panic, their mouths moving without Finn being able to hear or focus on what they were saying. He struggled against his restraints, his body and mind entirely consumed by a rage that wasn't even supposed to exist in someone like him.

"Swear you won't tell, Valerio. Swear it. Swear it, Valerio. Swear you won't tell," Cyd was saying over and over.

Sweat poured down the technician's face. "Brighton, I'll make a deal with you. We'll turn him in and split the money. Okay?"

"No! That's not the deal. You never saw him. We never came to you. This never happened."

Valerio kept licking his lips, his eyes enormous in his head, his whole body shaking. "He's a killing machine. And he's all torqued. And if we don't put him down, he's gonna kill you and he's gonna kill me. You don't understand what he is. Give him back, and we'll split the money. They'll take care of him."

"No, *you* don't understand what he is. He's human, Valerio. Deep inside, they are *all human*. You're not operating on machines. You're operating on humans."

Valerio rose off the floor and grabbed his comm device. He raised it to his lips.

"You're not going to make that call," Cyd said, her gun still trained on him. She knocked his comm to the floor.

"Kill him," Finn said. Cyd and Valerio both froze.

"Finn, no," she said, pleading with both her voice and her eyes.

Valerio took advantage of Cyd's shift in focus. He smashed his fist into the side of her face, leaped for his comm and started punching in a code.

The sight of Cyd hitting the floor ignited Finn's rage. "You don't control me!" he roared, bringing his right arm up, engaging the weapon. "*You don't control me!*" And he pulled the trigger. With the silencer on, it made only a tiny, inconsequential sound. The comm device fell to the ground, Valerio slumping to the floor along with it.

Sweat dripped down Finn's face and torso, stinging along all the sutures on his body. Half out of his head, he looked down at his deadly arm and slowly lowered it.

Cyd knelt on the floor over Valerio's body, her mouth open, her fingers searching for a pulse at his neck. When she finally looked up at Finn, every emotion in her face seemed to have vanished. All efficiency, all cold efficiency, Cyd Brighton moved to the control panel, flipped the restraints and threw his clothes at him.

"Listen to me. You've got to come down from this, or we have no chance of getting out of this complex alive. We walk briskly until we get to the main building." She turned around, grabbed some papers from Valerio's desk and shoved them into Finn's hands. Then she took the duffel bag and went to Valerio's supply closet. Pulling out a couple of bottles, she stuffed them in on top of the money.

Finn pulled his clothes on, watching Cyd through the

strange curtain of blue code and red light. Finally capable of putting two coherent thoughts together, all he could think was: I lost her. I've just lost her.

"Hey, Cyd, I've got some—"

"Important lead, Bridget. Gotta run," Cyd Brighton called as she came barreling down the hall with some guy.

Some guy? Bridget stepped out into the hallway and purposely collided with her. "I'm so sorry! Are you okay?"

"I'm fine," Cyd said tersely, trying to disentangle. The man with her kept walking. "I'll catch up with you," she called after him.

The man turned and looked back at them for a moment, pulling up short, and Bridget froze, seeing a thin line of blood trickling down the side of his face. The look of shock on her own face must have scared him.

"Wait!" she cried out.

But he just turned and bolted, taking the next corner too fast and stumbling against the wall for a moment before disappearing.

Bridget wheeled around. "Cyd, that's—"

"Just an informant of mine," she replied. "He didn't want to come here. He hates authority." She leaned against the wall, her breath still coming out in gasps from having had the wind knocked out of her.

But that face . . . No way. If anything, it was the other way around: Cyd was probably selling scoop to outsiders. Folding her arms across her chest, Bridget fished for more information. "Informants don't generally get clearance back here. I haven't seen that guy before."

Cyd glanced toward the exit. "What's your point?"

Bridget shifted, putting her weight on her other foot. "I'm just supposed to report things like this, that's all."

That got her full attention. Cyd stared at Bridget in silence for a moment, then said, "Maybe you should consider the likelihood of a reasonable explanation, given the unusual and frankly damn freaky subject matter I'm investigating. Do I need to remind you that you work for me?"

Wait a minute, diva. "I work for I-Ops," Bridget replied icily, dropping the secretarial nicey-nice tone that she had once used on a daily basis. She was more important now. "How about you? Don't you work for I-Ops? Are we on the same team, Cyd?"

Cyd's face paled. "You aren't what you pretend to be."

"Neither are you," Bridget replied. "And *neither is he.*"

Backing up slowly, Cyd maintained eye contact with her until she reached the corner. Then she spun away and disappeared.

Bridget's mind reeled as she stood there putting the pieces together. She'd seen that man's face in a different context. That had looked like the freelancer, Finn, the mercenary who normally held a table at Bosco's. But . . . she'd never seen Finn close-up, without sunglasses or a hood, and this guy . . .

Sucking in a quick breath as an idea struck her, Bridget ran to the nearest break room. There she flipped through the bounty notices that generally hung underneath the first-aid kit. Three quarters of the way down, she brushed aside a musty layer and found a photo. She studied it . . .

That was him. It had to be him. In the picture he was wearing a short-sleeved uniform, his mech components obvious for all to see. But there was a blank look in the eyes in this picture; the person she'd passed in the hall definitely seemed all there. The eyes she'd just seen were fired up, alive. He might be a machine, but he knew how to act like a man.

And Cyd Brighton was a liar. Which was too bad, because Bridget had actually kind of liked her.

Bridget followed Cydney's tracks back to where the three of them had collided, this time noting a fresh red smear on the wall where the man had leaned. Around the corner a little ways, before the double doors, was a bolt. When she picked it up, it felt warm to the touch.

Pushing her glasses up the bridge of her nose, Bridget turned around and walked back the direction Cyd and Finn had come. When she reached the courtyard outside, she started walking the perimeter, opening and closing each door.

With three more to go, there it was. On the inside of the doorknob leading to the Body Shop was another blood smear. Bridget stepped in and started knocking on doors and peeking into offices. The technicians must still be at training; most of the doors swung open freely, until she reached the office marked VALERIO DAGAMA. His door stopped short.

Bridget checked the halls behind her, then knelt down and stuck her hand through the crack, patting the floor until she felt what was preventing the door from opening completely.

She stepped inside. Dagama lay on the floor in a pool of his own blood, his pulse registering a big fat zero. Sticking out from underneath his arm was a small metal rectangle. BETA CLASS XG8.

For a moment, Bridget just stood there, paralyzed.

Cydney Brighton. Stupid, stupid, stupid.

She locked the office door behind her, pulled out some cleaning supplies from Valerio's closet and began to collect the forensic evidence.

Chapter Twenty

Two steps into the apartment, Finn was already tearing off his jacket and shirt, ripping the bloody gauze from his body. He buried his head in his hands. The fucking mechanic hadn't even got to his legs! His left eye was still going haywire. And he was back on the Grid with who-even-knew-how-long before Ops realized the connection was there for the taking. What a mess. The whole thing. Just a damn mess.

Cydney slumped on the couch in a kind of daze, completely blank. She wouldn't look at him. Now more than ever he felt the weight of her disgust. Finn closed his eyes and tried to block it all out—he never should have let her stay while Valerio worked on him. It was all so confusing, and he didn't know what bothered him more: that his longed-for cure-all, his appointment with Ops, had gone horribly wrong; or that Cyd saw him as more of a machine than ever.

He knew she thought the whole thing was a lost cause. He took her chin and gently turned her face up to his. "Do you think I'm giving up? I don't resign myself to this, Cyd. I don't resign myself to anything."

She met his gaze, and he searched her face, mining every detail. Her eyes: a fan of lush, dark lashes. The curve of her full lips. Her impossibly perfect skin. Thick, lustrous hair. Her beauty was truly extraordinary. Too extraordinary.

A wave of realization swept through him. If he couldn't get the humans to fix what they'd done to him, maybe he could look elsewhere. Perhaps to an entirely different species.

"I don't resign myself . . . " he whispered.

Ironic, that he had access to database files again, being back on the Grid. He ran a scan on Cyd's name. He looked in her file, at her photos. The first was a shot upon graduation from the Ops academy. Young, fresh, made-up, smiling. But imperfect. Then a second shot. In action. Hair in a ponytail. Serious expression. Not so youthful. Not so hopeful. Third shot: Full battle gear. Cigarette in hand. Rebellious look in the eyes. Don't-fuck-with-me body language. Her face, her eyes, jaded and drawn.

And last was the Cyd that stood before him now: the jaded air of her recent past, but a dewy, youthful physical package that outshone even her earliest days.

Where had she been for all the time she'd been gone? Had she ever said? She'd said she didn't know. Could it be as Finn imagined?

It all fit. It all made sense. The timing, everything. Somehow Cyd Brighton was part demon. Not vampire, not werewolf—they never would have let her into I-Ops like that—but part demon. And the demon side was perfecting her human-side. Regeneration. She was becoming a perfect specimen of the human body, while Finn's own human body degraded.

But did she know? Was she hiding it from him?

Cyd's connections to Ops were played out and couldn't help him, but maybe her connection to the demon world could. Whatever was making her body whole, maybe it could do the same for him.

You can't ask for more. Not now. Don't do it. . . . Don't do it. "I think there's another way," he blurted.

"You're looking for a miracle, then," she said grimly.

He looked down at her, searching her eyes, then stared at the side of his scarred hand next to her perfect flesh. "You . . ." He couldn't say it; he ended on a harsh breath.

But she was his miracle. Cyd Brighton was his fucking miracle.

Does she understand? Does she know? You've got to make her believe. If you can't make her believe in you, you can't make her help you.

He turned and grabbed her by the shoulders, trying not to scare her with his desperation. "You know my darkest secret, Cyd. Trust me with yours."

Her eyes searched his. She swallowed hard and looked away.

"Look at me," he said. "*Please.*"

She turned and looked at him, raising her chin defiantly.

"I think I know," he said. He took her arm, ran his fingers down to her hand, then curled her fingers into a fist. She resisted at first, then let him direct her. He raised her arm and brought her fist up to his face, below his eye. "When you hit me—that would have hurt," he said.

"You deserved it."

"That's not what I'm saying. Press harder."

She didn't move, and he took her by the elbow and pressed her knuckles harder against his skin. She stared at him for a moment; then, as he forced her to press her fist even deeper into his flesh, it was as if the lights went on. Her eyes widened as comprehension set in.

"It's metal plate, Cyd. You should have broken your hand when you punched me; your knuckles should have been scraped up, bruised at least. You didn't have a scratch."

Her fingers unfurled, and she tenderly tested the skin on his cheek, then suddenly pulled her hand away, her face a mask of defiance. She didn't speak.

"No one's quite *that* tough," he said gently. "I don't think you're entirely human anymore. You understand that, don't you?"

Cyd lurched backwards out of his reach, speechless. She wore a crazy look, terrified. He advanced on her.

"You're not a dog. You're not a fang. And yet somehow, miraculously, your body is regenerating whenever there's damage. That leaves only one possibility."

She was shaking now, her arms wrapped around her, and it wasn't cold in his apartment. "I don't know what you're talking about," she said. "You don't *make* demons. That's not how it works."

He'd never seen anyone look so desperately afraid, except for those who knew they were staring death in the face. "Are you so sure you know how it works?"

Cyd's mouth twisted in a snarl. "You selfish son of a bitch. You desperate, selfish son of a bitch. We are screwed. Can you comprehend what just happened? Not only are you back on the Grid where Ops can find you if they know where to look, but you killed the guy who put you there. Why couldn't you just accept what you are?"

"If it's so easy, then why the hell can't you?"

"You men are all the same. You always want something. It always ends the same damn way."

"I'm not like anyone else," Finn growled.

"Metal for a heart and wire for brains," she spat out. "What's the difference?"

He let her say her worst. He knew he deserved it. But he had to push. "I know about keeping secrets, Cyd. Fine, don't tell me anything. But think. Did anything happen to you while you were gone that could have changed you? Did you come into contact with someone, something . . . ?"

Her face went white. "We're done, you and I." She rose and ran to the door, flung it open and walked out.

"Cyd!" *Shit.* Finn grabbed his jacket and bolted after her. "Cyd!"

"Go to hell!" she yelled, breaking into a run.

He could have caught up with her easily, but instead he let her run. He trailed her to the Dogtown subway hub and headed after her, threading through the passengers standing on the platform as she tried to lose him once again.

Slowed down by the crowd, he could see her panting, stumbling a little, swiping her sleeve across her eyes. A train shot through the station, going express toward the city center. As it passed, Cyd looked anxiously down the opposite end of the tunnel for the one that was heading toward the outskirts of the city.

Blaring horns, blinking lights, the wind from the passing train whipping loose strands of hair around her face. In the chaos, Finn caught her around the waist, closing his arms tight around her as she struggled to get free.

She pressed her fists against his shoulders, but he pulled her close, the wind continuing to rage around them. He looked into her eyes. And then he crushed his mouth down on hers. She pounded her fists against him for only a moment longer before her body seemed to melt and her fingers went slack, curling slightly into his clothing.

The taste of her—so sweet, so dark, so tender and filled with dangerous heat—he couldn't have said whether it was the physicality of the union or the feeling of pure human emotion that moved him so deeply.

I need you, Cyd. In so many ways.

A train bound for the outskirts slowed to a halt, and Finn finally disengaged from the kiss. He lifted Cyd's hand in his and kissed her palm with all of the passion in his heart, then flicked out the blade that extended from his right arm and made a deep cut across it.

Cyd's face registered a woozy combination of confusion, desire, pain. She clenched her fist and swayed backwards, and Finn moved to steady her. As the train doors opened, he put his lips to her ear.

"We are *not* done, you and I," he murmured. Then he stepped away, unfurled her fist and showed her palm to her—uncut, unscarred and perfectly unscathed.

Cyd stared at her hand, then looked up at him dazedly. He had to reach forward and gently push her through the open doors of the subway car. She would want some time alone.

Chapter Twenty-one

Cyd stood in the train, her eyes fixed on the floor, both hands gripping the pole as the car jerked and swayed. Most of the riders were werewolves; some of them were probably her old informants. Either way, she knew they could sense someone who was human, someone who was werewolf . . . and someone who was something else.

She could have played off the wide swath of space they left around her as the same old thing, that she'd suddenly reappeared in the city and those who knew of her were suspicious. Maybe the word was out that she'd been involved in the death of that werewolf informant way back at the beginning of all of this. But the fact was, she made them uneasy in a way that clearly transcended mere suspicion. She could feel it, they could feel it, and though she wasn't willing to accept Finn's words at face value, the proof of something horribly wrong was present in the very absence of a wound across her palm.

The subway pulled to a stop at the next station, and a train bound for the beach cities pulled up across the platform. Without giving it another thought, Cyd slipped out of her car and sprinted for the opposite train, sliding through the closing doors just in time.

She'd tried to help Finn become what he wanted to be. That had failed. Now, his suggestion that she had demon powers that could be his salvation was like a dousing of cold water. His desire to save himself was clearly more important than any feelings he might have for her. Why should she spend one more second worrying about him? Because of him, there was a dead body in the Ops complex that would almost definitely be traced back to her.

She was tired of speculation. She was tired of wondering deep inside if what he'd suggested might be true. Perhaps the amulet was what had bound Griff-Vai to her. The simple solution seemed to be: Get rid of it.

The train pulled up to the beachfront station, and she headed along the ramp to the surface streets. The walk to the pier was quiet, with only a few packs of teenagers and a handful of couples; that was it. Quite a few animals roamed the streets out here, and every now and then a howl or bark pierced the night.

This area still hadn't entirely recovered from the demon attacks. Standing on the beach, Cyd stared at the tattered yellow caution ribbons fluttering off posts stuck deep in the sand. Giant craters along the shoreline remained unfilled. The ocean lapped at pieces of burnt driftwood and stray, spent ammo cartridges.

The pier itself was still mostly intact, though leaning dangerously to one side. The noisy, glittering amusements once lining the pier had gone silent. Cyd pressed the amulet in her hand to her chest as she gingerly made her way along the groaning wood slats to the very end of the dock.

An abandoned war zone, to be sure, but if you

looked up and out, if you left the skyline of Crimson City behind you and set your sights on the horizon, the purity of the water and the sky and the moon—well, it was nothing short of perfection.

"So, I'm coming to *you*, Draig," she whispered, wrapping her arms around herself. "Your turf. Air, earth, fire and water. This is as far away from the city as I can get these days. And as close to nature as I can get. Help me show Finn he's got it all wrong."

She pulled the amulet chain over her head and cradled the artifact in her palm. It pulsed with an unseen energy that yet seemed impossible for one attuned to energy fields to miss. "If you're what they say you are, maybe you can sense this, feel it here."

The wind picked up, and cold sliced through her clothes as she moved farther out over the water. "Please. *Somebody*," she said through gritted teeth. Everything inside her told her to get rid of it. If nature wouldn't come to her, she'd send the amulet back to nature.

You said we were connected, Griff. Well, just watch me break the connection. I'm not a demon. I don't belong to you, and you don't get to control me. Leave. Me. Alone!

She picked a spot far out in the ocean and took aim, the amulet chain dangling against her wrist as she cocked her arm. But just as she was about to throw, she was almost bounced off the dock by the pounding of feet against the aging wooden boards.

Cyd closed her fist around the chain just before it could drop, and in a whirl of muscle-bound tan skin, wet suit, and blond hair, she took a full-body blow so hard that it whipped her head back. She went flying off the edge of the dock, a man's arms wrapped tightly around her from behind. And as they plunged into the water, she watched the black fluid in the amulet's crystal glow red.

It was as if Griff-Vai was taunting her, but Cyd was more resolved than ever. Struggling in the stranger's grasp, she felt him pull her backwards underwater with his arms around her stomach, and most of her remaining oxygen vanished in a mass of bubbles.

But then, as if he realized what he'd just done, the stranger closed his fist tight around the amulet in her hand, gave it a squeeze as if to tell her not to let go, and pushed her upward.

Still gripping the amulet, Cyd swam for the surface, breaking through just in time and wading toward the shore, sputtering and coughing as she fell to her hands and knees. Exhausted, she looked behind her; wave after wave came in, but the rest was dead silent. Then a huge burst of water erupted from the ocean. Cyd yelped in terror, sloshing back in the ankle-high tide.

The stranger rose up out of the surf and pushed his hair from his face, climbing out of the ocean as if he'd just finished a casual swim. "You okay?" he asked.

"What the hell?" she sputtered.

"Sorry. I couldn't let you cast it away. The thought of losing it again . . . We've been looking for it all this time."

Cyd nodded dazedly, her head spinning. "Just tell me you're the Draig-Uisge," she said after she caught her breath.

He nodded. "I'm the Draig. Patrick."

"Cydney." She raised the amulet, not quite ready to hand it over anymore. "Still got it," she said.

"I can feel it," he remarked. He drew his sopping wet hair into a ponytail. "Outside of the city interference, I can definitely feel it. Come on. Let's take a walk."

He held out his hand. Cyd looked suspiciously at it, then up at him. "Tell me you have some answers," she begged.

"I have some answers," he said with a smile.

She let him help her up; then she followed him down the beach. Ahead, an elderly man in swim trunks lay down towels. A young Asian woman stoked a fledgling bonfire.

Shivering in the wet clothes plastered to her skin, Cyd welcomed the heat and knelt down by the fire. The old man settled on the opposite side, his weathered face turned to the ocean. The woman smiled and tossed Cyd another towel to wrap around her shoulders.

"Cydney, this is Xiao Fei," Patrick said.

Xiao Fei's eyes widened as she saw the amulet in Cyd's hand. "If you can use that thing, you're a powerful woman."

"Hardly," Cyd muttered despondently.

Xiao Fei gave her a strange look, then, recovering her composure, stuck out her hand. "So, it was you we pulled through the portal. Nice to finally meet you."

"No offense or anything, but I'm not here for the party," Cyd said. She held up the amulet. "You want this, and I want to get rid of it. It's like some homing beacon, right? He said something about us being bound together in his eyes, and at the time I couldn't imagine he meant we had a tie that crossed worlds. I couldn't imagine that he could get so far inside my head. But he did . . . he *has*. And I think it's because of what he did with this amulet. At first I thought it was protecting me from him, because it pulled me back here. But now I know that it's just been drawing him closer. Without it, he can't get to me. That's it, right?"

Patrick and Xiao Fei exchanged glances. Patrick sat

down next to her. "You're talking about the demons," he said.

Cyd looked down at her hands, not wanting to admit it aloud.

"You don't have to pretend," Patrick said softly. "We know you came from the demon underworld."

She stared at them for a moment, a crazy relief sweeping through her. "Yeah. I came back from the demon underworld," she repeated, unable to hold back a nervous smile. To be able to say that out loud, and to not be judged or to fear for her life—that was a wonderful thing.

"Do you know what we were trying to do with it when you came along?" Xiao Fei asked.

Cyd glanced down at the amulet; she was clutching it tightly in her hand. Then she looked up and studied their faces. "I think you must have been trying to do something good."

"Xiao Fei and I, we closed the portal that night in the park, the night you came through. But your return caused a rift in the fabric of the veil. If we don't close that rift for good, demons may still be able to return."

Cyd looked at the pair. "You two can close it?"

"We could have. We'll figure out how to harness the energy again," Patrick said, looking over at Xiao Fei. "This time without risking so many lives."

"You hope," Cyd said.

"We believe."

Cyd didn't try and bargain. Didn't haggle. Didn't even try and cut a deal. She knew that they would protect this talisman in a way that she couldn't, and she sensed that it was only harming her to keep it. "Take it," she said. "This can't help me; that much I know. If you think you can use it to keep the portal closed, it's all yours."

She hesitated for a moment more, but then she put the amulet down in the sand between them.

Xiao Fei and Patrick didn't grab for it; they just looked down at the artifact, and Xiao Fei's hand moved to his. Patrick took the necklace, gave it a squeeze, and the two held on to each other. Cyd looked away to the ocean, a little undone by the intensity of their feeling. She thought of Finn, how they'd failed each other, each so desperate to find the solution to their own problems, and an empty, lonely feeling clutched at her heart.

"Take it," Cyd repeated. "I just want to be free. Griff won't be able to get to me, and none of them will be able to get through."

Patrick frowned. "I don't think it's quite that—"

"Take it, already!"

The Draiz-Uisge took the amulet and placed the chain around his neck, resting the medallion gently on his chest. Cyd sat in the sand, waiting for the big moment. Waiting to feel some kind of change. Some kind of intense, personal relief.

"We're not bound anymore, Griff-Vai. I'm free," she said, as if just saying the words out loud would make them so.

She looked up at the two neo-druids, but their carefully measured expressions told a different story. A kind of swamping horror roared through her mind. "You said you had answers. Where are my answers? Nothing's changed, has it?"

Xiao Fei rose, moved closer and put her hands on Cyd's shoulders. "Please calm down," she said.

Cyd threw the woman's hands off. "Don't tell me to

calm down! You try living this way. I see him, I hear him in my head. He's doing things to me, and he's becoming more . . . present each time. Do you understand what I'm saying? He's trying to get to me, and he's getting closer. Something's allowing him to build up the strength to present himself in person. I thought that by giving you the amulet I would break the link that binds us together."

"Why would you think that?" Patrick asked gently.

"I was right there in that energy you created. Didn't you see? When I grabbed on to the amulet, Griff-Vai . . . he held it down to my forehead. He pressed it against my head, and he's saying this stuff I don't even understand. Some demon language or something. And I was struggling, and we were struggling, and I had him by the neck, and I guess . . . his forehead came down on mine, the amulet between us. Suddenly, I was just . . . out. I was back in Crimson City."

Cyd's whole body was shaking, and not just from the cold. Patrick and Xiao Fei tried to get near her to help, but she wouldn't let them.

"Are you listening to me? From that moment, he's been dogging me. It's got to be the amulet that binds us together. So, you take that thing, the two of you. Take that thing and walk away. I want it as far away from me as it can get."

"We'll walk away, Cyd. We'll walk away," Patrick said. "But listen to me carefully. The amulet itself did not create a bond between you and this demon. He simply took advantage of the unusual force of the energy it created to cast an incantation upon you. Still . . . there's something special about you now, right? You're not like a typical human anymore. Remember that there are advantages—some of his power will be inside you now. You'll have to find the courage to use it."

"It was the amulet," Cyd said stubbornly. "There's nothing of him in me. It was the amulet."

Patrick sighed. "I'm sorry. This demon of yours may have been dogging you long before the amulet, and he may be dogging you long after. The only thing left to do is to fight him in a way that uses all the power of our world. You need to transcend what just a human or a demon can do."

"Take it away," Cyd repeated in a growl. "Take it far away from me."

Nodding, Patrick stood. He took Xiao Fei's hand, and the two walked off down the beach. Biting back a sob, Cyd watched them go.

"Oh my god. What do I do now?" she whispered a moment later. She'd come here to find answers, and miraculously the Draig-Usage had been here. Why, then, had she learned nothing?

She suddenly realized that the old man was still there, perfectly silent on the other side of the bonfire. "He said there were answers. Do *you* have the answers?" she asked.

The old man turned to face her, his shoulder-length gray hair shifting away from a face marked by harsh weather and time. He said, "To fight your foe, you must be stronger in some way. So think. What is stronger than a demon?"

Cyd shrugged helplessly.

"A human?"

"No," she said.

"A vampire?"

"No."

"A werewolf?"

"*No,*" she snapped. She was losing patience.

"You can kill an individual demon, or you can hire someone who will . . . but there will still be a tear in the veil. You will be running for the rest of your life—unless you are stronger than all your foes."

She threw out her hands. "I can't be stronger than this demon. If I could be, I'd make myself so and stop him from coming for me."

The old man's eyes twinkled. "One power is not stronger. Two may not be stronger, either. Three, still not enough. Four? Now we're talking."

"I don't understand," Cyd complained.

The old man held up his hand and counted off: "Human, vampire, werewolf, demon. These are the races. One of their world, three of ours."

"That's helpful," Cyd said sarcastically. "Show me the individual who is all four."

"I cannot."

Cyd shook her head, furious. She stood up, and the aged druid reached out and grabbed her wrist.

"Part demon, but not born so like others. Torn from the clutches of he who would make you his, pulled back through the veil by one of the druid faith. It is a lot for anyone to handle. But only you have the power of two worlds. You have both. You need all the power of our world, however. With two more, you shall have all four species. I cannot show you the individual who is all four, but I can show you the individual who can *become* all four."

He closed her fingers around her palm until her hand was a fist; then he took that fist tightly in his hands, squeezing it to the point of pain. "Pure blood, Cydney. Or you will die trying."

Cyd wrenched her arm from his grasp and slowly

backed away, a dull roar in her head like the ocean's waves. "You're crazy, old man," she said. "You're crazy."

She turned and ran off down the sand. *Always running, Cyd. Always running from something.* She knew exactly where she was going. She'd been there a million times before. What surprised her wasn't that she was going back down that twisted road, but that she hadn't gone there earlier.

A couple rights, a couple lefts, a subway ride and a code word later; a flashlight in her face, a pat-down, a strange look or two, and an irony-tinged, "Welcome home." Cyd was in D-Alley, where you could buy anything, from anyone, at any time.

"Where's Dougan?" she asked the gatekeeper.

He pointed. "Same as always."

She passed over a couple of bills and hurried through the gate, flinching as the iron clanged shut behind her.

She counted off the doors lining the alley, and knocked. A set of eyes appeared through the rectangular slit. Dougan. He studied her face. "The usual?"

Cyd laughed bitterly. She hadn't been here for a long time, but when she had, she'd been a regular customer. How sad. How pathetic.

"For here or to go?" Dougan asked.

"To go. Please hurry." Cyd looked over her shoulder out of habit. This time, she wasn't paranoid about somebody on one of the Ops teams catching her. But . . . *Griff-Vai doesn't stalk you that way. For that matter, you won't hear him approach. He just appears.*

Dougan made a hand signal, and Cyd answered back using transaction code—not bothering to negotiate. She pulled a bunch of bills from her pocket and held them out, leaving her palm open as he whisked them away and laid two poppers in their place. She stuck those in her pocket and turned away without another word. Slipping into the alley, she pressed the back of her hand against her mouth in a futile attempt to keep herself from crying.

Don't think. Don't think. Don't think.

Down the same old road. Maybe you just couldn't change. Maybe destiny, fate, all that—maybe that's just how life went. She'd never even tried to get clean. All she knew was, when she'd returned from the demon underworld, she'd been better. Trouble was, it didn't last. Life in Crimson City looked a lot better when you were viewing it through a rainbow-colored mist and a human-engineered fantasy world—all available in convenient punch form.

Cyd found an empty corner and ducked into the shadows. She slid down against the wall, the cold of the concrete seeping into her flesh. "Fly away," she murmured as she pulled up her sleeve and pressed the punch into the bend of her forearm. "Rainbows and butterflies . . ." She closed her eyes and waited, letting the empty cartridge drop to the ground.

The tiniest edge of bliss began to unfurl inside her, and Cyd waited for the warmth to spread. But before it could take hold, the tentative fantasy evaporated. Cyd's eyes flew open, and she watched opalescent fluid drip off her elbow to the ground.

Please, just be defective, she thought.

Her hands shaking, she grabbed the second popper, aligned the punch and and pressed it in. This time she watched as her body rejected the serum, watched it leak back out of the tiny hole, impossibly cheating both her mind and her body.

Everything she'd tried to deny since she'd arrived—the burned flesh regenerating at Bosco's, the scar tissue fading, the bruises and cuts healing, the track marks disappearing—played in her mind. She thought about the inexplicable change as her face and body—her human shell—became more beautiful. All of the signs told the same story, forced the same conclusion.

With shaking hands, she pulled a knife from her boot and held it up to her palm—the same one Finn had cut to try to prove to her that she was not what she wanted to be anymore.

Bracing herself, she swiped the blade across her skin. The blood spilled out from the deep cut, and for once in her life, Cyd welcomed the pain. But it lasted only a second. The pinprick vanished and the wound repaired itself before her eyes.

No more denials. Finn had been telling her the truth, and she wouldn't listen. The amulet might have helped forge the bond she had with Griff-Vai, but it hadn't been what was causing all of this.

Trying to stop the tears pouring down her face was impossible now; the truth was exactly as Finn had put it. She wasn't entirely human anymore. She was part demon, bonded by the amulet in the energy surge of the portal. Griff-Vai had got in her in the end. He'd won.

I am demon.

She put her forehead against her knees and gave up.

She couldn't say how long she sat there before the sound of heavy boots along the pavement caught her attention. "I've been all over the city looking for you. I wanted to say I'm sorry."

Cyd picked her head up. Finn crouched down beside her, and though the last thing she wanted was to turn him into a babysitter like she'd done with Dain, like she'd done with other men, she couldn't even think about turning him away.

"Well, of course you're going to find Cydney Brighton in D-Alley when the bottom falls out," she said numbly. "Everybody at Bosco's will tell you that. I'm sure they did."

"Stop it," he said gently. "This isn't who you really are."

She laughed bitterly. "Apparently it is. Didn't you see?"

Finn reached out and pulled her hair out of her eyes. "I saw," he said.

Cyd looked up at him, and suddenly tears were again streaming down her face.

"Aww, Cyd," he murmured.

She couldn't hold back; loud sobs wracked her body.

"Get up," Finn said. All trace of humor vanished in the face of her anguish. "You're not giving up like this. Come on. Get up!" He reached down, literally picking her up and setting her on her feet.

Cyd slumped weakly against the wall and started to cry again. "I can't handle this," she rasped. "I can't handle it. I'm not strong enough to deal with this. I'm weak. I've always been weak. I just need to accept that."

Finn had one palm on either side of her face. She couldn't even look him in the eye. "Now you listen to me," he said. "You're stronger than you know. You have no idea what's inside of you, what you're capable of. Pull yourself together."

His anger just made her cry more. "You were right about me all along. I'm part demon, Finn. There. I said it. I'm part demon. Everyone keeps asking me where I've been? I've been in the demon underworld. I've been the lover of a demon named Griff-Vai. I gave in to him in a moment of weakness, and now there's something that links us, and it's not that amulet. It was just supposed to be the amulet. And now getting this out of me is as impossible as getting the machine out of you. Okay? So there, I said it."

Finn didn't say a word, and Cyd just shook her head. "I bet you're not exactly disappointed," she guessed. "What do you think is going to happen? You think if you kiss me enough times, you'll become pretty like me? If you sleep with me, you'll wake up with perfect skin? If you stand next me long enough, your wounds will heal? I can't help you. I wouldn't even know how. Can't you just . . . Can't you just—"

"What? Can't I just what?"

Can't you just love me for me? Because you want to, not, because you think I can save you. Can't you realize that I'm weak and don't deserve to be loved? Can't you just leave me alone?

"Nothing," she said. "I can't save anybody, Finn. I can't save me. And I can't save you. There's nothing about where I've been that doesn't come without a price. I can't give you a damn thing," she said.

"I'm sorry," he said haltingly. "I—"

"That's why you're here, picking me up out of the gutter. You just think I can help you." She couldn't see any other reason he'd have.

"That's not how it is."

"You think I'm the answer to your problems," she accused.

"Well . . . maybe I'm the answer to yours, too," he burst out. "Nothing's impossible. There's always a way."

Cyd pushed feebly at his shoulders and glanced off into the distance. "A way," she repeated. "You don't understand. I don't want to be like this. It's hopeless. To conquer him, to conquer the demon Griff-Vai, I must be stronger than he is. To be stronger . . . I have to get worse. They're saying I need to be all four species. They're telling me that I will have to chance becoming even less human to be free." Thinking about it made the panic and anger and tears well up all over again. "I can't do that. I can't do it. It's impossible."

He shushed her, clearly trying to soothe her pain, his arms moving around her shoulders to hold her up while she went weak in the knees and tried to lower herself back to the ground, where she could put her head down and curl up and try to block absolutely everything out.

At last, she turned and looked up at Finn. "Is this why no more demons have come after me? Because I'm headed toward the dark all on my own? Am I going under?"

"I won't let you go under," he replied. He shrugged, as if her situation was the most natural thing in the world. "We have a stake in each other now." He turned his head and met her eyes. "I can't let them have you. I won't. Put your arms around me."

Cyd wrapped her arms around his neck, and he lifted her up in his embrace and walked her back through the D-Alley gate. She buried her face in his shoulder and gave in. She allowed herself to be comforted physically if not emotionally.

He needed something from her. That's why he cared.

Yet in spite of her cynicism, Cyd was overwhelmed by two things: by dread of her circumstance, and by the knowledge that this mech was capable of a tenderness beyond what she'd experienced with any fully flesh-

and-blood man she'd ever known. As he carried her through the streets of the city, whispering words of comfort in her ear, Cyd ran her thumb over the perfect smoothness of her palm where she'd taken the cuts.

He's just a machine, Cyd. Get over it. Get over it. Get over him.

I can't.

Chapter Twenty-two

If pressure made Bridget cooler and more collected, it seemed to have the opposite effect on Trask. She could hear him pacing in her office as she got herself a glass of water in the kitchen. She didn't need the damn water; she needed to get away from him for a moment. If he asked her even one more time if she was sure her intel was good, she might have to knock him out cold and finish the job alone. As harsh as it might sound, she didn't really need him anymore; she'd taken advantage of all the training he had to offer and was even better than he was on the technological side.

And that wasn't the only justification for cutting ties with him. Trask's increasingly erratic and violent behavior was definitely beginning to freak her out.

"Are you sure this intel is good?" he called from the other room.

Bridget rolled her eyes. "I'm going to say it one more time: My intel is good. I think that tech triggered something before he got whacked. I'm telling you, the mech's on the Grid and he's live. And if he's on the Grid, we can hack in."

"What happens if he slips the Grid like he did the first time?"

"Then we can't really do anything as far as manipulating his behavior. Off the Grid, I guess he's . . . well, just another guy on the street as far as we're concerned. It's sort of like being in hibernation, with all systems running in the background undetected, waiting to be accessed. It's tricky. Until code is deleted from the network, there will always be the potential to manipulate him. And the only way you can delete the code is when a program is on the Grid." She took a deep breath and stepped back into her office.

Trask followed on her heels, crowding her, looking over her shoulder as she plopped into the chair and clicked to connect once again to the network. "Are you sure you understand how all this works?"

Bridget glared at him. "You don't honestly think I spend all those hours at the admin desk playing solitaire, do you?"

Trask shrugged. "Can we trace him?"

"I don't know."

"We're certain he's still in Crimson City?"

"I just *saw* him."

"I knew it," Trask said, falling heavily back in his desk chair. "I'm going to find him. And I'm going to get that money."

"I thought *we* were going to get that money," Bridget said through her teeth, again wishing she hadn't called him.

"That's what I meant," Trask said soothingly. "We. So, how long until you get access to his system?"

"You asked me that ten minutes ago. We're getting closer," Bridget snapped. "At least we've gotten to the log-in screen now." Hacking this was tougher than she'd thought.

Trask crumpled the printout in his hand and smashed it down into the garbage can. "We're so close!" He rose and stalked the room, rubbing his hand over his chin. "Look, Finn's not exactly the invisible man. Those free-lancers all hang at Bosco's. If he's in town, somebody there will know where he is; let's just go find him and bring him in."

"Not before we make this connection. We don't want him sabotaging his systems."

"Why does it matter?"

She heaved a frustrated sigh. "It matters because, if we want to control him, we need access to those."

"He's wanted dead or alive," Trask said.

Bridget glowered at him over her shoulder. "We're *not* killing him. And it's not like he's just going to tell us the password to his mind." She plugged in yet another username and password and hit enter. They were re-jected. Again.

Beside her, Trask slowly worked himself into a frenzy. It was driving Bridget nuts.

"Relax! What's the hurry? Nobody else has the intel I've got," she said. "I told you: I packaged up all that ev-idence, and nobody will figure this out. No one but us."

Trask made what seemed to be an honest effort, scooting his chair back next to her and resting his fore-head on his clasped hands. Bridget glanced sideways at him and forced herself to remain clam in the face of his almost overwhelming intensity.

But in the next moment, he stood and pushed his chair back, sending it careening across the floor.

Bridget moistened her lips and pulled the printout

from the garbage, smoothing it down. "I'll try working off these a little more." She glanced at the first sets of passwords she'd hacked out of the Ops system and started plugging in new variations. Trask paced behind her; she could hear him compulsively pulling his weapons, checking the ammo and reholstering them.

The guy was gonna blow.

A moment later, Trask grabbed his jacket and shades and headed for the door. "I'm going into the field. This is ridiculous. It's a nice idea, hacking into him, but it doesn't affect his value. If we want to get the bounty money, either way we have to get at him."

"He's worth more alive, Trask. Don't kill him. Think of what's in his mind."

Trask pulled Bridget's hand off his arm, a cold, dark look in his eyes. "I'm just going to check Bosco's. You keep trying. Meet me over there later if you want."

When she grabbed him by the arm again, he exploded. "We're *this* close!" he shouted at her. "I'm tired of these delays. I don't want someone else to bring him in." And with that, he stormed out.

Bridget watched the door close behind him. Slowly, she walked back to her computer and sat down.

Normally she would have been right by Trask's side, but not today. While she would have loved to keep an eye on him, if she was going to get at the mech before he did, it was better they should part ways.

Bridget waited a few more minutes, in case he came back, and then she pulled a scrap of paper from her wallet and stuck it on the counter. She copied the number on the paper into her comm device and dialed up. "This is the Club? Yeah. I'm looking for the boss. This is Bridget Rothschild. Yeah."

After she waited a few moments on hold, a voice came on the line. "Who is this?"

"It's Bridget. I have something I think you're going to be interested in. Do you have what I want?"

The man laughed. "What is that? If you mean money and power, I can guarantee you'll get more of that from us than you will from Ops. Especially with your only ally being Trask. That's not the best gamble in town at the moment."

"Are you saying what I think you're saying?" She felt a chill.

"Bridget, let's not fuck around. Trask is dirty. He's working non-official. If you knew someone was killing your friends, think about what you'd do."

Bridget took a deep breath. What would she do? Easy. She'd kill him. And that's probably what was going to happen.

"Look, you know we want you. It's why I've been trying to recruit you in the first place," her contact said. "If you're ready to switch sides, let's make a deal."

She didn't need any more time to think. "Done," she said. "I'm ready. Let's make a deal."

"Good. We'll be in touch." Her contact hung up without ceremony.

Bridget tossed the comm back onto her desk. She typed in a few commands, hit enter, then sighed and went to put on a pot of coffee.

Finn opened his eyes with a start, glancing over at the clock. He'd barely slept all night. The pain in his head came and went so suddenly; he would only just manage to relax before a twinge at his temple and a fresh sweep of code over his retina had him reeling.

Cyd lay fully clothed on top of the covers next to

him, tangled in an extra blanket, her face burrowed into his side. Resisting the urge to touch her face, he carefully slid off the bed before his body starting asking for things she wouldn't want to give.

On the desk, his rigged Ops scanner made itself known with muted squawks and static. He'd turned it down so Cyd could sleep, but he'd have it at full blast when she woke up, just as he'd had it since arriving back from the Body Shop.

Valerio had done a fine job, considering; and the longer Finn thought about the circumstances of the man's death, the heavier the guilt weighted on his shoulders. Finn was grateful for the work the technician had done—was impossibly grateful for every way he wouldn't have to hide from the world anymore. He'd given the man an unjust reward.

He felt another twinge of guilt, too. Cyd was right—he couldn't help but look down at her flawless skin and wonder if there was something she could use from her demon experience to help him. He didn't blame her for not understanding how it was possible for him both to care for her and still dare to wonder if he could use her; he didn't blame her at all.

Cyd stirred, a frown wrinkling her brow. Finn leaned over her and gently pressed his lips to her forehead.

"Cyd," he whispered.

"Mmm?"

"I've got some business at Bosco's. I'll set the alarm for another hour."

She didn't answer this time. Finn pulled the blanket up over her, then went for a quick shower and shave.

Half an hour later, he pushed through the front door at Bosco's. He sure as hell wasn't at his best, but on the other hand, he couldn't help but enjoy the freedom of moving around in public without so many layers, without cowering inside of a hood in a way that truly went against his nature. He ran his fingers over the wound at his temple, the wound that would soon heal into a seminormal-looking scar, then checked his watch and looked around for Hayden.

But it wasn't Wilks who suddenly plunked down in the chair opposite him; it was Jill Cooper. She put a small briefcase down by her feet along the aisle, and held out her hand. "Hi. I'm Jill," she said.

Finn forced himself not to laugh. What was this? He glanced around the room; quite a few people were watching. Some of them weren't bothering to hide their own amusement. He thought about it for a moment, then engaged in the handshake, trying to ignore the fact that if everything had gone well with Valerio, he'd be offering her his bare hand. Of course, if he had, he probably would have found her palm sweaty, judging by her obvious discomfort.

"I know who you are," he said. "Are you sure you know who I am?"

"You're Finn. Hayden Wilks sent me." She leaned down, opened her briefcase and pulled out a file, which she handed over.

"Right." Finn handed the file back without even opening it. "Sorry, I think there's been a mistake. I'm not getting involved in this."

Jill frowned. "You think I don't know what I'm doing?"

"I *know* you don't know what you're doing." He leaned over the tabletop, picked up her briefcase, swung it over her head and dropped it loudly in the space between the wall and her legs, where she should have put it in the first place. She flinched, and he shook his head at her. "Tell Hayden I need to approve our contacts. If he wants to train someone, that should be a cost on his side of doing business, not mine."

"I'm not an extra risk," she argued. "I have a reputation for being honest, trustworthy and totally loyal to my friends—and if you really know who I am, then you know that."

"Déjà vu," he muttered. Then: "You were also known for not taking sides. What gives?"

"I'm not a journalist anymore."

"Oh?"

She looked down. "I'm done with all of that."

"What are you doing, Jill? Seriously, what are you doing getting yourself involved in this stuff? You're a nice girl."

"And Cyd Brighton's not?"

He didn't allow his surprise to show; he smiled. "Cyd's special."

"We're all special," Jill said bitterly. "It doesn't seem to make a damn bit of difference."

Finn studied her face for a long moment. "If you're doing this . . . if you're teaming up with Hayden to make Marius Dumont crazy—you know that would be incredibly dumb, don't you?"

Jill leaned in close, her eyes narrow. "I may be a lot of things, but I'm not dumb."

"Okay. Maybe pissed and bored is a better description. Let me warn you that it might seem exciting, running around with bad kids . . . until you're staring at a dead body or about to become one yourself. That's all I'll say about it."

"Don't patronize me."

"Hell hath no fury like a woman scorned. Is that it?" Finn murmured.

"How is it you're so interested in what is or isn't happening between Marius Dumont and me?"

Finn wasn't about to tell her that if she and Marius were cutting ties, he was probably out of one of his regular paying gigs.

After a moment, her look softened. "Can't a girl change careers without all the gossip?"

"Sure," he said with a shrug.

She smiled. "I look forward to working with you then," she remarked, handing him back the file.

He didn't take it. "No offense. Really. But I'm still not going to take you on. Tell Hayden I only work with principals—and no newbies."

Her smile vanished. "I'd appreciate it if you would work with me," she said. "And let's just say it would be in your best interest."

There was something in her voice that made Finn freeze. "What exactly do you mean?"

She glanced over her shoulder, then back at him. "I know who you are, Finn. Beta Class XG8."

He stared at her. Just stared at her, suddenly unable to form any kind of reasonable response. Whatever she saw in his eyes made her look away. Finally he sat back heavily in his chair. "Damn. When you decide to start taking sides, you don't go by halves, do you?"

"Sorry, that's just the way it is," she mumbled, and put the file down in front of him. She added, "They want you to catch him on the streets by the end of the workday. Either that, or the dots between a wanted mech and one very private freelance jobber known as Finn will be connected."

He stared at her, his mind trying to figure a way out of this mess. "Who's testing me?" he asked.

She looked blank. He tried again.

"What kind of test is this? How did you find out?"

She still didn't answer.

"Who told you I was XG8?"

"You know I'm not going to tell you."

It was what he most worried about—that his true identity would become known to more than just the random mercenary who saw a piece of metal he shouldn't have; that his true identity and background would begin to spill out far and wide like this. It was the worst possible scenario.

"Jill . . . I've killed people for this," he said as nicely as he could. "Why shouldn't I kill you?"

She swallowed hard. "You'd regret it. I don't have it in for you. I swear."

"You swear it. Unfortunately Hayden doesn't. You should tell him it's not really kosher for one mercenary to blackmail another. Word gets out. It's kind of bad for business."

"Just do the job and everything will be fine," she replied, clearly stressed out.

"Is that so? What you know about me could very well be the end of me."

"It doesn't have to be," she assured him, swiping her sleeve across her forehead. "Finn, don't give me a hard time."

"What's in the folder? What could possibly be in the folder that would make you—and Hayden—play a card like this?"

"Does it matter?"

"Okay, how about: *Who's* in the folder?"

She stuck the material in the metal menu holder and pushed her chair back. "You'd have to do him anyway. He's on to you. He's trying to put you back on the Grid pretty much as we speak."

She stood up, and Finn grabbed her wrist, jolting her back down into her chair. It was all he could do not to unleash the full force of his fury on her, enraged as he was that it was happening all over again even before anyone had caught on to the fact that he was already back on the Grid. That he'd never left. "I do not like being cornered. I do not like being forced into things. And I particularly do not like being set up for a fall. You tell Hayden Wilks to expect a personal visit from me down the line. You think you can transmit that message for me?"

Fear flared in Jill's eyes, and she nodded and tried to pull her arm away. He held it fast.

"This was just supposed to be a subcon from Hayden Wilks. The message was that he'd double booked. He didn't double book; that much is obvious. So, tell me . . . who's 'they'? You said 'they' want me to do this—'they' would connect the dots. Who do you and Hayden work for?"

Jill blinked, clearly realizing that she'd slipped, given away too much information. "I'm not going to tell you, Finn," she growled.

"It's a little different on this side, isn't it? Can't hide behind your clever aliases or your reputed honor," Finn said cruelly. He shook his head; the earlier euphoria he'd felt just from having some of his more noticeable components removed had been erased by a familiar bitterness. Why the hell couldn't people just forget he existed? Why couldn't they just leave him alone?

He eased his grip, and Jill Cooper pulled away and stepped back from the table, her cheeks flaming. She looked over her shoulder then, glancing to the door as if she half expected someone to come in.

"Is Hayden watching you with me?"

"No. I just thought . . . I thought it might be someone else."

"Dumont must have broken your heart pretty bad."

At his words, Jill's face changed. Finn watched her curious disappointment disappear as she shrugged it off, picked up her briefcase and left the bar.

As the door slammed shut, he picked the folder up and pulled a knife blade through the file's security seal. It didn't surprise him in the least that the job was a hit. What surprised him was who Hayden Wilks wanted dead:

Trask Spalding.

Finn stared down at the picture of the government operative. Jill had said the guy was on to him. Trask was on to him. If that was the case, she was right: No one needed to persuade him he needed to get to the man first . . . and as soon as possible.

Another thought roared through him, as painful as ever: If he didn't get himself off the Grid, they'd be able to track him forever.

Almost as soon as the thought materialized, a blinding pain seared through the left side of his head. Finn dropped the knife and gripped the edge of the table as the blue code blinked and the encrypted gibberish with which he'd been dealing since Valerio had tooled around suddenly began to form actual words:

```
<Password, username, enter,
rejected.>
<Password, username, enter,
rejected.>
<Password, username, enter . . . >
```

Finn dumped some cash on the table and stumbled to the door. *Trask Spalding is on to me, all right. . . . I'd better hope this is him. Because if he isn't the one trying to hack into my head, then there's someone else out there who is.*

Chapter Twenty-three

I'm as beautiful as I ever was. As I was ever meant to be. It's the best trip of my life. My hair is glossy, flowing long and gorgeous. I walk in a walled garden overgrown with glorious green vines, bees and hummingbirds buzzing among a rainbow of flowers. It's everything I could have ever wanted to feel.

There's someone else here with me. I turn and raise my arms to welcome him home. He comes toward me, and he seems perfect. Perfection itself, in the body of a man. White shirt, black hair, eyes of the palest green—his beauty is breathtaking.

He comes toward me, across the lawn, butterflies flitting around his body, and he moves with a grace I've never seen in another.

And he looks at me as though I'm perfect.

The breeze picks up, and the temperature begins to rise. The flowers wilt and die at my feet. The birds are rendered silent. The butterflies whirl around his body faster now; then they fall from the sky as moths, smashing to dust on hard concrete. The vines shrivel on the walls, turning green to gray like bars on a cage.

Before me he stands, a windstorm whipping around us. The beauty disappears. He is the last thing to go. He is wear-

ing a white shirt, he still has luxurious black hair; but he is no longer a man. His smile is a grotesque snarl; his eyes are a fiery red.

Griff-Vai. He's not perfect anymore, and neither am I. But, oh god, I'm still his. This is the demon underworld. Here, I'm his. And I'm terrified. . . .

Somewhere in the midst of her dream, Cyd struggled.

Finn, are you there? You don't understand. I don't understand. I don't know what, or how or why, but . . . I love you.

"Is that so?" came a husky male voice. Then: "Come now, open your eyes, Cydney. I know you're awake."

Cyd flew straight up in bed, her breath coming out in a surprised gulp. Part of her knew she'd been dreaming, and she expected the quick relief of reality to set in. Except, when she blinked, the image of Griff-Vai sitting formally on a chair across the room didn't go away.

"We have something of a dilemma, you and I," he said.

"I'm still dreaming," she whispered.

"Not anymore. Look what you made me do." Griff-Vai seemed amused as he gestured down at his body.

She blinked, trying to make sense of his form. He was neither a wholly physical presence, nor just a thought in her head. "How are you doing that?"

He glared at her. "It seems that we are somewhat cleaved together, you and I. You know, when you spiral down, it brings me closer. And I miss you. In fact, I have a project in mind. I want you to do something for me."

She gritted her teeth and waited for the axe to fall.

"I want you to indulge. I want you to embrace your demon side, to find out what you are capable of."

"And what's your suggestion?" she asked dryly.

"Kill for me."

Cyd laughed. "What?"

"It's a simple enough request. And it's not as random as it sounds. I think you'll like the circumstance. There's nothing quite like a truly definitive conundrum."

Cyd nervously licked her dry lips and clutched a pillow to her chest, as if it could somehow protect her from Griff's power. "I'm not doing anything for you," she whispered.

"I think you'll consider it."

"Consider what?"

He shrugged, a slight twitch of his shoulders. "Killing someone you know." He grinned.

It was so ridiculous; the fact that he'd even proposed it scared her to death. "I'm not doing anything of the sort. And there won't be a dilemma. It's just a no-way." She shook her head in disbelief. "You're insane. I did a lot of things in B-Ops long ago, but what you're talking about is a whole other level. I'd never do that."

"Never?"

"Never."

"What if your lover asked you to?" Griff purred.

"My lover?" she repeated, stumbling over the words. "Someone who loved me wouldn't ask me to."

Griff-Vai shrugged. "I'm asking you to."

"Love has nothing to do with things when it comes to you. This is about control."

His face turned sulky. "I really dislike it when you negate my feelings for you."

Cyd just rolled her eyes.

"Well, I'm certainly not here to argue." Griff-Vai stood up from his chair, and light rippled and warped around his half-present body. "I'm fond of dilemmas myself, you see. The man I'd like you to kill . . . his name is Trask. I think you know who I mean."

Cyd's mouth dropped open. "Trask? My old B-Ops teammate Trask Spalding? Go to hell!"

"He's hardly a pleasant person."

"And a crazy fuck, to boot. That doesn't mean I should kill him. You might as well make him a demon. He'd fit right in with the rest of you."

"But I want you to *kill* him, Cydney," Griff ordered, his voice hard and brittle.

"That's . . . such a very random request," she said. "Why him?"

Griff-Vai smiled. "If I tell you the answer to the puzzle before you get a chance to play—well, that's simply no fun."

Cyd's mind went into overdrive. "If my lover asked me to . . ." Her stomach dropped. "Does Trask know about Finn?"

She didn't get a verbal answer, but the pleased look on Griff-Vai's face said it all. Trask knew about Finn, and it must have been because of Bridget. When she'd seen them together in I-Ops after the Valerio disaster, she must have finally put the pieces together and told Trask. Cyd hoped she'd told him only.

The alarm beside the bed went off. Cyd turned to silence it, but when she turned back, Griff-Vai was gone.

"Griff?"

No answer. He was just gone.

Shit. He was close to becoming a physical presence in the city now. Very close. And she remembered how he'd always tracked her, from the very first moment, waiting for her to reach her lowest point, her most debauched state. Then he'd come for her and taken her away. Which was exactly what he was trying to do now.

Except she wasn't going to kill Trask for Griff-Vai. She wasn't going to fall into that trap. Finn would help her figure something out. She wouldn't let herself sink to that level; she was taking charge of her life.

First she and Finn needed to make sure Trask was really a threat. Then they would figure out what to do with the operative.

Cyd dragged herself off the bed and found a comm device on the table. She tried to use it to contact Finn, but there was no connection. She tossed the device away and looked around at the room. Okay, fine. They would get around this.

Trask couldn't track Finn if he wasn't traceable. And the only thing that could make Finn untraceable, at least for the short term, while they figured out a solution, would be a signal jammer. Such drugs weren't made for something so serious, for mechanicals embedded and interconnected the way Finn's apparently were; but if they could temporarily jam microchips implanted under human skin, as she knew they could, the pills could temporarily jam any of his outgoing signals.

Cyd rummaged in her duffel bag for clean clothes, cursing under her breath that a black skirt and tightly fitted black T-shirt were all that she had left. She dressed quickly and was out the door mintues later. She could buy a signal jammer in D-Alley. And the ludicrous thought of Dougan assuming she would ever become a regular again made her smile.

Finn made it back it his apartment with what seemed to be the worst migraine of his life. Cyd met him at the door, releasing a panicked stream of consciousness that would have been challenging to process even on a normal day.

"I'm half blind, and my head feels like it may explode," he growled, slurring his words.

"Holy shit. I don't understand a word you just said. Get inside."

He tripped over the threshold, and Cyd caught him before he totally keeled over. "Serious pain," he murmured.

"I know. I see. I have something for you."

She got him to the bed, and Finn pitched forward onto the mattress, holding his head, groaning in pain as a fresh set of input scrolled down his eye; then the whole screen refreshed.

"Take this." Cyd handed him a glass of water and held out a silver capsule.

"What is it?"

"It's going to save your life. Take it."

He looked up at her, the outline of her beautiful face fading in and out of focus. He gritted out: "I've got to do a job. Got a job. *Now*."

"You took a job for this afternoon?"

Finn stared woozily at the capsule in Cyd's hand. What was it? "Will that make the pain go away?"

She was silent for a long time, then finally handed it to him. "It will save your life," she said.

Even better. He would trust her. Finn downed the capsule and then rolled to a sitting position. "I'll feel better after a shower."

She got in front of him. "No shower. No job."

"Yes, job."

Cyd put her palm on his chest and pressed him down onto the bed. "No job. I'll take care of it."

Suddenly warmth began to expand through his body, though the pain did not subside. "What did you give me?" he asked, his tongue too thick to pronounce the words properly.

"A signal jammer. It's supposed to block output from bio-broadcasters."

"A signal jammer?"

She ran her hand over his brow. "Finn, they know you're back on the Grid. How long before they trace you? They're going to find you, and then they're going to kill you. If this works like it's supposed to, they won't be *able* trace you. Someone's on to you."

Finn angrily pushed her hand away. "I *know* someone's on to me. That's why I have to go out tonight. Cyd, what have you done to me?"

She took him by the shoulders. "I wouldn't have done this if I didn't think it was critical. You asked me to trust you that first day we did a job together. The blind. Now it's my turn. Do you trust me?"

"Yes, but—"

"Do you trust me?"

"Yes! Now tell me what the hell this is doing to me. For god's sake!" His head lolled back, and he put one hand to his temple, staring up at the ceiling. "Tell me what you just gave me is going to wear off within the next two hours. I've got a deadline."

"Four hours or more," she said. "Give me the specs of your job."

Finn winced. A bead of sweat slid down his neck as he stared helplessly at the ceiling, his arms splayed out around him. "I don't want you doing it. This isn't your problem."

"Whatever."

" 'Whatever'? Why are you doing this?" He couldn't wrap his mind around her sudden intractability.

Cyd frowned for a moment, as if she were just now asking herself that question. Finally she said, "You literally just picked me off the ground, Finn." And that was it.

A moment later she sat down next to him and cradled his head in her hands. "Listen to me. There is no way you're going to be in any condition to do a job. That's the end of it. I'm doing it for you. Where's the info?"

"The . . . the kitchen counter," he gasped. "It's a hit."

Cyd froze and looked back at him.

"I *know*. Don't try to do it. Just help me up."

"Lie down." She checked her weapons, grabbed some ammo and her jacket, and went into the kitchen for the file folder. She crashed back through the room.

"Cydney," Finn barked angrily as he heard the door open. He could barely move. "Hold on."

"I'm still here," she said softly.

"The second this shit wears off, I'm coming after you. Be careful."

The door slammed shut.

Finn lay immobilized on the bed, getting more and more angry that he was lying at home like a coward while Cydney Brighton was going out on one of the most dangerous jobs he'd have ever done—and all on his behalf. The minute she opened that file, she was going to wish she'd never volunteered. Would she come back hating him? Would she come back at all?

He felt guilty. Angry. Tricked.

Struggling up into a sitting position, he grabbed the glass of water she'd left. A fierce pain shot through his head, and the vision in his left eye went completely dead in a sheet of blinding white light.

The water glass slipped from his hand, smashing on the floor. Finn doubled over and dry-heaved.

As he pulled himself off the bed, his knees were jelly and he had to crawl across the floor to the bathroom.

Note to self: Confirm ingredients of mystery capsules prior to ingesting. The cure hurt worse than the injury.

It took all his strength to pull himself up to the bathroom sink. Finn opened the medicine cabinet and grabbed for a bottle of aspirin, missed and fell backwards in a hailstorm of medical supplies. Curling his legs up under him on the floor, from that position he reached out and limply dragged the bottle of aspirin over. The lid wouldn't come off. Finally, clutching the bottle to his chest, he let everything go black.

Chapter Twenty-four

There was no such thing as a coincidence like this. In a kind of daze, sitting on the steps of the church a short distance from her old B-Ops depot, Cyd finally understood what Griff-Vai meant. If the man she needed to kill to save Finn was the same man that Griff-Vai had already told her to kill, if they were one and the same, for whom was she really doing it? She wanted to do it for Finn; somehow, she knew that Griff-Vai would be just as pleased.

She stared at the front door of the depot through a pair of field glasses. Every so often, the door would swing open and the field operatives would head out in groups and pairs, chatting about business, pleasure, whatever. At last, Trask and JB bounded down the stairs and headed across the sidewalk.

"Peel off, JB. You don't want to be around for this," Cyd murmured to herself. Tucking the glasses away, Cyd waited for a safe distance to stretch out between herself and the two men, then stepped out into the sidewalk and followed, her hands stuffed casually into her jacket pockets. The right hand curled around her pistol.

It was one thing to be on the job, taking care of business and firing a weapon in the course of duty; it was something else entirely, this business of going out to do a hit. Maybe it did happen every day in the city. Maybe Trask had gone off the deep end. Maybe he was making hits of his own on the nonhuman population. And maybe he wouldn't be missed when he was gone. But none of that made the prospect of killing him any more palatable. With every step she took, the less certain Cyd was about being able to see this thing through.

She'd followed the two men a few blocks when, to her relief, they stopped at a corner and, after a brief conversation, abruptly separated. Cyd watched them head off in different directions: then she set off after Trask.

He walked with purpose, obsessively checking his watch, slamming back against buildings and ducking into alleyways every time he glanced over his shoulder. The reality of Cyd's purpose sank further in.

Would Finn really have seen this through? She didn't believe for one second that he would outright murder a guy unless he had absolutely no other choice. Meaning, unless he had reason to believe the guy would kill him first. Was that true? He'd killed those vampire leaders, the Dumonts. But he'd been controlled at the time—hadn't he?

"I don't know if *I* can do this," she whispered.

"Yes, you can."

Cyd wheeled around. There was nothing. No one. Then her mind gave Griff-Vai the physical outline that seemed begging to manifest itself to her. "This isn't for you," she growled.

He actually smiled. "Deep inside, how will you ever be sure?"

"I'm already sure."

"Mm-hmm. We'll see." He raised his arm and pointed down the street. "He's getting away from you."

Cyd glanced around the corner and saw Trask turning down another street. Swearing under her breath, she ran out of the alley and moved quickly down the sidewalk.

Trask continued to look over his shoulder now and then, but he showed no signs of sensing her tailing him. She almost laughed. But after walking several more blocks, he simply stepped into a side alley and vanished from sight.

Cyd slowed down, approaching the street carefully, one hand on the pistol in her pocket, the other reaching down to unsheathe her knife. He could be waiting to jump her. He could be going up the fire escape. He could have taken a back door leading away from the alley.

She drew in a deep breath and then exhaled, forcing herself to calmness as she crept along the side of the last building in the row, toward the mouth of the alley. There were voices—two of them.

Okay, he was still in the alley. Hadn't gone up or down. She studied the inconsistent sounds, the wild swings in volume, the interruptions. . . . He was arguing with someone.

She relaxed a little, knowing she wouldn't have to act in the near future. She wasn't going to off Trask in front of anybody, and she certainly wouldn't want to take the chance of murdering an innocent party if she did. Rather than making any sudden movements, she took advantage of the dark shadows and curled her body around the corner of the building, gingerly placing her feet between the cans and trash bags nearby to avoid any sound. And then she was in the alley with them, her body pressed flush against the wall.

So far, so good.

Trask stood with his back toward the alley entrance, in heated conversation with a fang Cyd recognized as a rogue—one who had sometimes provided information about the inner workings of the Dumont regime. It was hard to see the details of his expression, but the angry gestures and the loud voices made things clear enough.

And then suddenly Trask punched the rogue in the face. The vampire stumbled back.

"What are you waiting for?" Griff-Vai purred. "You have a clear shot."

Cyd didn't move. The rogue recovered and returned the favor with a punch to Trask's gut. The two men began grappling, the rotation of their bodies providing a clear shot only now and then.

"Time's running out, Cydney," Griff-Vai hissed.

Trask had the rogue against a wall, his hands around the fang's neck. As the vampire struggled fruitlessly against Trask's grip, he caught sight of Cyd at the far end of the alley. She sucked in a quick breath as they locked eyes.

"Do it for me," Griff-Vai purred. "Do it for yourself. Come closer to your demon half. Do it, Cydney."

Cydney thought of Finn. Of the kind things he'd done for her, of the way he made her feel. There had been no one else like that. And here she was, taking care of his needs. What did that mean? What did they mean to each other? She thought, and still she couldn't pull the trigger.

"Oh, Cydney. You don't even understand what you are. You don't understand what you're capable of. If you stay here in Crimson City, there will be no place, no outlet for what you could one day achieve. If you come with me, you will be celebrated. Come with me."

"What am I capable of?"

"Come with me."

"What am I capable of?"

He shook his head. "You must take the risk to find out."

A knife in one hand and a gun in the other, and there was a rage so intense in her soul that it seemed it might consume her completely before she finished her task either way. "I hate you, Griff-Vai," she whispered.

She said the words, meaning them as a final casting-away, as a message to the demon that he could never have her again, body or soul. But it was as if the very words created more of a bond between them; they gave Griff-Vai more access to her, allowed him to draw her even closer.

Her lips curled back as she snarled, a sound she'd never made in her life, and it thrilled her to the bone. She wasn't *that* crazy, this sad girl from Ops who'd been too scared and too fucked up to really be of use. She wasn't that person anymore. She was powerful.

Griff-Vai whispered something in her ear; all she heard was the delicious, seductive sound of power. The words themselves dissolved in thin air. Legs braced apart, her coat billowing out behind her, Cyd aimed her pistol. She thought of Trask. She thought of Finn. The rogue's desperate eyes trained on her face and . . . she pulled the trigger.

The blast ricocheted off the alley walls. For a brief spell, no one moved. Then Trask's body slipped away from the rogue and fell backwards to the ground. The man himself never made a sound.

I'm a fucking superhero, Cyd thought.

And then her adrenaline varied. All that was left was the rogue, gasping and coughing, his hands at his neck, staring at her from the other end of the alley.

"Where . . . where is . . . ?" he rasped, finally just making a motion with his hand, thanking her, it seemed, as he staggered past and away.

Cyd stared down at the body lying heavy on the cement, gun smoke wafting up in the dim light of a streetlamp. The acrid smell of gunpowder burned her nose.

After a moment, she shook her head. She felt another surge of power. She blew the muzzle of her weapon clean, and stuck her boot on Trask's chest while she holstered it. A smile was on her face; Griff's encouragement was ringing in her ears. And as the demon congratulated her, she . . . looked down and fought back to the fact that this wasn't just some piece of scum lying on the ground.

She took an uneven step. "What are you doing to me, Griff?"

She'd been enjoying this too much. She had changed too much. She even wanted more. She wanted the surge of adrenaline; she wanted a frenzy. She wanted to feel what the dogs and the fangs felt when compelled to a violence beyond their ability to control. And she wanted a part of the sexual ecstasy she'd seen that the demons felt.

She wanted more. She wanted this moment to last forever. And she knew it was wrong. She knew that some part of her was now pure evil.

"What happens next?" she whispered.

Suddenly his full figure manifested—his strong, powerful body—and he came to stand over her, seducing her with his flesh, touching her burning skin with his.

It was a kind of diabolical lust that gripped her. She

was both dying at his hands and experiencing a mind-boggling arousal. And as the demon who would again have her began to win control, taking what was easiest to get at, her basest feelings, she tried to cut the connection by turning her thoughts to Finn. He was why she'd come here in the middle of the night, to this dank alley.

Finn's not here, a voice said.

"Shut up, Griff."

The demon's hand moved up over her face, and she had an undeniable sense that he meant to suffocate her. Then his hand stilled, and the only answer he gave was a weighty exhalation full of sex and darkness. He took her mouth hard, kissing her . . . but Cyd's mind kept calling out for Finn.

Finn's not with you, the demon's voice repeated in her head. He pulled his mouth away. "You are mine," he said aloud.

Sweeping his fingers across the open air above her eyes, he closed her eyelids, but Cyd could still see his face as if she was staring right at him. "You are mine," he repeated.

She brought her fingers up to wipe her mouth, and spat, "You're not the one I want."

Chapter Twenty-five

Finn met her at the door, the intensity in his eyes suggesting that though he might be recovered from the side effects of the jammer drugs, he hadn't recovered from the experience. Wearing nothing but a pair of trousers slung low on his hips, he stood just inside the apartment, the light glinting off the metal on his right arm.

Cyd leaned against the door frame, her chest heaving, her body still gripped with its black desire.

Finn reached out, put his hand around the back of her neck and pulled her over the threshold—and into his arms. His heart pounded into her as if it were her own.

"Do you have any idea how it felt to send you off to do the dirty work while I played invalid?" he asked, unable to conceal his rage. "Do you have any idea how it felt to know you were out there trying to save my ass? I'm out of my head. I hated it, Cyd. I *hated* it."

She looked up at him, wondering if he could see either the guilt or the lust burning inside her. "I liked it," she growled, pounding her fists against his chest, pushing him back into the apartment. "For a moment, I liked the kill. And that's exactly what he wanted. 'Indulge.' That's what he told me. 'Indulge.' I walked right into his trap."

Finn shook his head. "Who? Griff-Vai? He's not going to get you. I won't let him."

"He's all over me," she said, running her palm down her sweating skin. "And I want . . . I want his touch, his scent, all of him gone." I want you, she didn't say. But he had to know.

They circled each other like wild beasts, Finn's eyes narrowing. "What did he do to you?"

"Nothing and everything. He's trying to get control," she said, reaching out with a lightning-fast grip and grabbing him by the waistband, meaning to haul him in.

Finn knocked her hand away easily, the metal leaving a pink scratch on her wrist. She looked into his eyes, and they both bent slightly at the knees, stalking each other. The adrenaline was pounding through her body, a kind of intense want that no one else had ever inspired. Griff-Vai had inspired lust, but he couldn't inspire desire. That made no sense; but it was true. And everything the demon had tried to force upon her had seemed to channel right through into this moment. It was as if Cyd was turning something dark and unwanted, something she couldn't control, into something she could. It was a heady feeling.

It was like some kind of sexual exorcism. Everything the demon wanted of her, some things she'd even given to him that one time in the very beginning—she could take it all back. She could win the day by giving everything inside her, every powerful emotion inside her soul, in concert with this physical need to release her power and anger with the one she really wanted.

Cyd moved to place her mouth on Finn's, reeling back in the next moment as a vision of Griff's mouth on hers filled her; of his body moving to cover hers, of his voice telling her what he wanted her to do. Caught up in the intensity of the moment, in a mistaken eruption of rage, she turned and unleashed a powerful roundhouse kick, striking Finn cleanly in the chest and sending him flying across the room.

He rebounded immediately with an acrobatic twist. And as she raised her leg once more, he grabbed her ankle and held it, dragging her leg over his shoulder and hooking it there at the knee. Her skirt rode way up her hips, her black panties exposed.

She felt Finn's body react; the taut muscles flexing, his desire spurred on, the pulse of his cock against her other leg. He gave her a look that was almost angry with want, and reached out and ripped the panties off her body.

"Every time he touched you, everything he made you feel . . . ," he said through gritted teeth. "I will erase him."

Her body completely open to him, the dark romance of his words drawing her under and into the most glorious haze, Cyd swooned in his arms.

Finn picked her up by the waist and threw her against the wall, powerfully but without hurting her. One hand caressed the leg hitched up high, the other running a thumb up her inner thigh.

Cyd gasped, pressing back against the wall as he moved his fingers in a light caress over her slick core. He touched her so slowly, so delicately. It was as if he was experimenting with the sensation for them both.

Her body began to dissolve into the swirl of ecstasy. The metal, the scars—she didn't really see them anymore, if she ever had. She didn't see him as a machine; she only saw the man. She saw Finn.

She wanted to scream at him to take her. To just *take* her. *I'm yours. Can't you feel it?* She said with her soul.

She moved her mouth to the side of his head, her tongue licking hot at his ear. "I want you inside me, Finn. I want you to take me." She pushed hard at his shoulders, desperately trying not to give in to such an easy climax and have it all be over so soon. She couldn't have it over so soon.

The emptiness she felt as he took his hand away and slowly let her slip out of his arms almost became regret; it would have but for the expression on Finn's face. The corner of his mouth turned up in the barest hint of a smile, all the confidence of a man who knows he's got his prey in his sights and it's only a matter of time. It was a heart-melting smile.

He backed slowly across the room, one foot behind the other, his right palm faceup, light reflecting off the metal as he beckoned her forward. Cyd slid down the wall until she was on her hands and knees, pounding her palm against the floor in protest of such cruel deprivation.

Then she pushed off the wall and began crawling toward him.

Finn leaned back on his haunches, watching, doing nothing else, deliberately letting her desire build to the breaking point. His own was more than evident. At last, in a hurried movement, he released the drawstring on his trousers and pulled them from his body to reveal his gorgeous, erect cock.

Never breaking eye contact, he fell to his hands and

knees and slowly advanced. Cyd didn't try to escape; she wouldn't have wanted to for the world. Like a flash, Finn leaped at her, taking her rolling across the ground with him and giving a kind of war cry.

His mouth couldn't seem to get enough of her body; Cyd couldn't get enough of his passion. His tongue swirled over her breasts, taking her taut nipples into his mouth. He was pressing kisses to her skin. . . . It wasn't enough. She wanted more, and he wanted the same.

Moving around her, his cock pressed up against her ass. She arched back, pushing against him, and he groaned.

His hands came around her torso to take her breasts, and the head of his cock found where it needed to be, began to press inside her. Finn seemed to release every emotion he'd been holding inside. On a roar of sheer pleasure, he plunged himself in up to the hilt. Her slickness welcomed him.

Powerful in his eagerness but still somehow tender, he wrapped his arms around her and worked his body over hers. She had the sense of being completely engulfed by him. Desire, anger, joy, safety, chaos—the intensity was overwhelming, so many emotions thrumming through her body all at once.

Bucking against him, Cyd couldn't hold back. She cried out as the budding arrival of ecstasy threaded through her body. And to add to her joy, Finn was fulfilling her hope—he was owning her without controlling her; he was taking her without binding her. He was everything Griff-Vai wasn't. He was everything the other men in her lives had never been. He was . . . everything.

Before she could control herself or even try to make

the moment last, she felt delicious sensation blooming at her very core; and as Finn thrust inside her, Cyd mouthed his name and let pure happiness explode through her body.

She turned her head to look over her shoulder, searching for his mouth, wanting a connection in the moment of this feeling. Finn's eyes were closed, his face completely free of self-consciousness, almost angelic in its expression of ecstasy. And when he opened his eyes on a cry of wonder, emptying himself inside of her, Cyd knew in her heart that he'd been a virgin and that his dominance wasn't something practiced. It was animal instinct. Something base. Something pure. At the heart of the human species was just another animal, like the dogs or the fangs.

Suddenly Cyd knew without a doubt that, for all her fears, for all her need to understand and control what and who she had become, she'd found a reason to pursue the impossible, the unthinkable. The Draig-Uisge's old friend had told her the only way to conquer Griff-Vai was to become a power of all four species, and that she'd have to find a pure-blood vampire and a purebred werewolf to sink their teeth into her to do it.

There was a line you crossed that could not be redrawn in a different place just to suit: Just as Finn had explained that, once he'd tapped into his human side, he could never live in his shell as a mech, Cyd knew that to save them both from horror, she had no choice but to call on the one thing she most wished to rid from her body, mind and soul.

Finn pressed a kiss to her neck, and she closed her eyes and turned her face to his scarred chest. All her life she'd been waiting for something worth taking a chance on. At last she'd found it. She would free herself from Griff-Vai's bond for a life with Finn, or she'd die trying.

And at the same time as she made that decision, she realized she had to give warning: "He's here in the city, Finn. Griff-Vai is finally here."

Finn lowered his body to the floor, keeping Cyd curled in his arms, heat still roaring off his skin from their lovemaking. He cradled her in his arms, his heart beating madly; and when she looked over at him again, he took her mouth with his, slowly now, savoring the lush, full taste of her. She looked strangely innocent, though she'd proven herself anything but. At least, part of her.

Waiting for her to return from the hit had been torture. When he'd regained consciousness and recovered enough to think straight, all he could do was pace and check the time every other minute. And he had sensed her as she neared. The key in the door. The doorknob swiveling. He'd stood up, his heart pounding, knowing she was right on the other side. He had felt her there, had felt her energy, her passion. It had practically seeped through the door itself.

She'd stepped over the threshold, her teeth clenched, her eyes overly bright, a glorious creature of both light and darkness, unspeakable lust rolling off her in waves. He knew they both had been slightly out of their heads, but he wouldn't take anything back—and he wouldn't stop himself from doing it again if he had the chance.

His right arm was resting above their heads, out of the way. It was exactly the same. The same metal, the same scars, the same skin. With a rueful smile, he realized that having sex with her wasn't the cure, if he'd somehow thought it was. Nothing was that easy.

The thing was, it didn't really matter anymore: the physicality of his condition. There was no more trying to convince anybody he was more man than machine. He *knew* he was a man, and the only thing that mattered anymore was staying alive. If his fate was to keep the metal parts he still had, so be it. All he wanted now was to be off the Grid and off the wanted list so that he wouldn't have to spend the rest of his life watching his back, so that he could start the rest of his life. Finn looked down at Cyd. A *real* life.

Cyd looked back at him and met his gaze. "The last thing Griff told me was to go to you if that's what I wanted, because it would only bring him closer to me."

"What do you think he meant?"

"He's here now," she whispered. "He's actually here, through the veil, and it's the bond with me that brought him."

"He would have killed you by now if that was the case."

She laughed sardonically. "If only. He doesn't want to kill me, Finn. He wants to take me back to the demon underworld." She sat up, and Finn pulled the blanket down from the couch, laying it over them. She pulled the fabric close as if she needed the comfort.

"I told you what happened to my research team. We were experimenting, thinking we would form an alliance with the demon underworld to join in our eternal fight against the werewolves and the vampires. But I never really explained how I was spared when the demons killed everybody else.

"Griff-Vai saw me and had me spared. He had lost

his soul mate to a human who turned her against him. And humans . . . don't do well in the demon world. But Griff had a plan. He watched me fall apart in the aftermath of the experiment, watched me fall apart as I tried to cope with what I'd seen, what I knew. And eventually he came for me." Cyd looked away. "He said he waited for me to corrupt myself, and then he came for me.

"He was trying to create a special bond between us when the keepers of that amulet I showed you conjured the energy to close the portal. I was caught up in it. He tried to keep me with some kind of spell through the amulet—he did something that bound us together. But I grabbed the thing and tore through the portal as it closed, and got away from him. He's come after me, as I knew he would. He believes that I owe him because he wouldn't let the others kill me along with everybody else on that development team. In a way, he's right. He saved my life. He might have fucked it completely up, but he did save my life."

"I know that you fear him," Finn said, running his fingers over her flesh—flesh that was flawless and perfect, flesh that healed itself as he wished his own could. "But he has never been physically present. Apart from that agent—"

"Until now." Cyd didn't speak for a minute. Then she found her voice. "Because I hadn't embraced my demon side until now. Tonight . . ."

"The hit?" Finn asked. He felt pained. Responsible.

"The hit was the trigger. Of course, there would have been something. I could feel it. I've been changing all this time."

Finn's pulse raced. "If he's here, then where is he?" he asked softly.

Cyd looked him straight in the eye. "Oh, he's around. And he's coming."

Finn sat up slowly, confused by her seeming calm. "You already have a plan," he guessed. "Are you aware of something I don't know?"

She picked at a loose threat in the blanket. "When you picked me up in D-Alley, I'd been to see druids. To see the Draig-Uisge, the keeper of that amulet. I'd done some research in our old files. I thought if I got rid of the thing, he wouldn't be able to find me again; that it was what bound Griff-Vai and me. But I was wrong. The amulet itself isn't a tool I can use. And the druids gave me some advice." She shook her head. "I ignored it. I didn't think I could do it."

She fell silent. When she looked up at him again, he saw that her apparent calm was a mixture of both fear and determination.

"I couldn't have killed Trask before Griff-Vai was in my head," she said. "I know that. He's . . . changed me. But I still have hope. I've got to get rid of him once and for all. I've got to take my chances. The druids told me that I am already demon and human. To vanquish Griff-Vai's power over me, I have to become even more powerful—the power of four species. And I'll need the pure blood of vampire and werewolf to do it."

She was silent again for a long time. Finally she looked up at him and searched his face. "Finn, I'm going to do it. Because if I don't, Griff-Vai is going to win. It's the only way. And I'm going to beat this."

Finn thought about Cyd's words for some time, wanting to tell her not to put herself into any further danger—but knowing that she really had no choice. Instead of arguing, he told himself that he would stand by her, that he would fight all the upcoming battles alongside her. "Do you have any idea who might be able to give you what you need?"

"I have," she said. "Maddox and Dumont. Those are the purest lineages in Crimson City. The question is . . . will they help me?"

Chapter Twenty-six

The boss, Will Gaviola, was at the window in his office in the B-Ops depot when Cyd pushed open the door. "How's it going?" he asked without turning.

"Slowly. But there are leads. I've been doing a lot of street work. In fact . . . I don't plan to be in the office for a while. I need to chase some things down. I just wanted to run that past you."

Gaviola turned and looked at her with a dead expression. At first, Cyd wasn't sure he'd even heard.

Then he sat in his chair and slammed a fist down on his desk, swearing a blue streak. "Cut the crap, Brighton. Just cut the crap!" He shook his head, raising his clenched fists in front of her. "Will somebody in this godforsaken city just be straight with me for once? I'm trying to fix things. The whole damn system is falling apart, and I'm the only one trying to fix things."

Cyd slid heavily into the chair opposite him. "Is the whole system falling apart, or is it just that humans are losing power?"

Gaviola went completely silent, slouched back in his chair and clasped his hands on his empty desktop. He rubbed his eyes, then stared at her, obviously weary.

"Were we right not to kill you?" he asked. "Not that you'll tell me. This place is crawling with people hiding their true agendas. I'm pretty sure you're one of them. Are you human, Cyd? What are you really trying to accomplish?"

Without missing a beat, she said, "You want the honest truth? I promise you that I'm not a double agent, and that I'm not trying to bring this department down."

He shook his head and stared at her, clearly doing his damnedest to keep up the impression that everything was under control. Finally he said, "It doesn't matter. We're flushing the whole system."

Cyd's heart skipped a beat.

"Meaning what?"

"The government has decided on a total overhaul. Our means of addressing the species situation in Crimson City are . . . 'no longer viable.' " He smiled wryly at Cyd. "This department is being purged. You'll have to reinterview for your job along with everyone else."

"Or not?" she suggested with a laugh.

"Or not," he said. He almost seemed amused. Almost.

Cyd did a double take. "Do I dare ask why?"

He frowned, becoming serious. "Did you hear about Trask?"

Cyd looked him straight in the eye. "What about him?"

"He's dead, Cyd." Gaviola spoke matter-of-factly, but watched her. "I know you two were teammates once. I'm sorry."

"I'm sorry, too," she whispered.

"He's the eighth Ops employee killed this week."

Cyd stared, thinking of Valerio and wondering about the other six. She could only account for two. "Man," she said lamely. She sat there, growing more and more uncomfortable under the weight of his boss's stare. "I'm really . . . sorry."

"Don't beat yourself up over it," Gaviola said at last. "Trask was a demon agent."

Cyd froze. *Drop a bomb, why don't you?* The boss waited for her reaction; again, almost as if he was testing her. Cyd didn't know what kind of reaction would work best. She didn't even know how to feel about this. Either way, she was the one who'd killed the guy.

"Why didn't we do something about him?" she finally asked, her voice carefully measured.

"Number one, we didn't figure it out until recently. Number two, the things he was doing weren't necessarily at the top of our list of worries."

"What did he do?" Cyd asked, curious to know the boss's version of which crimes weren't at the top of the list of worries.

"He murdered rogues."

Cyd arched an eyebrow. "Rogues murdered by a B-Ops agent aren't a major concern? I thought the Battlefield Ops charter was centered around paranormal crime."

Gaviola pointed a finger at her, his eyes blazing. "Don't even *think* about judging me."

Cyd put her hands up in surrender. "Whoa. I'm the last person to judge."

And she meant it. It might be some kind of karmic justice that she'd killed Trask, but she hadn't known it at the time.

The boss's face turned pink, then red, then headed towards a nice enraged shade of purple. "Do you have any idea how out of control things are in this city? It's coming from every direction: demons, vampires, werewolves, other humans, the mechs. We're under attack in more ways than you can even fathom. The file of suspected rogue retaliation against humans is pretty thick, so forgive me if a few less bitter dogs and fangs didn't seem as significant as our concerns at having the entire human species possibly eliminated or enslaved. We didn't come out of that last demon battle so well. Now, if we'd realized sooner what Trask was up to, we could have done something more about it. If we'd figured out that his agenda really was designed to undermine the entire human species, I can guarantee you we would have done something about it."

"Killing rogues was going to do that for him?"

"That was the idea," Gaviola said. "We think his mission was to set the rogues even more against the primaries of all species. And I think we all know that there's no group more unpredictable and less concerned with the ethics of warfare than those guys. The demons would like nothing more than to get them going." He pressed the pads of his fingers into his temple and sighed. "That, and I think Trask just liked the killing. Bottom line, he turned out to be a problem for a lot of groups in this city. Now that he's gone, you'll be hard-pressed to find someone who's sorry."

Cyd blurted a cynical laugh before she could stop herself. "The demons are probably pissed his mission didn't quite work out."

"Oh, yeah. Probably." Gaviola pulled a cotton handkerchief from his pocket and wiped sweat off his face, his coloring returning closer to normal. "But I can guarantee you, Trask was just one cog in the wheel."

"I believe it," Cyd said grimly. "You know, demons, fangs, dogs, rogues, I get. But you mentioned mechs. How can we possibly be concerned about the mechs? Only one ever got out."

The boss just shook his head.

"What?"

"We've let more out," he said. "Or they've escaped. It's not going to be a secret much longer either. That's part of the purge. To be honest; the entire cadre of mechs will either be reprogrammed and released, or destroyed."

Cyd forced herself not to blink. "You're bullshitting me."

"It's gotten out of hand, and there's no money for the program anymore, Cyd. Not after all the incidents. No money for invention, no money for repairs. The demon war wiped out the budget. The people in charge are losing power. Their system isn't working anymore." He laughed wryly. "Maybe it never was. And with all the reports of dirty agents—"

"What about the first mech? The one still out on bounty?"

Gaviola shrugged and straightened a pile of papers on his desk. "I haven't been given that information. "It's likely dead. We haven't had contact since it disappeared. Periodically, I've heard a bounty hunter has a lead, but nothing's ever panned out. Those hunters were probably just grifting for cash."

Cyd shook her head, confused. Gaviola looked so honest, sounded so sincere. This was one of the reasons she'd come: to get a little bit more information. She and Finn needed to know their danger before they went after Griff.

Dead? Why are you pretending you don't know that he's on the Grid? You must know he's on the Grid; you've been trying to break into his head and get things started again. Because if you don't know about this, and it hasn't been you . . . then who the hell is doing it to him?

"I'd be more worried about the other machines roaming the streets," Gaviola said.

Cyd snapped, "They aren't machines. They're humans. Inside, they're human. We've locked them up in a kind of prison, stolen their identities. We've made them slaves." She huffed angrily. "You know something? I would think that you would support anyone or anything that wanted nothing more than to be recognized as human. Isn't that what this administration was all about—humans? Isn't that the Ops charter, fighting for human survival? But shouldn't we be trying to include rather than exclude?"

The boss narrowed his eyes, studying her face. "Why so hung up on the mechs?"

She made a decision: Gaviola had been incredibly blunt about the failings of Ops, about the failings of the human strategy in general, and not only did that make her respect him more, it made her trust him more. "I want to make a deal with you," she said abruptly. "Call Ops off him. For good."

To Cyd's surprise, the man gave a small smile. That wasn't a good sign, but she pressed on, went for broke. "I want the bounty cancelled and any network connections deleted from the mainframe so he can't be put back on the Grid even if someone wants him to be."

"Cydney, I personally don't give a crap about the mech. He's just a detail. Okay? He means nothing to me."

Cyd gritted her teeth, forcing herself to let him finish.

He leaned forward, his fist clenched. "What I care about is the demons. At the end of the day, we can learn to live with everybody else. They want to be here, to live. These demons just want to use us to make their own world better. And the last few months proved that they're worthy of our fear. That's why I brought you back to Ops in the first place." Eyes ablaze, he shook his fist. "I wanted to get the demons. And now . . . now it doesn't look like I'm going to get to do that, because once I get done taking the rap for being the guy who's going to dismantle B-Ops as we know it, I'm assuming I'll be out with the rest of them."

"If you really mean that, if you really care about taking down the demons, do what I ask for the mech, and I guarantee you that I will do everything in my power to keep up the fight."

He shrugged. "It's not—"

"Look into my eyes," Cyd said.

After a moment's pause, Gaviola looked into her eyes. "Son of a bitch," he whispered. "Didn't they used to be a much darker brown?"

Demonic. The accusation hovered silently between them. Cyd felt a bolt of fear that she'd overplayed her hand, but the boss just exhaled slowly as he studied her face, nodding and tapping his fingers against the top of his desk. Finally he said, "I can probably get the mech bounty removed. The network . . . I don't know. I'll do what I can to have his file deleted as soon as possible. As for you, today is your last day of work. Take your things and get out of here."

The look of fear on her face made him smile. "Do what I brought you here to do. Go out there and do something about those demons."

"I'll try my hardest," she said. "And if you really believe your days are numbered in Ops, then make deleting the mech a priority. Please."

He turned his back to her, his attention already on his computer, the black and red Top Secret login screen flipping up.

"Sir—"

"Come here."

Cyd hesitated, and the boss beckoned her over. "Come here."

She moved in behind him as he typed through a few layers of network files, somewhere in the depths of the Ops system hierarchy. Up popped a list of names. Using the Find tool, he typed in XG8 and Finn's record appeared. An audible gasp escaped her mouth before she could stop it. With his fingers poised over the keyboard, the cursor blinking at the ridiculous dollar value next to Finn's code, Gaviola looked over his shoulder at her.

"I'm one of the good guys, Cyd. I hope you are too."

And with that he pressed delete, typed a few sentences into a pop-up screen, and Finn's record vanished from the bounty file.

"Is his record completely wiped out?" she asked nervously. "Is that it?"

"No. There's no bounty on his head anymore. But that's not the same as clearing out the record. Let me . . ." He moved out of the bounty file and switched from the B-Ops drive to the I-Ops drive. After a few moments of typing, he just shook his head. "Two people can't be in the same folder at once. Avoids accidental override. The admin's already in there. Huh. She called in sick, though."

"The admin?" Cyd said. A cold horror crept over her. "Bridget Rothschild?"

"Yeah."

Cyd took a step backward. "I've got to go." Bridget was trying to hack into Finn's database. It was Bridget.

The boss grabbed her by the arm. "I just want to make sure we're clear. I'm letting you go . . . but if I ever need to call on you to help against the demons—"

"I'm there," Cyd said. "I'd be there." She slipped from his grasp, turning back to him at the door. "Boss? You *are* one of the good guys. We don't have enough of your kind in this city. Thanks."

They exchanged a look, and Cyd finally escaped the place once and for all.

Cyd couldn't help feeling shocked at the sight of Finn walking briskly down the sidewalk toward her. He'd insisted on going with her. He'd made love to her that night, she'd told him what she'd planned, and he'd insisted on going with her. This was the part when he was supposed to let her down. Yet, here he was.

The look in his eyes was so intense it almost scared her. He simply walked up, cradled her face in his hands and said, "You're ready then?" As if his presence were the most normal thing in the world.

"I don't want you to come with me," Cyd said, half-lying. "You need to—"

"I need to go with you."

"You need to go find Bridget Rothschild." She handed him a slip of paper on which she'd scrawled the admin's address. "She's the hacker, Finn. She saw us after we killed Valerio and she's the one who's been in your head."

The expression on his face shifted from anger to confusion.

"The boss clued me in."

"But . . ." His voice faded away.

"The thing is," Cyd said, tucking a loose strand of hair back behind her ear. "I wouldn't mind having a go at this on my own. Kind of . . . take care of my problem on my own." She looked up at him, searching his face, and while he clearly didn't like it, he seemed to understand.

But then in the next moment, he growled. "You're not going to the Dumonts without—" He suddenly grabbed his head and cursed.

"Finn?"

"It'll pass." He took a step toward her, but Cyd shook her head and pushed him back. "Go take care of your business, and I'll take care of mine."

"Cyd. Not the Dumonts. No way, the Dumonts alone."

He again winced at some unseen pain.

Watching him experience agony and being unable to do anything about it was torture.

But *Bridget* could do something about it, if Cyd could get him to go take care of her. "Okay! Okay! I'll ping your comm before I go to the Dumonts. Just go."

"Anything happens with Maddox and you need me, you call me. Got that?" He took her by the shoulders and gave her a little shake. "Got that?"

"I got it."

His last word was intermingled with a kiss, hectic and wild, but oh, so sweet, with his hands rough around her face, his tongue sweeping her mouth without a hint of hesitation. Finally, he pulled away, brushing his lips across hers one more time, and then he simply took off running.

The loss of his heat made his good-bye that much harder to take. Cyd pulled her jacket closer around her body and forced herself to concentrate on her mission here in the heart of Crimson City. In the end, anyway, if she managed to pull this off, this idea of the power of the four species, she'd finally have a little peace.

And then maybe, just maybe, she could think about Finn as something more than a temporary fixture in her life.

Really, when you had to come to terms with the fact that you already had demon blood coursing through your veins, other scenarios such as being made into a dog or a fang didn't hold the same horrific lustre. So what if she became a dog? There were thousands of werewolves living in this city.

Becoming a dog? Not so terrible.

A fang? Not so terrible.

Living the rest of her life in the demon underworld with a diabolical mate that she loathed? She definitely had issues with that.

She had a couple of choices. Finding purebred nonhumans in this city wasn't going to be that hard. Convincing them to bite her might be a little harder. At the top of the list were the cousins, Keeli and Tajo Maddox. It was an easy choice: Tajo Maddox was a purebred *and* a rogue. She'd gotten him a message, and received a reply.

Of course, she hadn't tried asking a dog for a real favor since she'd accidentally gotten that werewolf informant killed. "Accidentally" being the operative word. It had been Fleur Dumont's fault, so as far as Cyd was concerned, that was a fang who owed her something.

How ironic this all was. She had to become her worst nightmare to become a stronger person.

She reached the area in which she'd been given to understood Tajo headquartered, and stopped to take a look around. She was back in the Triangle with the quarantine signs all still there, the barbed wire, the silence. And the dark.

It wasn't exactly what she'd expected to find, but she

separated the barbed wire and slipped through. Once inside the quarantine zone, she picked up the pace, sweeping occasional looks over her shoulder, then switching forward again to scan the streets and alleys ahead.

"There's no such address," she muttered. She looked around at the dilapidated buildings. Her heart started to pound. Maybe it was a trap.

After a moment of total silence, she took some comfort in the fact that no one had jumped her yet. Staring down at the massive metal doors in the ground where a storage facility had once been, it suddenly dawned on her . . .

These rogues did it in style. They did things in their own way, but always in style. She took a step forward into the middle of what looked like an orange fluorescent construction code sprayed months ago onto the pavement. Looking up, she spotted a small camera mounted on the side of the nearby building, and stared straight into the lens. An infrared flash and a few minutes later, the buzz of hydraulics sounded, and the metal doors began to slowly open even as an elevator gurney began to rise.

With a clank, the motor stopped. Cyd stepped onto the platform and the system lowered her down, closing the metal doors above her.

She hit bottom and nothing happened for a moment. Then she reached out and gingerly pressed her fingers against the plain whitewash wall. Nothing.

There came a clackety sound, as if a communication was being sent via Morse code, and then the sound of sliding doors. The white wall behind her slid to the right. Cyd stepped out onto polished parquet floor and the wall slipped closed behind her.

"Welcome to the club," a voice said.

A young vampire Cyd recognized immediately as a rogue gestured to the back of the well-appointed space. "They're waiting for you," he added.

She wended her way through a cluster of tables, Cyd recognizing most of the faces. Rogues. All of them were rogues of one species or another. She wondered how they all got along.

Finally, in the back room—apparently a conference chamber of sorts—the rogue werewolf Tajo Maddox and rogue vampire Hayden Wilks were sitting at a table loaded with beer bottles, as if they'd been in discussion for some time. It didn't surprise her to see the two men together, a fang and a dog who were supposedly from warring species but who had instead found a logical partnership in their expatriate status. If she had it right, Hayden would be the blade of this group, Tajo the hand that guided it.

Cyd gave a low whistle.

Both men sat back. Hayden was lean and dark, sported smears of black eyeliner. Tajo was much bigger, burlier—in jeans and T-shirt, and looking as though the only thing he'd do with eyeliner would be borrow it to take phone messages.

Tajo tipped his head and studied her face. Then he stuck out his hand. "I hear you're applying for membership. What the hell took you so long?"

Hayden was less abrasive. He raised his hands and gestured all around. "What do you think? It's like a gentlemen's club, except we don't accept anyone who qualifies as a gentleman."

"A gentlemen's club for nonbelievers. Perfect," Cyd said. Hayden nodded. "Gentlewomen, too. We don't discriminate."

"That would sort of be against the point."

Cyd gave Tajo a look and started to pull her hand away. He kept it firmly in his grip.

"Is it true what they say?" the werewolf asked.

"Which rumor would that be?"

"That you baited a werewolf informant and let Fleur Dumont have at him."

Cyd wasn't about to lie. "I didn't know the fang would pop. It was supposed to be a routine info exchange."

Hayden spoke up with venom. "I'm sure Fleur Dumont doesn't feel guilty about biting a dog. She probably wished she had a wine spritzer to chase."

Tajo laughed. "How many thousands of years is it going to take you to get over her?"

The rogue vampire just glowered at his drinking partner and lowered his piercing eyes.

Tajo glanced up at Cyd with a shrug. "Hayden can be quite charming when he feels like it. He just never seems to feel like it." He laughed again.

Cyd studied Hayden's face. The vampire looked like an ordinary street punk, but he was actually much scarier. People were more dangerous when they stopped caring about what happened to them. Cyd understood; she'd once been like that. "I could care less about Fleur Dumont. I'm no fan of hers," she said.

Hayden gave Cyd a curious look. "That's right. You're the ex," he said.

Cyd ground her teeth. "Ex-*partner*."

"I'm sure," Hayden said, ducking into his drink.

"So, you wanted to see me," Tajo interrupted.

Cyd studied him. Tajo wasn't an unreasonable guy. He didn't seem to have many revenge issues, though word was, his current refusal to play ball with the werewolf primaries was more personal than philosophical. Still, he was a purebred Maddox up to the top of the family tree.

Cyd leaned over the table, her voice low. "I need a purebreed to bite me."

She was expecting a big reaction and didn't get it. Tajo just smiled. His teeth were white and looked sharp. "Why?"

"I'd rather not say."

"Well, then. I can't help you."

Cyd folded her arms over her chest. "I don't suppose you could take my word for it that it's a good thing?" she asked.

"I don't suppose," he agreed. "I'd never want to make you my responsibility without a damned good reason."

Cyd shook her head. "Biting me will not make me your responsibility. You bite me, I walk away."

The levity in Tajo's voice disappeared. "I don't think you understand," he said. "If I bite you and you're without a clan, you're my responsibility. It's an honor thing."

Cyd moistened her lips and considered a new tack. Before she could say anything, Tajo took a walnut from a bowl, set it on the table and smashed his fist down on it. He sorted through the shells for the nut meat. "In several cultures, if you save someone's life, they are your responsibility until death," he said.

Great. He was going all spiritual on her.

Clearly in spite of himself, Tajo couldn't contain his curiosity. "So, you want me to just up and bite you? Just like that? This isn't the vampire strata; you're not going to be issued a instant credit card along with your bite marks."

Hayden looked as if he was about to remark on his own conversion, and its lack of perks, but Cyd cut him off. "Yeah, I realize that. Who the hell asks to be bitten by a werewolf unless they have a damn good reason?"

Tajo's eyes narrowed, but that was fine. She wanted him to take her seriously; she wanted him to realize her desperation. He took his time chewing the nut meat, and looked around at the rest of the occupants of his "club."

"There's something I need to tell you," Cyd said. "But it's hard. It's hard to say, and it's hard to accept."

She had their full attention now. Tajo and Hayden looked at each other. Hayden took the cocktail straw he was chewing out of his mouth and leaned his chin on his hand. He looked unsympathetic. "I'm a vampire. I got made," he said. "Asked for it. Regretted it. He's a dog. Born that way. Pure-blood, like you say. Let's just say it didn't suit. We're rogues. We don't apologize. And in this clubhouse, we don't have to hide who we are. No one does. Either tell us the truth, or get the hell out. Go play by yourself in the cold." He splayed his hands, palms up, like easy-does-it.

"I'm part demon," she blurted. Swallowing, she added, "I've got demon blood in me. I don't know how much. I'm some kind of anomaly. And I'm . . . I'm trying to do something that's going to sound fairly insane."

She expected some big reaction. She expected at least a jaw to drop. Hayden just raised an eyebrow and Tajo leaned forward.

"Connect the dots for me," Tajo said.

Cyd took courage from their willingness—or their seeming willingness—to accept what she said at face value. "I've been told that the only way I can stand up to the power of the demon who is trying to take me back to the underworld is to become something more powerful than the sum of my human and demon sides."

"Did you say take you *back* to the demon underworld?" Hayden asked.

She nodded.

"Damn," he said. "So it's true."

"Damn," Tajo echoed.

"Yeah. And the thing is, they say the power of four is what it will take for me to stand up to the one who took me there. He's one of the Vai."

"The power of four. Human, demon, vampire, werewolf," the rogue vampire clarified. He looked thoughtful.

Tajo cut through the silence. "Uncontrollable frenzy of lust, or uncontrollable frenzy of anger?" he said calmly.

"You'll do it?" Cyd asked.

Tajo shrugged. It was an assent.

Hayden laughed. "And don't tell me! You're going to hit Fleur up next."

Cyd sighed. "One at a time, if you don't mind. This is a lot for anybody to handle."

Tajo stood and walked around the table, putting his hands on her shoulders. "Should we sign out a room?" he teased.

"Uh, I'm going to go find Jill, see how she's doing," Hayden said.

"Jill?" Cyd asked.

"Jill," Hayden confirmed. "We needed more girls," he added with a wink. Then he left Tajo and Cyd to do what needed to be done.

"Are we doing this or not?" Tajo asked.

Cyd nodded. "Go ahead and bite me."

"No foreplay?" he said, his voice full of mock disappointment. His hand slid over her shoulder and down to her collarbone. "Ah, I think your heart is already beating double-time."

Cyd looked at the dog and thought of Finn. "We're doing this," she said. "We're definitely doing this."

Tajo smiled and pulled Cyd's hair away from her face, sweeping it clear of her neck. He said, "Just close your eyes and think of your boyfriend."

Chapter Twenty-seven

"Mulberry's Pizza!"

The door opened a crack. One cinnamon brown eye looked through, then narrowed. "I didn't order any—"

The sole of Finn's boot on Bridget Rothschild's apartment door cut off the last part of her sentence. One kick, and the door splintered, the brass latch shearing off the wall. Finn walked calmly over the threshold.

Bridget Rothschild stood before him in her tennis whites, her legs braced apart, an enormous gun in her hands. It was pointed directly at him.

I'm not in the mood for this, he thought. Not at all in the mood.

With a karate-style chop to her wrist—his reflexes were faster than she could possibly have anticipated—the gun flew out of her hand and flipped end over end to smash on the floor.

Finn removed his jacket, the mech components on his arm clearly visible. Bridget's jaw dropped slightly, but then she recovered herself. Still, she whistled as she surveyed the scars and gleaming metal buried in his arms.

"You think you know," she said in wonder. "But you don't know until you see."

"You still don't know," he said. He stood there, unarmed save for how he was physically engineered, and aimed that deadly weaponry on his arm at the space between her eyes. Fury coursed through his veins. He was done with this. Done with people like her. Done with everything. "I'm not hiding anymore."

She walked toward him, taking her time.

"You hear me, girl? I'm not hiding anymore. And I'm not going to let you take me down."

Bridget swallowed audibly and shook her head. "If you're really human like you claim, don't kill me. Please. Of course, if you're a machine, you can't justify not putting a bullet in my head. I guess the question is: Are your impulses man . . . or machine?"

That had always been the question. This wasn't at all how he'd imagined it, this scenario. This final showdown. There was no Ops swarm, no sirens. No rush of adrenaline-filled communications over comm devices. No team of scientists watching through double-glass, or secret cameras. It was to end as it often started: with a single girl, on an otherwise quiet night, in the dark. So be it.

"After everything I've been through," Finn said, "you are not the girl I will get down on my knees and surrender my life to."

She backed up, arms in the air. "Finn, look—"

He reached out and grabbed her by the wrist, spinning her around until he had her tucked neatly against his body, the weapon in his arm up to her temple. "I guess I should be flattered you know my name."

"Could you just let me—"

"No," Finn said. "Until I ask a question, just shut up."

God, how easy it was to revert. Tunnel vision, intimidation, disarming, deletion: the old instincts, coming back so easily. Especially with the code in his head now, making him feel as though he was slipping away into the machine shell he'd been trying so damn hard to shed.

"Where's your console?" he asked.

"Behind you," she replied. "In the office."

He could feel her heart racing underneath his arm, which gripped her diagonally across her chest. Good. She should be scared. He'd taken people out for much less than what she'd done to him.

Finn dragged Bridget over into the other room, to her computer, pushed her down in the chair and wiggled the mouse to kill the screensaver. *Bingo*. The code running across his retina matched the code on her screen.

It was a surprise but, rather than getting even angrier, Finn nearly choked on the lump in his throat as tears stung his eyes. The evidence of his mech side had never been clearer. The pain from the electronics in his head aside, it hurt more than anyone could ever know. Except Cyd. Cyd would know what seeing this did to him. Griff-Vai had messed with her head the way Ops continued to mess with his. And now, while she was taking care of her problem, he was going to take care of his.

"Can I say something?" Bridget asked boldly.

"Sure, but don't ask me for a cigarette later, because this will be your final request."

"Okay." She paused for a moment. To her credit, she

didn't panic, scream or beg. "Okay, so the thing is . . . this looks bad."

Finn cocked his head. "Keep going."

"It looks bad. That code on there, that's me trying to hack into you. Trying to put you back on the Grid, fully operational."

This was surprising. Admitting it straight up was not at all what he'd expected. But he'd known she was a slickster, a trickster, a mover and a shaker. Cyd had told him, had warned him.

"I have no choice but to hack into you so I can put you back on the Grid and . . . whoa, there!" She reared back, ceasing her explanation as Finn cocked the trigger of his arm component. "You have to go on the Grid for your account to be deleted!"

Ah, here was the panic he'd expected. "Cyd went in and got her boss to promise to remove the bounty on your head. And that's been done. Her boss took the bounty off you and took you off line. But, can I just . . . lemme . . ."

Finn gestured to the keyboard with his hand, indicating that she could proceed, but he kept his hand on her shoulder and his weapon by her ear even as she tapped into the Ops mainframe. After a few minutes, she accessed a database file and opened it. The Wanted list. He'd seen these faces before. His used to be one of them. But now . . . his face was no longer on the Wanted list; under every bounty dollar range listed, he looked for his name and came up empty.

She had to be lying. Tricking him. "If there is no bounty on me anymore, then why are you still messing with my head?" he asked quietly. "There are only a very select few who know what I am and have lived to keep the secret. None of them has ever made an effort to hack into my brain and run code through my mind. I've killed people for less than what you've done. What do you want? Who do you work for?"

She hesitated. Finn jammed the metal muzzle of his weapon against her temple. Bridget squeezed her eyes shut.

"Who do you work for?" he repeated. "You can either take me to your boss, or I'll kill you right here."

"It's complicated!"

"Try me."

"Originally, I was working for Trask, off-hours stuff. He was training me to do operative work. But . . . I changed sides. And when I changed sides, my plan for you got changed."

"What was the plan then, and what's the plan now?" Finn felt a surge of adrenaline making him crazy.

"The plan was to find you using a mixture of intel Trask got from Ops, and then to take you in for the bounty. To split the money. But the guy was nuts. He killed just about anyone who said boo. Especially the dogs and the fangs. He's dead now, and his partner JB's being retired—sent off to some assignment out of the city. You're safe from them."

"What's the plan for me now?" Finn growled.

"You're a brilliant operative. Everybody in the business will vouch for that. And that's without knowing what you can do with your mechanicals. Those I'm working for . . . they didn't even know about you being a mech until I told them. They always thought you'd be good for the team. They've been testing you, Finn. And part of my deal is to try and get you completely off Ops radar." Bridget looked up and a bead of sweat trickled down the side of her face. "What they're doing—what *we're* doing—is a good thing. I'm trying to help you."

"What team?" Finn asked.

"The rogues."

Finn blinked, thrown for a loop. "Which rogues?"

"The ones you already know."

Feeling totally out of control, Finn exploded. "I don't know anything!"

Bridget broke, cowering away from him, and Finn saw that the serrated edge of one of his retractable knives had cut through her skin. He took a step back. Just a step, to put a little space between them. She exhaled loudly, as if she'd been holding her breath.

"I have to get you back on the Grid, Finn. Do you get what I'm saying? If you're not part of the network, your file can't be deleted. And if you're not deleted for good, even if you stay off the Grid, you'll just be in a kind of hibernation, waiting, wondering about the day the lights are going to suddenly go back on. Like today. The way we're trying this, you'll be off for good. No one will be able to track you. No one will trace you. And no one will be able to get any money for your head. So—"

"Why are you so concerned about me? Why go to the trouble?" he interrupted.

The corners of her mouth turned up in a little smile as she looked him over. She shrugged. "It's not what you might think, or for same reason as Ms. Brighton. You're a hell of guy, but . . ."

"Yeah"

"Power. Leverage. Control. The same thing everybody in this city wants. We're building a group to rival the primaries. You were valuable before as an operative. You're gold as a mech. And you'll command plenty of fear as the mech that killed two primary vampires. You know, there are plenty of fangs and dogs in this town. There aren't a lot of mechs . . . and there aren't a lot of demons that aren't hardwired to maintain their allegiance to the demon underworld."

Finn stared at her, taking stock of the pointed nature of her comment. *Cyd? Was she talking about Cyd?* "How do I know you're not bullshitting me?" he asked. "I'd say just about anything if I were you, if thought it might save my life."

"They were going to tell you. They were going to bring you in, make you an offer to join. It . . . it wasn't supposed to come down to you and me. It wasn't supposed to be this complicated," Bridget went on, talking faster and faster as if she had a sense her time was running out. "You were just supposed to be a machine. You weren't supposed to have . . . feelings and stuff."

Finn found himself smiling a little at that. It was a hell of a story, but . . . possible. He deactivated his weaponry and moved his arm away. "Us. How about I give you an opportunity to prove you're not lying? How about you take me to meet 'us'?"

Bridget's body finally relaxed. "That," she said in a voice of pure relief, "is something I would be more than happy to do."

The "clubhouse," as Bridget called it, wasn't exactly crammed with members. But it had a sizable attendance. The group had legitimacy as something tangible, something real. And it had the one person Finn was willing to trust in this world: Cyd lay sprawled out on a couch, looking pale and frail. But she was laughing about something with the men gathered around her, looking as if there was nothing more important in the world than beer and bad jokes.

Jillian Cooper was pouring her a glass of water, and fussing around with a damp napkin that Cyd clearly didn't want stuck on her forehead. Hayden Wilks was arguing about something with another rogue vampire whom Finn had seen at Bosco's. Tajo Maddox was sitting quietly, deep in thought with pencil and paper in hand, a sniper rifle leaning up against his chair.

As Finn approached with Bridget, he caught Cyd's notice. She sat up, eyes wide and a huge, surprised smile spread over her face. The others turned to look and fell silent.

"What do you know," Finn murmured. He looked at Tajo. "You get it done?"

Tajo answered with a beer-bottle salute.

"What do you know," Cyd echoed. She looked at Bridget and then back. "You *didn't* get it done."

Finn shook his head. "We'll be doing a little code cleanup later." *After you and I get done with Fleur Dumont and Dain Reston.*

Bridget collapsed into the nearest empty chair, and half laughed. "Talk about a close call. This is one dangerous guy! Somebody get me a drink." She looked at Cyd. "We all square?"

"I . . . guess so," Cyd said.

As Finn sat down beside her, she said to him, "It's nice to stop being so serious for a second." She raised her own beer.

"Are you okay?" he asked.

"I'll be fine."

"You don't look so fine. Are you sure you want to go through with this? To get a vampire to—"

"I'm going up there, Finn. No matter what. I've got to get Fleur Dumont to sink her fangs into me. But there's more than that. I want to . . . square things with Dain. And maybe you can square things with Fleur."

Finn nodded. "I was wondering about that. I wanted to come with you, but if I was going to be a liability . . ." He wouldn't be surprised if Fleur Dumont had trouble getting past the fact that he'd killed her half brothers. He didn't want to create a fight where there didn't need to be one. On the other hand, he'd spared Fleur's life. And besides, he wanted to meet Dain Reston, the man they said had once been a mech but was converted back to a wholly human state. Cyd's old partner was the only other mech Finn knew of who lived off the Grid.

Tajo looked over at them both sitting on the couch. "You guys want some backup?"

"Backup, huh?" Finn shook his head with a smile. "This is really something." They probably didn't know what he meant. This feeling of belonging, the camaraderie in this strange hodgepodge of a team . . . it wasn't something he'd ever had.

Cyd must have felt the same thing. "What does this all mean?" she asked, waggling her fingers in a circle to include everyone.

Hayden looked over and shrugged. "We're prepared to trust you. That's all it is. We're prepared to trust both of you. We're hoping you will trust us."

"It means you can call us if you need someone to watch your back," Tajo added.

Bridget held up a beer. "To the new family," she said.

Jill nodded, a little shyly. "To family."

Finn looked at Cyd and smiled, and they both held up their own drinks. "To family," they said in unison. But Finn still wondered where this journey would end.

Chapter Twenty-eight

"You really didn't have to come with me," Cyd repeated as they stood before the doorman at the entrance to Dumont Towers, the headquarters for the primary vampires of Crimson City.

"You're still weak from Tajo's work," Finn said gruffly. As if he wouldn't have come otherwise. As if he hadn't sworn to come earlier. Cyd just smiled and appreciated it.

A gilded plaque greeted them with the words COME NOT HERE IF YOU DO NOT BELONG, and Cyd shook her head to think that Dain had once read that very phrase and shuddered. Now he lived here, was a vamp. He belonged.

Whether or not *she* belonged here was another story. But she was going to find out.

Dressed in red and gray finery, with a machine gun strapped over one shoulder and an umbrella in the opposite hand, the doorman made it clear that he was all business. He remained stone-faced as they approached, and cocked his head only slightly to speak into the microphone at his lapel.

Cyd shot Finn a sidelong glance. "Just to keep things

straight, Dain and I never had a . . . thing. I've said it before, but . . . some weird things might be said in here."

"He was important to you."

"Yeah." She sighed. "He was. Very important. It all seems like a very long time ago."

They introduced themselves, though it was likely unnecessary. The doorman just nodded. For a moment, Cyd had the peculiar idea that perhaps her old friend wouldn't see her. That Fleur might convince him she wasn't worth seeing again. But after a moment, the doorman said, "Miss Brighton, he'll see you and your guest now," then stepped to the side and ushered them past. "The elevator is in the back."

"Thanks," Cyd replied.

The lobby alone could have housed a museum exhibition. It practically did. The soles of their boots squeaked as they walked along the heavily polished wood floor, and kings and doe-eyed Madonnas watched all comers from the walls like painted sentries of another age. The crystal strands of the chandelier trilled faintly as Finn and Cyd passed through the foyer to stand at the bottom of an enormous velvet-covered staircase that curled up into the heart of the vampire world like a crimson ribbon.

The doorman called from the door, "Miss Brighton?"

Cyd swiveled around. "Yeah?"

"Mr. Reston said to relax."

She stared at him for a minute, then laughed and joined Finn at the elevator bank. Dain would have said that.

Once they were inside the elevator car, the doors closed, and Finn ran a palm over the polished woodwork. "I can see the appeal of this place," he said. "If you're going to stop being human, might as well go fang."

"Maybe," Cyd said. But she'd never been a huge fan of the species. She wiped a thin sheen of sweat off the back of her neck. Finn put his hand on her shoulder and gave a comforting squeeze.

The doors opened, and a manservant appeared to lead them down the hall. Using both hands on the double doors, he ushered them into the room beyond, then backed out and disappeared.

Cyd immediately recognized the figure at the window. The broad shoulders, the dark hair. He turned around, and Cyd sucked in a breath. Dain. He looked so fucking . . . upscale. Still dangerous, still handsome.

His eyes widened as he accepted the truth. "Cyd?" he asked, his voice betraying intense emotion. "Is it really you? When I heard you were here, I . . ."

Cyd swallowed the lump in her throat and forced herself to keep things light. "Holy crap, Dain. What's with the suit?"

He stared at her, and Cyd knew he was trying to process her appearance. The last time he'd seen her, she was pretty ragged. Pretty damn ragged. He crossed the room in an instant and wrapped her in an enormous bear hug. She stood there in shock, then brought her arms up and hugged him back with all of her strength.

"I missed you," he whispered.

Blinking back tears, Cyd responded, "I missed you, too." And just like that, the rift between them was mended. She realized she could have come to him earlier, should have come to him earlier. But then she wouldn't have solved things herself. And there was always Fleur.

"This your guy, then?" Dain asked, turning to Finn.

Cyd nodded. She felt a brief moment of fear, as if Finn would deny it, but that didn't happen. "Dain, this is Finn."

The two men shook hands, obviously sizing each other up. When Dain went to pull his hand away, Finn held on. With his other hand, he slowly rolled up his right sleeve. Dain stared down at the mech components, not even trying to mask his look of wonder.

"Any friend of Cyd's is a friend of mine," he finally said, "but I think we'd understand each other even if she weren't here."

"Agreed," Finn answered, letting go. His sleeve unfurled, covering his arm once more.

Cyd cleared her throat. "Where's Fleur?"

Dain lifted his hand to his face and stroked his jaw. "She thought I'd like to see you alone first. Since you two . . . don't . . ."

"Really get along?"

"Right," he said. He looked at Finn and gave him a *women, can't live with 'em, can't live without 'em* look.

"Well, I'm glad you two are hitting it off," Cyd grumbled, noting the wordless exchange.

Dain laughed. "Look, I'd like nothing more than to see you two patch things up." But his eyes didn't convince her it was likely.

Cyd looked around the room, stalling. The fancy décor only made her uneasy, made her feel more out of place. "The thing is, it's more than just friendship. I . . . I need a favor from her."

"From her? Specifically?"

"Specifically."

Dain looked surprised, then reached out and chucked Cyd gently under the chin. "Never a dull moment with you. Are you ever going to tell me what the hell happened to you? I . . ." He got misty for a moment, and Cyd did, too. If he only knew.

"Yeah. I'll fill you in. Some other time, though. Okay? This thing with Fleur is kind of important."

He studied her face. "Okay."

Dain went behind the desk, turning his back for a little privacy while he made the call. Cyd looked at Finn. "It isn't going to be easy to convince her," she said. "When it comes to me and Fleur, we're still working on even liking each other."

"I caught that," Finn said. "Be careful."

Fleur entered the room in a stylized feminine version of a charcoal pinstripe gangster suit, complete with a fedora tipped at a perfect angle. Her makeup looked professionally done. The men looked bedazzled. She smiled, crossed the room quickly and stuck out her hand. "You look fantastic, Cyd," she said.

Well, to Fleur's credit, it wasn't exactly bullshit; Cyd knew she looked better than ever.

"Hello, Fleur," she replied. She looked at Finn and Dain, who suddenly snapped out of their trances. "You guys must have a hell of a lot of questions for each other," she suggested.

The men looked at each other and, each sending warning looks at their respective woman, headed out the door. Cyd breathed a sigh of relief that there hadn't been a confrontation about the murder of Fleur's stepbrothers; but maybe Fleur hadn't recognized Finn.

As soon as they were gone, the vampire leader turned on Cyd. "I don't imagine we're going to be able to be friends right away. Not with our history. But for Dain's sake, I'm willing to try—if you are."

Cyd shrugged. "Well, yeah, sure." She hadn't imagined this would be so easy.

It wasn't. Fleur went on: "But while I'd be happy making peace, I'm not going to pretend to be something I'm not. I have to confess that I rather enjoy this change-up. I like that you're a bit muddled in my world rather than the opposite."

Cyd smiled weakly. "That's . . . nice."

"So, Dain said you had something you wanted to ask me."

"Yeah." Okay, this wasn't going to be fun. At all. She'd never been a big fan of vampires, she and Fleur had shared an adversarial relationship, and in the end, Fleur had converted her partner. Now she needed this favor. There was only one way to go for it: full force. It was not the way the old Cyd would have acted, but there was no way around it. Griff-Vai was coming. She wouldn't be his again.

She clasped her hands and put them down carefully on the table, then leaned forward. "I . . . need a vampire to bite me."

Fleur's face was completely blank.

"I need a—hell, what would you call it—a 'thoroughbred' to bite me. A pure-blood."

A flicker of confusion passed over Fleur's glamorous face. "Dain said that. I thought he was joking," she said, her voice all wonder.

"So, you knew? He prepped you?"

"I laughed."

"He was telling the truth."

Fleur went silent, searching Cyd's face. She was shaking her head.

"What am I going to have to do to convince you?" Cyd asked. "This is serious."

Fleur scoffed. "There are too many risks. I know I changed Dain, but . . . you don't even know that story. You could go rogue. You could . . . I won't do it."

"Yeah. You will." Cyd had to convince her. She advanced on the vamp.

Fleur didn't seem impressed. She folded her hands across her chest and cocked her head. "You act like you're asking me to invite you to closed party. Well, guess what? It *is* a closed party. With everything going on in this city right now, I can't think of a worse reason to turn someone vampire than because they miss their crush."

Cyd reeled back. "You're kidding. You think that's why I want this?"

Fleur just looked grave.

"That's not it at all. This is serious. I told you that."

"Whatever reason you've got, I can't imagine it will convince me. I can have Dain explain the way things are to you if you like."

"Dain is a vampire now, an accepted primary—so I don't think he's going to be able to come up with an explanation I'll buy."

Fleur shrugged, an elegant undulation of her shoulders. Standing next to her made Cyd feel like a troll, even with her newfound demon-blood beauty. That made her mad.

She decided to come a little clean. "Look. Here's the thing. This isn't a normal bite. You're not going to turn me. Not exactly. It's not an issue of that." She took a deep breath and just spit out: "I'm not even entirely human. Okay? So, that's not the moral dilemma here. The moral dilemma is that if you don't bite me, every single one of us, human or non, is in deep trouble. It has to do with the demons."

Fleur swept her gaze from Cyd's scuffed boots to the top of her head. After a moment, she said, "You know, there's this one phrase that Dain always uses that might apply to this situation."

Cyd narrowed her eyes, not quite liking her tone. "Go ahead."

"Give me a fucking break."

"Yeah. That sounds like something he'd say," Cyd agreed.

Fleur smiled coolly. "For Dain's sake, I'm doubly sorry I can't help you. But I'm not going to bite you, and I'm not going to direct you to another—what did you call it—'thoroughbred' so that you can try to convince them to bite you. Frankly, I don't buy your story. You just aren't the type to care much about saving the world. I've never trusted you, and I'm not going to start now. Demons? Right. I know you're working for B-Ops again. So why don't you run on home to them."

Cyd bit her lip and deliberated. Finally, she said, "You know something? We've had something to settle for some time now, so I guess I don't have to feel bad."

"Feel bad about what?"

"This." And Cyd hauled back and punched Fleur in the jaw. This was the new Cyd. She wasn't waiting for others to save her anymore.

The vampiress was off guard to begin with, and she took it badly, losing her balance and falling to the ground. She was up in a second, though, hovering above the floor, a trickle of blood at one corner of her mouth and an unbelievably pissed-off look in her eyes. She gracefully swept the blood away with her fingers, then looked at it.

Cyd readied herself.

Fleur looked up. "You must be joking," she said. "This is how you plan to convince me?"

"I'm desperate, Fleur Dumont. I throw down."

Fleur rolled her eyes. "That's a vampire thing, Cyd. You're not a vampire."

"I throw down," Cyd insisted.

Fleur crossed her arms over her chest and smiled. "I think you've gone completely insane."

"Mano à mano, Fleur. Let's have at it. You've always had it out for me anyway." Cyd launched herself forward, slamming Fleur into the wall. "Do it," she growled.

Fleur's lip curled, revealing a perfect set of fangs. But she did nothing.

Violence began to course through Cyd's blood, making her nearly delirious. She reeled back, dragging Fleur with her until she hit the other wall. "Do it," she ordered again through gritted teeth.

Something horribly foreign was welling up inside her. A destructive force. Face-to-face with Fleur as Cyd was, the combined anger of the two females was boiling between their bodies, creating a rush of energy. It whirled through them.

Suddenly Fleur had the upper hand. Literally. She was choking the life out of Cyd. Cyd only had a moment of doubt before her survival instincts took hold. With one hand around each of Fleur's wrists, she pulled the vampire off her with a supernatural strength far beyond what she'd ever had. Everything faded, but Cyd had never felt more conscious of her surroundings. She wasn't losing consciousness; it was more of a reorientation, as if a hole had been wiped in a swiftly fogging window. Even Fleur, who'd been so vibrant in the deep emeralds and crimson reds of her opulent jewelry and cosmetics, had faded to a pale version of the former vision; and it was as if the two of them were locked in battle in a silent movie that ran only in shades of gray.

Something in Fleur registered the change; her eyes widened. Cyd wondered if it was just surprise, or if there was also an element of fear. After a brief respite, the two women ratcheted up the struggle.

"Bite me, Fleur," Cyd hissed, her smoky voice taking on a level of danger she'd never heard from herself.

Fleur's eyes locked with hers, and the vampiress spoke some sort of mantra in a foreign tongue. Her look seemed to beg for strength. It got worse when Cyd's skin was raked by one of her nails. Fleur seemed to smell the blood.

"Give in to your bloodlust," Cyd said. "You can't make me vampire. I'm already gone elsewhere. Do your worst."

With her eyes narrowed to angry slits, Fleur struggled. She opened her mouth to fire off a retort, when suddenly she froze. Her nose twitched, smelling the blood again. "You weren't lying," she said, a look of comprehension dawning in her eyes. Her head cocked, she was clearly using all of her senses to understand what exactly it was with which she wrestled. "Human, demon . . . and werewolf? You're not lying. You need the fourth." The two women released each other.

Cyd stood, chest heaving, mind reeling. Silently she begged Fleur to do her this one favor, without anymore struggle. The vampire puzzled over the situation in silence.

Finally she looked Cyd straight in the eyes and, to Cyd's surprise, it was almost a look of respect.

"For Dain," Fleur murmured, stepping nearer. Then she took Cyd's face in her hands, the perfect crimson of her vampire mouth flashing with white teeth that lowered toward Cyd's neck. The pain was momentary.

Chapter Twenty-nine

Finn knelt on the floor, gently stroking Cyd's hair. For the past ten minutes she'd stayed curled in a ball in a weakened state, mumbling one name over and over: Griff-Vai. That was a strange experience. It had made him realize how much he cared for her. How much he hated the demon.

Dain crouched down beside him. "They're bringing a car to the door for you. Look, we can take care of her here. I'd prefer it. Are you sure—?"

"She wants to go home," Finn said firmly. "But thanks."

Dain nodded and handed Finn a comm device. "If she needs anything at all . . . if you need to turn around and come back . . . just call."

Finn took the device and stuck it in his pocket, then held out his hand. They shook, and Finn couldn't help thinking that, if he were Cyd, Dain Reston was what he would have wanted for himself.

"Take good care of her," Dain said.

"I will," Finn replied. He leaned down and scooped Cyd up into his arms.

Dain led him to the elevator. Finn got in with Cyd, the door closed on them and they were alone.

Finn thought of the blood on his hands: the dried blood from Cyd's neck that had wet his skin while he was tending her. She'd been right before; it was foolish, the business of him hoping she would somehow make him more physically whole. What the hell had he been hoping would happen—that he'd somehow become demonic by osmosis? That she would share her strange blood with him? There was nothing Cyd could really do about his situation, about making him more "human." And if he was honest with himself, he would realize that he'd known that for some time. Maybe humanity was a state of mind. Like the way "rogues" were not always loners out for themselves. Hadn't he learned that tonight, too?

No, there was nothing in Cyd that could take the machine out of him. And there was nothing in the world that could make him more human than his own actions and thoughts.

He wasn't going to take any more of the implants off. He wasn't going to chip away at the metal anymore. He wasn't going to dismantle the last weapon, comprising his right arm. He wasn't going to try to become something he wasn't. He was going to embrace what he was—all the things he was.

It's over.

The doorman cleared the way as Finn carried Cyd to the waiting limousine. The driver reached over Finn's shoulder and opened the door. Finn gently laid her down on the long seat so that she could stretch out, and he took the shorter horizontal seat for himself, his hand stroking her hair.

"Get me out of here," she murmured.

He bent down to her and whispered, "You're safe."

"Take me home."

He was surprised by her command. Did she mean her abandoned base apartment? It would be difficult, but all he cared about was making her comfortable. "Where's home?" he asked.

"With you," she slurred, opening her eyes.

She kept them open only briefly, and Finn sucked in a quick breath—as much at the look of them as at his fleeting moment of joy. Her brown irises had gone so pale they were nearly white. But when she smiled before drifting back into a blur of unconsciousness, he knew that inside, at least, she was the same. She was his Cyd.

"You're already there, then." He took her limp hand in his and leaned back against the seat.

She was still alive. Changed in some incalculable way that remained to be seen, but alive. He was thankful for that.

Dain and Fleur had offered to take care of her. They'd tried to insist, really. But every time she drifted back from the edge of oblivion, she'd begged Finn to take her away, and he knew she wanted to wake up somewhere safe and comfortable. So he'd taken an offer of a ride and escaped the vampire skyscraper.

Holding Cyd's hand, Finn looked out the window and watched the city pass by. It took him fifteen minutes to realize they were going the wrong direction. He looked around for the window divider control, and when he couldn't find it, he tapped on the glass.

No answer.

He raised his fist to tap once more, and the glass began to slide open just as the comm device Dain gave him went off. He held it up to his ear and switched it on.

"It's Dain. Don't tell me you walked. Not with her in that condition."

Finn frowned, struggling against jealousy. That this man would feel protective, would feel the need to check up on Cyd . . . "Actually, we're in the car right now."

"The car is still waiting downstairs, man. Uh, is everything okay?"

Finn's eyes flicked to the car's rearview mirror. Pale lilac eyes met his. "Not okay," was all he had time to say before dropping the device in favor of attacking the door locks. The locks wouldn't budge.

"Cyd, wake up!" he hissed. He turned his body and started brutally kicking at the door.

There were two figures in the front seat, and neither seemed perturbed as Finn went ballistic, using the heel of his boot to try to break the glass out of the windows. Inexplicably, though he'd only kicked one, every window in the back of the limousine shattered.

Finn lunged forward, pulling Cyd to the floor and under his body as the shards of glass swirled in slow motion inside the vehicle. Most embedded themselves in the upholstered sides and seats of the car.

The sound of brakes and the sharp swerve of the vehicle had Finn and Cyd rolling across the floor. Finn rose to his hands and knees, his arm braced on the limousine's bar as the driver ramped up the speed and careened down several new streets. Cyd was still facedown on the floor, arms and legs limp, apparently in the deepest sleep of her life. One too deep to be believed natural, in the face of the chaos swirling inside the limousine.

Suddenly Finn felt as though someone had grabbed the back of his shirt and pulled him up into his seat. He reached out for Cyd, but a palm in his chest slammed him backwards.

"Hello, Finn," a voice said.

Finn stared at a man sitting on the side seat where Cyd had been, and his foreign look gave him away immediately. The demon.

"I'm Griff-Vai," the man said. "You and I meet at last. You do know who I am, yes? I'll be very angry with Cydney if she never talks about me."

"Leave her alone," Finn growled, every muscle in his body primed for attack. "You shouldn't even want a human."

Griff-Vai laughed. "She's not exactly human, is she? In fact, she's less human now than she is everything else combined. I created what she is. The very core of her. Of course I want her."

"She's human where it counts."

"I suppose you're going to say her heart. How sentimental."

"I was going to say her head."

"You're standing in my way. You've got your"—he looked down at the metal of Finn's arm and smiled wryly—"hooks in her. Turn her away, and she'll come to me."

Finn shook his head. "You can't make me give her up."

"I think I can. What if I offered you the one thing you really want—the only thing you've ever wanted?"

Finn narrowed his eyes. "How would you know what I want?"

"We all want the same thing. Completion. Perfection. Fulfillment."

Finn couldn't deny it. And the demon had a particularly seductive way of speaking. Something you couldn't spell out. It was like a kind of magic, and he finally understood what Cyd had struggled so hard against.

Griff-Vai smiled. "You haven't told me to go to hell yet. Interesting. Perhaps we can make a deal. What if I offered you perfection of body? Though you wished it to be so, though you've stayed with her on the thin premise that it would be so, the fact is that Cydney does not have it within her formidable powers to change the quality of your beauty. But I am a full demon. I have that power. What I gave to her can be given to anyone I choose. I gave Cydney her beauty, that perfection of human form, and I can give it to you as well. It is not in her power to give you what you want, what you crave . . . but it is in mine. Everything you've wanted can be yours. I can give you flesh that no one will wish you to hide; in fact, the very opposite. All I ask is that you give her up to me."

Finn curled his fingers and squeezed his hands into fists, trying to suppress his rage, to remain lucid. "So. You beg me to betray her so she'll have no option but to turn to you. You can't get her to come to you of her own volition. No matter how deep you got your *claws* into her, she hasn't crossed the line. That must make you crazy."

"If it weren't for you, she'd be mine by now," Griff-Vai growled. "She'd be with me in the demon underworld. I made her what she is," he repeated.

"You've helped her accept what she is. That's all."

Griff-Vai's eyes glowed bright red. "Without you, she would have nothing here. Nothing to sacrifice. I can kill you in a second. Give up willingly, and we both shall reap the reward we deserve."

Finn slowly shook his head. Griff-Vai was spinning a pretty web of words . . . which only managed to remind him of Cydney's worth. "All I've ever wanted was to get rid of this," he said, holding up his arm and running his fingers over the scar at his temple. "And the rest. But I've realized that doing so won't make me any more or any less a man."

"But it will change the appearance of what you are—a machine in a human shell."

Finn shook his head. "Thanks for the offer, my friend," he said in a menacing whisper. "At one time this would have been tempting, but it doesn't even register now. I'd rather have Cyd here and in my heart than be alone in the most perfect shell you have to offer. I will never give her up—to you or to anyone else."

"So be it."

Griff-Vai drew back his fist and delivered the opening punch. Finn turned into the blow, taking satisfaction in the sound of flesh hitting the metal plate buried on his face. He might not have the benefit of magical power on his side, but he'd put up a hell of a fight in hand-to-hand combat.

No, he hadn't absorbed all of that Ops training for nothing. With every ounce of strength in his body, he turned toward the demon and attacked, raining systematic blows down on him, the metal edges of his right arm blades merciless.

But as fast as he dispensed injury, the demon healed, just as Cyd's body had done, but faster. The whole scene threw the demon's physical perfection in Finn's face like a weapon.

Looking into the demon's eyes as Griff-Vai's fingernails tore at his skin, powerful knuckles bullying his bones with every blow, Finn felt warm blood well up from the cuts, and the dull pain of the impacts. His fate was sealed. There would be no perfection of human form for him; he would never be fully delivered from his mech past. He would die a machine. And Finn was willing to accept that.

"It's over," he said. "You can kill me, but she'll never choose you over me, no matter what I look like on the outside. You know it."

The demon's cry of rage sounded like a siren in Finn's head. The demon rose up to lash out once more.

Knowing he was about to die, Finn threw his strength right back at his assailant. He would go out fighting.

A bloodcurdling cry, the unforgettable sound of Griff-Vai's rage, jolted Cyd from the semiconscious state in which she'd been swimming. One look over her shoulder told the story: The two men in her life who most wanted her were squared off in the confines of the limousine, grappling and exchanging brutal blows.

Yes, Griff had finally come through the portal for her as a complete physical presence. He was a force with which to be reckoned. That force he'd already demonstrated, judging by the glass shards lining the interior of the vehicle.

Blood dripped from cuts on Finn's face. But Griff-Vai was not untouched; his chest heaved from the exertion of trying to fight a human designed specifically to participate in all kinds of warfare.

For a moment she was surprised that he hadn't destroyed Finn outright. But then she realized it wasn't just about the killing for Griff. He'd try to batter and humiliate Finn without killing him, enjoying it as much as an animal. He was playing cat-and-mouse. He would enjoy fighting to the death over a potential mate.

He turned to her and smiled. "I've missed you, Cydney."

She rose to her knees on the floor, catching a glimpse of the city blurring past through the open windows of the speeding car. The limousine took a corner too fast; Cyd lurched toward the glass spikes buried in the door next to her. Both men reached out, one on each arm, and pulled her to sit between them.

Neither of them asked her to choose; it was a simple matter of turning her body, an almost imperceptible motion. But Cyd turned toward Finn—and she could feel the ugliness of her rejection hit the demon hard.

He didn't say a word. He went one better.

Finn's arm had reached out to cradle her shoulders, but suddenly he slammed a hard backhand into her sternum. Cyd gasped and fell backward on the seat as Finn's hand found her neck and curled around it. A thin rasp of air was all she could manage as she begged him with her eyes.

"Cyd, he's making me. He's trying to turn you against me," Finn said, the veins in his neck bulging as he strained against the force that had made him hurt her. "We need to fight him together. *You* need to fight him—on his terms."

As she struggled, Cyd saw Griff-Vai in the corner of her eye, sitting silently in his seat, his eyes trained on Finn's arm. Suddenly Finn's fingers released. Both he and Cyd stared in agony as his palm slid down her shirt, where his fingers splayed over her heart. The blade fitted to the top mechanism in his arm rattled in its casings, sliding back and forth, a hairs-breadth from embedding itself in her body.

"I'm not doing this to you," Finn said, his face desperate. "I'm begging you . . . Use what you can of the powers you have in you now."

"I don't know how," she cried out in gasps, pushing feebly at his arm. "I don't know what to do!"

Her answer seemed to satisfy Griff. Still nestled in the corner, with a smirk playing on his lips, he eased off: Finn's arm relaxed.

"Get the comm!" Finn yelled.

Cyd did as instructed. Sliding out from underneath him, she grabbed for the comm device lying on the floor. She managed only to clear the signal and plug in a contact number for the Rogues Club before Griff kicked it neatly out of her hand.

But Finn took advantage of Griff-Vai's preoccupation. Leaping across the span, he stuck his arms through the divider to grab for the wheel. The driver looked back at him, and Cyd saw the same supernaturally pale eyes she'd seen on the demon agent who'd attacked her during that first job with Finn.

The glass divider started to move up, to crush Finn against the ceiling of the car. He swung out and demolished it with his arm. A jagged edge or two cut into him, though, leaving red streaks on his flesh, as he struggled to commandeer the limousine from the demon agent.

Careening wildly to the side, the car jumped a curb and sideswiped a row of parking meters. The metal posts punched holes in the side of the limousine. Cyd dove the opposite way . . . and Griff-Vai enveloped her in his arms. She remembered just how seductive his words could be, how persuasive his touch. He was almost sheltering her as Finn struggled with the demon driver in the front seat.

The car weaved left and right, twice nearly flipping. Griff grabbed Cyd back before she could slide onto any glass.

A blade punched straight through from the front seat, and Cyd screamed. Keeping relatively calm, Finn regained control of the car and made several motions with his other hand. All Cyd could see was one of the demon's hands opening and closing, as if he were trying to pump life back into himself, and then a swath of long, pin-straight hair slipping into view as he slumped over.

Finn crawled through the divider, over the demon's body, and braked the car. The limousine lurched and stopped. Then Finn turned his body and jammed the sole of his boot into the passenger-side door, smashing it open.

He came around and pulled the back door open, holding out his hand to Cyd without a glance at Griff-Vai.

"Come on, Cyd," he said, holding out his hand. Wrapped in Griff's clutches, Cyd could only stare at him.

"She doesn't want to go with you," the demon said.

Finn showed no fear. No fear whatsoever. He beckoned her again with his fingers. "Come on, Cyd," he said, his voice low and quiet. "Show him what you're really made of."

Cyd tried to push herself away. "Let me go," she growled. But Griff-Vai wasn't having it; he held on that much tighter.

"Stay with me," he whispered, equal parts temptation and desperation.

"Show him," Finn begged.

Cyd closed her eyes, not quite knowing what she meant to do. *I don't want you, Griff. I'll never want you.* She threw up her arms in despair. "I don't know what I'm doing!" she moaned.

But something in Griff-Vai took a step back. She and the demon looked at each other. And in that moment of hesitation, Cyd grabbed Finn's hand. He pulled her out of the shell of the limousine, and they fled.

She staggered weakly behind him down the street, taking in the neighborhood. They were near the Triangle once more, running along the last city street bordering Griffith Park. Her demon had meant to return with her to the place she'd come through the portal. It seemed she was retracing her steps.

As she ran down the sidewalk, her hand in Finn's, she could see a faint glow over the park, and she felt a familiar rush. She could sense the amulet nearby. Patrick and Xiao Fei, trying again to close the portal?

The farther into the park they moved, the closer they came to her point of entry, the site of the tear between the two worlds. She stopped in her tracks and turned around. . . . Griff-Vai wasn't there. She and Finn were alone. Too alone.

"We have to get away from here," she said. "We're heading exactly where he wants. Something's not right. He wouldn't give up like that. It's too easy."

Cyd understood why everything had converged on this moment: The Draig was wielding the amulet, the tear would be sealed tonight and the portal would be closed. Griff-Vai had no desire to be in this world, he intended to have her back in Orcus when that happened.

Silence again, except for the intermittent *drip-drop* of a leaky pipe that snaked along the side of the nearest building. A piece of cardboard tumbled down the middle of the street.

"It wasn't easy at all," Finn said, giving her hand a squeeze. But he didn't look like he thought it was finished, either.

They were both right. From the streets of Crimson City, figures began to assemble. There came the sound of voices, a vibration in the ground. It seemed Griff-Vai was marshalling an army of his supporters from every corner of the city—all those remaining who'd been hiding their allegiance to the demon underworld. Cyd recognized people from all walks of life. And yes, there were members of the police department, Ops and once-trusted informants.

A hideous sense of dread began to well up inside of Cyd: These numbers alone would make any fight a losing proposition. But as the demon agents assembled en masse before them, from behind Finn and Cyd another team came running through the park.

Finn sucked in a breath; she could feel him tense beside her. But instead of more agents, the members of the Rogues Club began to assemble.

Tajo appeared, ducked his chin in greeting. Cyd looked at the others. Bridget, Hayden . . . and the rest. She even thought she saw a flash of Jill Cooper's face in the back.

"No cops, no Ops, no Guard," Bridget muttered. "We're all we've got." Tajo bent at the knees, balancing his weight like a boxer ready to strike.

Hayden's lips curled back in a snarl as he sized up the opposition. The sound of metal on metal filled the otherwise silent streets: both sides readying their weapons.

There was no real signal; no real go-sign. Someone flinched first and then all hell broke loose. The rogue vampires leapt straight into the sky and then plummeted down toward their foes; the dogs and the humans just barreled straight ahead.

Finn was immediately using every weapon in his personal arsenal as the mobs converged. Swords, guns, lasers, fists—and the grunts and cries of battle demolished the silence.

As she and Finn fought side by side against the onslaught, Cyd saw Dain and Fleur descend into the heart of the battle, unsheathing swords and diving straight into the fight. She caught Dain's eye and he nodded, but then both he and she were forced back into the action.

The battle edged toward the park almost as if the rogues were being purposely pushed in that direction. On both city sidewalks and grass bisected with concrete paths, the small armies struggled for dominance and for their lives. The air was clogged with the frenzied sound of violence, and with the taint of both fear and adrenaline.

Griff appeared in the midst of the melee. Staring at him, Cyd knew that no matter what else was going on—no matter the other demons' agenda with the portal, if they had one—for him this was personal. He might have timed it with the larger effort, but all this, right here and now, by which she and Finn were surrounded, was personal and not official business. That's the way Griff-Vai wanted it, and that's exactly what he would get.

"Let the others handle each other," she said to herself. "Right here, right now, demon . . . this is about settling this thing between you and me. Let's get it on."

Chapter Thirty

For the first time since she'd met Griff-Vai, Cyd shook off her fear completely and went on the offensive. Rushing forward, she slammed the sole of her boot against his chest. He pitched back, grabbing the front of her shirt just in time to take her down with him.

Grappling and struggling, they rolled from grass to paved pathway, gravel crunching and skipping around them in their wake. Griff's fist swung out, connecting in a solid blow to her jaw. Cyd's head snapped back, her arms splaying at her sides. She went limp.

The demon pulled her to her feet. She was still woozy from the hit, and for a moment all she could do was stand and sway. She was no match for him. Not if she fought him as a human. So how could she beat him? Her mind raced.

She could regenerate flesh. She could communicate with demons using only her mind. She could hold a sacred amulet known to be demonic in purpose. And now she had the power of the vampire and werewolf worlds in the mix. She was a combination of all the power Crimson City had ever seen . . . but Cyd didn't know how to harness the sum of all of her abilities into something she could direct, control or use. And without that understanding, she would never break the bond with Griff-Vai.

"Do you have anything else?" the demon asked dismissively, backhanding her across the face. "Is that it?"

"Griff-Vai, I have something I want to tell you."

"By all means."

She stared at him, finding her courage, refusing to give in. Through gritted teeth she said, "That's the last time you're going to hit me and get away with it."

Griff-Vai simply laughed, gesturing to the scene behind him. "I think I'm already getting away with it."

Cyd glanced over her shoulder at the park-turned-battlefield, and at her friends struggling in groups and pairs against the onslaught of demon power. Finn looked like a man possessed, battling two demons at once, with his left fist and the blade from his right arm. This shouldn't all be in vain. His loyalty to her, his love. It shouldn't all be in vain.

Think. What does Griff do? He works with energy. He uses energy and is used by energy. He took the energy of that amulet and bound us together. . . .

"Cyd?" he purred. She looked up at him and could see on his face that he was beginning to believe he'd won. He knew that if she couldn't break the bond, there'd be no possibility of keeping him away.

Focus.

She closed her eyes and tried to mold the powers of the four species within her together, to combine them in the center of her mind.

Focus!

Maintaining her intensity, she centered her energy and leaped up, one leg bent. The other struck out at Griff-Vai's neck.

This time, her kick landed straight and with greater force, her reflexes so quick that she had hardly made up her mind before the action was under way. She sucked in a breath, anxious to temper her abilities into something less chaotic. Something with which she could control and conquer.

Griff-Vai was not impressed. Or, at least, that was what he wanted her to believe. He laughed, a sound as smooth and as ominous as any. "This is just sport. Tell me you've got something more than this. If this is all you have, this physical violence . . ." He shrugged, wiping the blood from his mouth, all injury seeming to vanish. "You may as well save your strength. This is too easy, and I'd rather not hurt you before your trip back."

"There isn't going to *be* any trip back for me," she cried, and in her intense anger, she found her elusive focus. She prepared to strike.

His next move was surprising; Griff knelt on the ground in front of her. "What is the one thing you've always wanted, Cydney?"

She didn't answer.

"Control. You've lost it so many times, in so many ways. I can give it back to you. Do you realize the kind of power we'll have together? Unheard of." He stood and took her by the shoulders, swept her hair from her face.

Cyd refused to look at him.

"All right. I have another offer. If you come with me, I will complete Finn's humanity. I will save him for you. Imagine his joy. The metal gone, his skin perfectly smooth. Perfectly smooth like yours. *Human*."

Cyd stared at the brilliant green grass beneath her feet. "He wouldn't want that," she said simply; and she knew it was true. They'd found something better, she and Finn. "He wouldn't want that anymore. And how would that be love for you? Why would you want someone so badly who loves someone else?"

"I made you what you are. From the first moment years ago. I can't stop that portal from closing, not alone. But I can make sure you're on the right side when it does."

Cyd locked eyes with Griff-Vai. "I'm *on* the right side."

And, summoning every power in her body, she pressed her energy against his, physically pushing him away from her. He struggled, stumbling, and Cyd couldn't help feeling strangely guilty as she latched on to her abilities and confidently sent him tumbling backwards, tripping and stumbling away from her as she walked slowly forward, her mind's eye on his. Matching power to power, she was coming out ahead.

The entire park was lit with the glow of energy. It came from the amulet, from Patrick and Xiao Fei somewhere out there, and Cyd was able to harness it. "Can you feel it?" she asked quietly, masking the intensity of her rage. "Can you tell?"

Griff-Vai could. She could see the confusion in his eyes. Almost as if he was afraid to wait any longer, he raised his fist into the air, speaking in the same tongue he'd used the night she slipped through the portal tear, the same tongue he'd used when stealing her out of Crimson City the first time around.

The wind picked up around them, disturbing sticks, loose grass, dirt and debris. Cyd ducked her face into her hands. She'd been through this before, though it had been fire and shards of glass whipping like a tornado around her. She screamed as he brought his fist crashing down to the pavement. Fiery sparks and concrete tornadoed around them.

And suddenly Griff-Vai had her at the rift. He stood on one side; she stood on the other. Curling his fingers around her wrist, he tried to pull her through.

Her focus wrecked, Cyd stumbled, nearly falling headlong after him. She lost her focus, panicked and threw a reckless punch with her other hand, catching him on an angle. It deflected harmlessly. She dug in her heels.

That's just physical violence, Cyd, just like he said. It's not going to work. Find it again. Find your strength. Take control.

He caught her other hand; Cyd twisted her body, desperately trying to pull away. Finally she and Griff-Vai were facing each other, palm to palm, fingers entwined.

She mustered up everything she could in her body and closed her eyes once more. *It doesn't matter if you don't understand it. Find your power and use it.* But . . . her craft was such a new thing, and Griff-Vai was so experienced at his. He took control of the situation before she could get her mind into it.

"Walk through of your own volition," Griff-Vai said, his beautiful hair blowing out around him in the maelstrom of energy. He didn't beg. He didn't have to. The tone of his voice was a seduction all its own.

It worked. Her mind slipped. She went hurtling into wide-open space, bright white light hotter than hell—if it wasn't really hell—her arms and legs flailing in free-fall, as if she were swimming through a supernova.

Clawing at a surface she couldn't see or touch, pulled by a magic she couldn't understand, Cyd panicked. She sensed the change in the atmosphere as the demon underworld itself seeped out through the tear and mingled with the park mist in Crimson City.

She felt herself losing ground to the image of Griff-

Vai hauling her back home with outstretched arms. *Home?*

Finn wouldn't give in. He could have traded her in for a demon's promise of everything he'd ever wanted in his life. He'd laughed in the face of the deal. He'd *laughed.*

He didn't run, and he didn't trade her away for a chance at perfection, and Cyd knew that he would die for her without a thought. That was true love.

Finn, I'm sorry. You know that I love you, don't you?

But she'd never said it. And now she was losing ground, giving in. . . .

You never told him, Cyd. You never said the words. And that haunted her.

What saved her was the strain on Griff-Vai's face. He was using so much power and energy to get at her, he could no longer control himself. She watched him shape-shift out of control; one moment wearing a human face, the next something more monstrous to match those red eyes.

His rage mixed with despair. Cyd knew that feeling well; and sensing it in him spurred her on all the more.

She looked into Griff's eyes and, as she stared at him, not even certain how she was doing it, it was as if the power behind her emotions burst against him. Griff-Vai's eyes bored into hers and then, suddenly . . . he blinked.

Cyd saw Finn's outline; it surged in an energy flash of darkness and light. And suddenly she and Griff were back in the park, in the battle. And Finn was there.

Finn raised his right arm and released the spring-loaded knife there. It flew through the air and buried itself in Griff-Vai's chest, pinning him to a tree. But when Cyd looked over at Finn, he was backing up, turning the demon over to her; he understood this was her fight. It had to be.

What is it I've become? The power of all species. Griff-Vai was but one; she was all four. She realized the power of that—and of accepting it.

"Don't do this, Cyd," Griff said.

Do what he does, but fourfold. Do what he does.

She looked at Griff-Vai one last time. His body was straining as he tried to pull Finn's knife from his flesh.

Sorry, Griff, but I'm not yours. Never was. Never will be. You should not have kept trying to control me.

Then she closed her eyes and hung her head, forcing herself to go limp and to let her arms hang freely. She imagined herself and Griff; one on either side of the veil, the rift between them.

His body remained still, but his mind took shape, took her hands. He took the two streams of light suddenly in her grasp and tried to seal them. She shrugged him off and began to pull the seams of the invisible veil together. She could and would heal the rift. This could and would end here.

Griff's face was ashen, his powers no longer any match for what she was conjuring, as inexperienced as she was. He saw his fate written in her mind's eye, and he gave up the fight. The rift closed between them.

Cyd stared at the energy in her mind and felt his fingers slip away. The veil was turning opaque at the seam. Cyd ran her fingers down it, symbolically resealing what she'd already accomplished.

Blood ran from the wound in the chest of Griff-Vai's human avatar, but he didn't struggle. She slowly walked up to the demon. His breathing was labored; his eyes burned an intense red. The sound and fury of a growing energy surge rumbled.

The wind picked up, and the world all around paled to a white light. The ground trembled, leaves falling all around from the trees. And then there came an intense sound like an explosion.

So intent was she on watching Griff-Vai's final moments, Finn had to pull Cyd to the ground and cover her body to protect her from the storm. And still, she turned her head to watch. Griff-Vai looked at her one last time; and then, as blinding white light seared through the air one moment, it was pitch black the next. By the time the black faded enough for her to see, there was nothing left but Finn's knife stuck into the tree.

She and Finn sat up. All around the park were the rogues, scattered here and there, still ready to fight, though they were duck-and-covering. Slowly their heads began to rise . . . and their weapons lowered.

The demon agents were gone—returned to the demon underworld by their true allegiance, once more contained behind the veil.

Over to Cyd's left, Tajo held out a hand to Bridget and hoisted her to her feet off the grass. Hayden stood, too. Jill came out from behind a tree, with a crossbow of all things. And there were others. Many others. Cyd looked around and saw Fleur and Dain. Dain gave her a quick salute, and the couple stepped away, likely not wanting to deal with the Rogues—not when there were so many; not when there was still so much politics unresolved. In Crimson City, there were few moments of true unity. But she was glad that they'd come, that they'd somehow known she was in trouble and come to help.

"Holy crap." Tajo finally said, as the survivors assembled on the grass.

Hayden released a shaky whistle. "Would've got more to come, but I didn't realize we were talking about the end of the world."

Cyd turned to Finn, who looked shell-shocked. And suddenly, seeing all of his cuts and bruises, she realized what this meant for him. The demons were gone, and with them his best chance to change himself. He was the same beautiful mess of a man he'd always be.

But he didn't seem sad. He pulled her away from the group and scooped her up in his arms.

"Well, this is all just really special," Tajo remarked.

Cyd broke away from Finn and regained her feet.

As Tajo threw his arm around Bridget's shoulders, he nodded at Finn and Cyd with a ridiculously self-satisfied smile on his face. "Just like a normal family," he remarked.

Hayden took Jill's crossbow and slung it over his shoulder. "Let's not get excited," he said. "I'm not sure I like my family that much."

Tajo threw a punch at the vampire, who dodged it by a hair. "Exactly," he said, laughing. "Just like a normal goddamn family. So, what do you say we all get something to eat? If the girls sit on the guys' laps, we six can all fit in one car."

Bridget slammed a playful elbow into his gut. "Not a chance, perv. I'm driving." The two of them started off toward the street, the other rogues following.

"We'll catch up," Finn called out. He turned back to Cyd, and finally they were alone in the park. But something was bothering her.

"Finn, I have to tell you something," she said. "Griff offered to help you, and I didn't take him up on it. I couldn't do it," she said in anguish. "I just didn't believe—"

He shushed her, pulling her back into his embrace. "It doesn't matter," he murmured, pulling her closer and burying his face in her hair.

"But—"

"Leave it. I *know* I'm human," he said.

Cyd's hand touched his cheek. He had a nasty cut under his eye. So much so that a thin strip of metal shone through.

"Cyd, just leave it," he said softly. "It's okay. If you love me, that's enough. It's more than worth it."

She couldn't process what he was saying. She wanted him to be happy.

"It's *enough*," he said, taking her wrists and holding them. "Just tell me you love me, and that will be enough."

Her voice choked with tears. "I love you, Finn."

He reached out and cradled her face in his hands, then kissed her almost desperately. It was all there—the relief, the joy, the passion, the danger . . . everything they'd been through and everything they were to each other; it was all there in one kiss.

Cyd pulled away. "But, Finn . . ." She took his hands in hers and tried to explain what she meant. "It's insane. The whole thing. I'm some kind of hybrid. I've now got human, demon, werewolf and vampire blood. And you, you've still got metal in you."

"Hey, Cyd," he whispered in her ear. "You know what they say?"

"What?" she asked with a frown.

Finn gave a huge smile, and he started to laugh. "Nobody's perfect."

Cyd smiled, too, and started to laugh with him. Loose dirt and gravel whorled around in minitornadoes at their feet, and the streetlamps lighting the park blinked and sputtered . . . but it was only an aftershock. Nothing else followed.

Finn took her hand, and they headed across the grass to where the others waited, many sprawled on the hood or against the sides of Tajo's car.

Cyd glanced behind them to the tree where she'd last seen Griff-Vai. There was nothing left of him for her. No connection, no sense of that woolly darkness in her mind. He was gone. And Finn was still here. Everything was just as she wanted.

She reached up and pulled Finn's head down for another kiss as they walked. Then she pressed her lips softly against his neck. "I suppose you're right," she murmured into his ear. "But if I'm yours, and you're mine . . . I guess that's about as perfect as it gets."

Epilogue

Marius Dumont looked down from the balcony high up on Dumont Tower to the streets crisscrossing the human strata below. *Jillian.* Once he'd made up his mind to marry someone else, he'd expected to find the strength to just let her go. It wasn't turning out that way. This was . . . torture.

In a perfect world, the engagement ring on his fiancée's finger would have been Jill's. So silly to even think that way; he and Jill had only ever kissed. But the Dumont vampires had a code. He was not to make a human vampire. He had put his cousin Fleur through hell over it. They all had.

Also, even if that family code was eroding in the face of outside pressure, he was still a Protector. With that came responsibilities.

"Will she choose duty? Or will she choose danger?"

Marius wheeled around. His brothers, Ian and Warrick, walked onto the balcony, bearing three champagne flutes and a magnum.

"Well?" Ian asked as he passed the flutes around.

"Yes—what do you have to say, Marius?" Warrick asked, pouring out champagne.

Marius answered by immediately downing his entire glass, and his brothers arched an eyebrow.

Ian said, "Hmm. Hayden seems to know how to push all of your buttons."

"Perhaps that is why he won't be bringing the rogues to the latest peace talks. There's no peace in him," Marius suggested tightly, gesturing for a refill.

"Pace yourself, or everyone at the Assembly will think you're heartbroken and taken to your cups for solace," Warrick spoke up, refilling his glass.

Marius managed a chuckle. All the same, he set the champagne aside and gestured out over the railing. "Can you feel it?"

"Ah, Marius, can't you just relax?" Ian asked. "Let's spare a night to recognize how far Fleur and Keeli have brought us toward the peace accord."

Marius nodded. "Of course, of course. It's just . . . that peace doesn't include the rogues. Fleur said that fight she and Dain were in . . . she said they were working well as a team. As an organized team. How many of them still have revenge on their minds?"

"I don't know," Ian said. "But we should focus on the positives. The demons are put down and the human government has changed—with luck, for the better. Things look good. It's been very, dare I say, quiet."

The brothers exchanged knowing glances.

Marius looked down at the lights blinking above the damp layer of mist that enveloped the lower level of the city. The multicolored bulbs illuminated the gray, which shifted in a slight breeze. "There's no such thing as quiet in Crimson City," he predicted, looking over the ledge at the deceptively silent world below. "No such thing at all."